Murder At Any Age

Murder At Any Age

By

Tony DeMarco

ISBN 978-1456458393

Printed in the United States of America
First American Edition
10124111292288385419-v4

Dedicated to those who unselfishly live to help

others—in that regard, pray remember:

No one is perfect.

Murder At Any Age

CHARACTERS

The Italian Side

Antonio & Maria Fazio

|

Frank & Bernardine (*Campbell*) Fazio

|

Dolores, Alex, Maria, Francine

Aunt Catherine
Frank's sister

Uncle Bart (*Frank's cousin*) &
Aunt Margaret

|

Bart Jr.
Victoria (Vicky)
Robert, Ron

The Irish Side

Jack & Mary (Donahue, called *Mommy*) Campbell
Alex's Grandmother

|

Rev. John (Jack)

Aunt Hannah (*Mary's sister*) &
Uncle Pete

Aunt Anna &
George Doyle

|

Georgie

Aunt Anne Donahue
(Mary's aunt)

Bernardine &
Frank Fazio

Veronica & Paul Netti
(Aunt Ronnie)

The Orphanage

Priest
Fr. Mike Monahan & Mrs. Corbett, his housekeeper
Nuns
Sr. Kostich · Sr. Barbara · Sr. Josephine · Sr. Claire · Sr. Hortense
Inmates
The Steeters: Robert and Maureen - true orphans;
also: Nancy and Joan Norbert & Albert Venden
The Costellas: Samuel and Estelle (not wanted by parents)
Ryan Goodwin & Arlene Stern (no fathers) | Kathleen Sprague (slow)
Peter Christian & Eliz St Ann (infants found on church steps)

After the Orphanage

Rosita (Alex's guardian) | Sara (Alex's wife) | Tom (Maureen's husband)
Eric (Maria's husband)
Parishioners: Judge and Jean Reilly | Rose McGinty | Gladys Rumpf
Sgt Arrondondo | Detective Randy Stillerman | Chief of Police
Jordan Saydorf, Med. Examiner | Bill Nelson, D.A.
The Tully Family: Rose & Joe Tully; their daughters: Katie, Linda, Patti
Katie's husband Paul and his parents Erica & George Bateman

Convent Layout – First floor

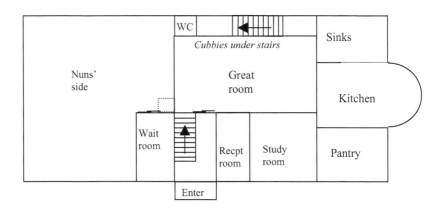

Convent Layout – Second floor

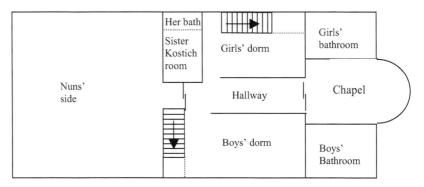

Church & Wall

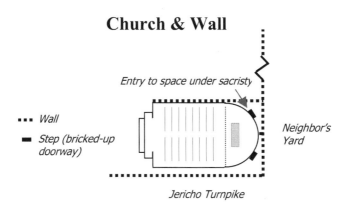

BOOK ONE

Nineteen Forty-six

1

The bed was soft—he remembered it well. The room darkened, because back then the shades were drawn until you got up—a holdover from WWII air raid drills. The sounds coming from the living room were muffled and sounded dark, like the drawn shades, way too dark. It only added to his realization that his mother was dead.

He lay on his back, stiffened, his large, wide-open eyes looking straight up. On each hand his middle finger was twisting around its index finger, untwisting again in a rhythm with his cadenced breathing. His aunt, in whose house he was staying while his mom was in the hospital, came in. She had on the dress reserved for serious Sundays. He could feel her smiling at him as she held her warm, clean smelling hand to his cheek but he didn't want to look at her.

She whispered, "You've been crying, is everything all right?"

"Where's my mom?" he asked. He could see his mother in his mind, dressed in her apron, sitting on the kitchen chair and he wanted to be safely on her lap again, but he knew she wouldn't be there any more.

"She's in the hospital with your baby sister; babies take a long time to be born." She moved her finger to his lips as if to stop any difficult questions.

"Then why are all these people here, why is my dad crying, I can hear him; and it sounds like everyone's ready for church, she's dead, isn't she?"

Aunt Margaret took way too long to answer.

That's all he remembered, he doesn't know what happened next. Why didn't he just get up, go into the living room, see who was there. Isn't that what you'd expect him to do, an eight year old?

But now his memory turned blank except for one tiny scene, sitting on his mother's lap. She was a big woman, round face with dark hair, a little curl plastered to her forehead. No conversation, no recollection of what was going on around them, just sitting there, on her lap, the only thing he remembers about her.

✦ ✦ ✦

Little Alexander Fazio was almost eight years old when his mother died. He was left with his father Frank and his sisters: Dolores age eleven and Maria age six and now Francine the newborn. None of the children went to their mother's funeral.

Over the next several weeks Alex figured it all out. Each morning and again after school as he walked by the Donnelly and Parcel Funeral Home on the corner across from Blessed Sacrament Church, he knew that's where the wake had been held. He'd slow and steal a glance whenever the doors were open. He would try to imagine what went on in there. He wanted his mother to be inside but he wasn't sure and didn't know where she was.

The church, school and funeral parlor were within walking distance from their flat on Autumn Avenue.

"Where is my mother?" he asked the nun who was his teacher. She was kind to him and he felt safe asking her—rather than his dad, or anyone else in his family.

It is difficult for an eight year old to comprehend her answer. "She's in heaven, with God. She is very happy, although she misses you and your sisters a lot, and your dad too, but God called her to Him. She wants you to be a good boy and when you die—we all have to die eventually, don't we—you all will be together again. Now run along and play outside, young boys are supposed to be outside playing during recess. Don't think about it too much. Everything will be okay, won't it?"

"But she's in a coffin. Where is the coffin? The door was open to the funeral home and I walked in and saw a coffin. That's where she is, I saw it."

"No Alex, that was someone else God called to Him. Your mom is in the cemetery. Her coffin is buried next to your Grandma, your Uncle Carmine...and she is keeping a place next to her for your dad, your sisters and you. I don't want you to be thinking of such things. When you say your prayers ask God to bless you and keep you safe until you join Him and your mother in heaven. Now run along, I've got work to do."

2

Aunt Margaret and her husband Bart were two of the finest people on earth. Surely there is a place reserved in heaven for them. They aren't pretty, not by a long shot and in fact Alex's dad always said, "She is as homely as a mud fence." She was short, not fat at all, but her build was funny. Her stomach stuck out and she had no ass whatsoever. Seemingly always dressed in a black dress with a white lace collar, her torso was way too large for her short stubby legs, accentuated by the ridiculous brown lace-up shoes that looked too large for her tiny feet. Then the face, the face said lots of things:

It said, "I love you no matter what."

It said, "If you need help, don't ask me, just let me know what it is."

It said, "Life is good, I am so happy. God has blessed me with my husband and my kids.

It said, " I am grateful to Him for letting me take care of little Alex."

"Poor Alex," she often said to her lady friends when they met at the store or chatted for a few minutes on the front stoop, "losing his mother at such an early age. I don't think he realizes it; it hasn't sunk in. He never mentions it, or cries, or asks for her. It worries me a little."

Aunt Margaret had a thick Brooklyn accent but her voice was soothing, even when she called to Bart Junior, her oldest. Everyone except her just called him Junior. He too was nice enough to Alex; had two younger brothers—younger than Alex—to pick on when the mood caught him. Margaret's only daughter Vicky was Alex's age, just a few months older.

"This is my new brother," when she would introduce him, "he's only part Italian." Why that was so important was not very obvious on the surface but if you knew more of the background it was understandable.

Alex's mother was Irish, his father Italian. This was Brooklyn in the mid thirties where Italians could marry Irish women but Irish women were not supposed to marry Italians! Or seemingly that is what was behind the friction with the Irish side of Alex's family.

Margaret and Bart didn't care; they liked Alex's mother—a lot. That's why they took Alex in when she died in childbirth.

✢ ✢ ✢

On the Irish side was Aunt Anna, Alex's mother's oldest sister; a traditionally built woman, rather tall at six feet, who had pinkish skin and wore her grayish hair in a bun. Alex's father was six feet...but weighed fifty pounds less and had jet-black, kinky-wavy hair. Anna took the newborn baby and had a conniption fit when Alex's dad would not let her change the baby's Italian last name to their Irish last name.

"After all, we are adopting her, aren't we? Wouldn't it make more sense, be easier on her if she had the same name as her 'sister and brothers?' " Referring to *her* kids who were the baby's cousins of course. But Alex's dad refused, there would be no "adoption" and the flying sparks were not lost on anyone.

"That man keeps his brains where he doesn't wear his hat," was one of Anna's favorite expressions about Alex's father. She didn't like him, never did, and blamed him for her sister's untimely death.

You could just picture her thinking—it was unholy to say anything like this out loud but it was okay to think it—if he wasn't such an animal, wanting to do it all the time, getting her pregnant, she'd still be here; Italian men are such animals!

✦ ✦ ✦

Alex's mother came from the large Campbell family. John and Mary Campbell had four children, the oldest was Jack the priest, followed by Aunt Anna. Alex's mother came next, then the youngest, Veronica—she was called Aunt Ronnie.

There was also Aunt Hannah, Grandma Campbell's sister, and she and her husband Pete lived above Bohack's Butcher Shop on Fulton Street. They took in Dolores while Alex's younger sister Maria went to live with Aunt Ronnie in Patchogue, a little village three quarters of the way out on Long Island.

As a result of this splitting up, Alex and his sisters didn't all get to see each other very often. Most weekends his dad would pick him and Dolores up, but it was too long a distance to get Maria out there on Long Island, so they only saw her about once a month. Visiting the newborn was a different story. Alex's dad hesitated to go to the Doyle house. Besides, every weekend was too much for Aunt Anna to handle; it interfered with her and her family's activities to have to wait around for that "dago" and his kids.

Maria was too young to remember much about this time in her life but she cried a lot. Dolores, on the other hand, being eleven when her mother died, still has all the details firmly imprinted on her mind. To this day she can remember what it was like on certain rare occasions when the three kids got together with their dad. Alex, on the other hand, remembers nothing, everything has been stolen from his memory.

Aunt Margaret and Uncle Bart, when they took Alex in, lived on Autumn Avenue, just three quarters of a block down from where he lived before his mother died and where his dad still lived; a few blocks from Dolores at Aunt Hannah's flat, and not many more from Grandma Campbell.

A grandmother, and especially an Irish one, is special to everyone.

"Mommy," Aunt Anna would say into the telephone when she called Grandma Campbell religiously every morning; this particular Friday asking, "what were you planning on serving this Sunday because I have a nice new recipe we can try out? And are you inviting Frank's kids as usual? Maybe we can skip them this weekend, have a smaller group if you want to try out this recipe I found?"

"Sure," answered Grandma Campbell who was called Mommy by everyone, but tell me what is in it and of course we cannot skip Frank's kids, they are my grandchildren and I will not hear of it. Ever again!"

Hers was the invitation the family could not refuse.

She lived in a brick house on Hemlock Street and would frequently pick a specific Sunday, then command that all her children along with their Fazio charges come to her house for dinner; she wanted *all* her grandchildren there. Aunt Margaret or Bart Junior would walk Alex to Blessed Sacrament Church where he would meet up with his aunts, uncles, cousins and his sisters.

Grandmother Campbell made it a point to have everyone meet for eleven o'clock mass at Blessed Sacrament, then walk together the few blocks back to her house for the afternoon meal.

Her house was fairly large and, as I mentioned, built of brick, so obviously grandma wasn't hurting. Who knows what happened to Grandpa John; he died a long time ago and was out of the picture soon after Alex's mother married Frank. The only outward appearance, besides the brick house, of whatever wealth he left Grandma Campbell was some flats in the black ghetto of Brooklyn.

Ancient Aunt Alice, Grandma Campbell's aunt, not only lived in the brick house but was like the maid. She wasn't treated that way; it was just that she took it upon herself to act like one and seemed quite content with the arrangement. She was referred to in private conversation as "the old maid aunt," and was probably a little "slow" because she didn't say much, although she had a grin on her face all the time.

These Sundays were about the only recollections Alex had of this time in his life other than going with his dad to Brooklyn to collect the rents from the black people. It was fun to sit in the blue Oldsmobile and listen to the radio or get out if the iceman with his horse drawn wagon happened to be there at the same time. He'd watch as the great big iceman used the large iron tongs to carry a huge block of ice up the long, outside stairs to his customer's house.

If it was the house his father was in, collecting rent, Alex liked following the iceman in to watch him put it into the wooden icebox with the chrome handles. There was usually a payback here; he'd get ooh's and ahh's from the black folks; they'd say what a fine boy he was, and perhaps he'd get a cookie, a piece of pie, always something to eat. He always felt so good because he could see that these people liked his dad so much. It made him so proud.

Later on, photographs filled in the blanks so that his memory was like an old-time film; scenes that jerked in and out of view.

3

It must have been difficult for Alex's father. You lose your wife, you've got three kids to look after plus a newborn. It wasn't like today where perhaps you'd get a nanny or a live-in housekeeper. This is Brooklyn remember, and except for grandmother in her "brick" house, everyone was just making it. Alex's dad worked two jobs as it was—accounting clerk at Republic Steel during the day and a soda jerk at Nedick's Orange Juice Bar several nights a week. But the kids were too young to realize the implications of his working so many hours.

Alex was the luckiest because he didn't remember anything, and Dolores was stoic, acting grown-up by not saying too much. Maria just cried a lot. But the relatives couldn't keep the kids forever, could they? Except for the baby, that is, who might as well have been adopted...but not legally.

Six months was as long as it would work. Alex became a nuisance to Aunt Margaret and Uncle Bart's household—too many boys; and Vickie, the only girl, for some reason looked at Alex as her plaything. She stood up for him no matter what he did, which caused a great deal of envy among her brothers, and as a result, fights became more frequent and more rough.

Aunt Hannah and Uncle Pete's place above Bohack's was tiny and getting tinier. Dolores had to go. Besides, they were older, much too old to have an eleven year old to watch. They figured that five lived in their apartment: Hannah, Pete, Dolores and two canaries. They never had children and treated the canaries like their offspring; even the canaries were old and

Hannah made a point of telling her friends that she was worried, they were acting strange.

"I think they are jealous."

Yes, it was time. Dolores would have to go.

Aunt Ronnie—it was bad enough that she lived way out on the Island, far from her family—was getting fed-up with Maria's constant crying. Ronnie was skinny and nervous to begin with and Paul her husband was no consolation. Besides, she had four kids and was beginning to feel the extra expense with a fifth who "wasn't even my own."

She and Aunt Anna had many a conversation about asking Alex's dad to pay a fixed amount for room and board; the occasional groceries he bought, or dollars he left on the cupboard, apparently were not enough.

"He hardly ever comes to pick her up, take her out, blow the stink off her, give me a break from that constant crying," said Ronnie. "You'd think we beat her all the time; it's embarrassing. My neighbors are wondering; beginning to not believe me when I tell them she cries for no reason. Do you blame them?"

"It's all his fault," Aunt Anna would commiserate. "He needs to put them in a home or something. Father John" —the two sisters often referred to their older brother as "Father" in his absence— "and I have been checking with Catholic Charities and there is a place in New Hyde Park that is just the place. Run by nuns, and they take in little orphans."

"But his kids aren't orphans," Ronnie countered, "would they take the little dagos anyway?"

"Well, Father John says it is quite nice, and him being a priest and all, he should know, shouldn't he, whether they will take them? He says he'll take care of everything; he knows the pastor, but I need to figure out a way to bring it up to that Frank. I don't want it to look like you and Aunt Hannah don't want to take care of them anymore. I'll keep the baby. Besides, she is too young to go with the others. I don't know about Alex, living with the other dagos, but I hear he too's becoming difficult."

She paused to take a breath and continued, "I had him and Dolores over for the weekend last week and he put up holy hell that he had to sleep up in the attic with my Georgie. Said he was afraid, wanted to stay up until my son got home. What? What did he expect me to tell Georgie...he's a teenager for crying out loud...'you can't go out,' or 'you have to be home early so little Alex isn't afraid?' Of course not."

"I know," Ronnie added. "He was at my house and the same thing. He's a sassy boy, won't do like I tell him and constantly picks fights with my kids; says they tease him, call him a dago. I don't look forward to him coming anymore. He's becoming that father of his."

"I'll talk to Mommy. The father listens to her and she has a way of putting difficult things nicely, don't you think?"

"Yes, but do it soon. My diabetes is kicking up and every time I take that damn needle it makes me irritable."

4

What is it like to be almost nine years old, having no memory of anything that happened to you before that terrible day when your mother was taken; driving up to a dark-red, brick building, with heavy wooden doors; a huge tower over the entrance, and a concrete-block fence surrounding what would now be your new home? It must have been terrifying.

He closed his eyes for a tiny second; then wiped each one in turn with his sleeve. He didn't cry though, but deep inside his nose, he had that strange, itching feeling that comes when you are trying to hold it all in. Even at that young age he figured, what's the use? He had no options and perhaps that was the worst feeling of all—resigned to this forbidding place forever.

Kids can't process the future, that eventually he'd be released from this foreboding place. Even if he could visualize a long time off, what would happen then, where would he go, who would take care of him? Resignation was the only option, horrible, heartbreaking resignation. His mind couldn't fathom what was happening to him. He was beyond sad; he just gazed out the car window at *Holy Ghost Convent;* he could see the name of the place chiseled over the doorway. He didn't move a muscle except to close his eyes for a second and give a barely visible shiver.

"We're here," his dad said, trying to cheer things up. "I think you are going to like it. From everything I've heard from Uncle John, there is a lot to do; you'll make friends..." but he started to cry. The three kids in the back seat sat there and just looked at him, not knowing what to do. Keeping terribly still as their father, both hands on the steering wheel, cried.

"Everything's okay, I'm just going to miss you a lot," through the tears, "that's all. But we'll be together on weekends, won't we? I can't promise every weekend because I have to go to Cleveland some of the time, but maybe not too often. If I can't be here your Aunt Catherine will come and take you to her place. You always like going there, don't you? And she looks forward to seeing you too...she told me. Yes, she told me, 'you make sure I get to see those children of yours...often. I like when they stay with me, they are such nice kids, fun to be around, and so well behaved.' "

He turned around and looked at each of them with eyes that little Alex never forgot; hollow eyes, glazed over, like there was nothing behind them, a torn-apart man, but oh how Alex loved him in that second; but now his dad was being taken away too, wasn't he? He stole a glance at each of his sisters and realized that he would have to take care of them, protect them. Neither of them had a mother or, for that matter, a father any more; Alex would have to be both. He raised his chin ever so slightly and said, "Don't worry Dad, we'll be all right. I'll take care of Dolores and Maria."

✦ ✦ ✦

This is the place where it all happened. This night should not have been much different than any of the previous nights during the almost four years the Fazio kids had been boarded at the convent.

Maria, now ten, had been told by Robert to meet him and her brother in front of the church. Robert was a bully. Again tonight, he knew he would get pleasure in making the two younger kids watch as he took his pack of cigarettes from the hiding place behind the church and light one. He would make Maria watch as he forced Alex to take a few puffs. It made him superior.

This night he was going to do more, he told them so. Robert and Alex were altar boys, and being the two oldest boys, they served at Wednesday evening devotions. Maria and a few other convent kids usually went along so they would get brownie points for going to evening church services. This night, when the service was over, she would do exactly as Robert had told her. She'd tell the others to go on ahead without her; she'd tell them she was going to wait for her brother.

"Go on, you'd better start heading back to the convent, and if Sr. Kostich asks where I am, tell her I'm waiting for my brother."

She didn't like waiting for her brother only because it meant going through misery with Robert. She was scared of him, especially tonight, scared for Alex but figured that just being there would offer some little bit of protection for both of them; she could scream, or run, but she was still really scared.

They had already been through this ordeal with the cigarettes a few times before and it frightened Maria and she knew what would happen to her brother if she told anyone. Earlier in the day Robert told her she'd better be there and to be ready because he was going to pull down his pants and show her something.

"You are going to like it," he told her. "You are going to like it a lot." She was petrified.

"And you are not going to tell anyone, are you?" he added. "I told you what will happen if you say a word, didn't I?" Maria could only nod her head up and down.

Now she was waiting for them to come out of the church. The old church building was situated on the corner of the two streets, with a wall starting three quarters of the way up the right side of the church, where it then made a left turn and continued along the rear.

Tonight as they'd done before, they would sneak along the sidewall, and then they'd go through another narrow space to the left side of where the sacristy of the church—which was curved and contained the altar—butted up against the rear brick wall.

On the outside, during the time the wall was being built, the original doors leading to the outside quadrants on both the right and left sides of the sacristy were bricked up; but inside they were plastered over so the only evidence of their former function was a lintel over the place where each door had been. Outside, once you squeezed through the space between the side of the church and the wall facing the street, you'd end up in the tiny right quadrant. Then, being careful to step over the narrow doorstep that remained, from there another squeeze got you to the left quadrant.

On the left side and under the other doorstep, was an opening quite hidden because the rear wall butted so closely against the curve of the sacristy, and was very narrow. The dirt by the step had been dug out long ago, and the overhang from the church roof prevented any rain from getting in.

Robert was sure no one knew there was a hole under the step. For some unexplainable reason, no one ever went behind the church; the town kids didn't hang anywhere around, it was too close to where the orphans were! They played in the parking lot, a block over from the convent, while the convent kids were confined to their walled-in playground.

Robert's cigarettes were safe. He could easily crawl into the small, hidden opening under the step and stash his treasure; and once inside—the space under the altar was quite large—you could sit cross-legged, and since the dirt was hard-packed you didn't even get any on your trousers that couldn't be slapped off with your hand.

Several months ago he had shown the secret hiding place to Alex and Maria, warning them of the consequences if they as much as breathed a word to anyone about it.

"You can't go in though," he told them. "Only I can go inside. If I find out you went in I'll kill you and hide your body in there. No one will ever find you; no one except me knows about this opening. That old janitor showed it to me. Sometimes we still come back here and I let him fool around with me—for money and cigarettes, but he got fired from his job here, didn't he? See what I made happen to him? I can do the same to you, if you tell anyone."

Now she saw them as they came out of the church door. Robert darted his eyes at her, the signal to not let anyone suspect they weren't going directly across the street to the convent. The look scared her. Robert always scared her. He was big, tough and scary. She trembled a little, almost more afraid for her brother than for herself.

They stood around, Robert stalling until everyone dispersed.

"You did a good job Alex, the priest didn't have to remind you of anything; neither did I. You did everything right," he was saying all this so anyone nearby would think they were just having a normal, after the service conversation about altar boy stuff.

But anyone who really looked would see Alex and Maria were scared stiff; their eyes wide open and their mouths tiny slits.

"Let's go," Robert said as soon as there was no one in sight any longer, "follow me and don't be looking all around."

They slipped back along the side of the church and squeezed through the wall towards the rear. There was all kinds of stuff that had been thrown over the wall and into the right quadrant: pieces of lumber, pipes, part of an old broken pew; you had to step carefully over and around everything. You could not see this spot from the front of the church, so it made a great place to throw things that someone unrealistically thought might be useful one day.

Robert continued on, through to the left quadrant, then Maria; Alex took up the rear.

"Come on, and be careful you don't trip or fall down, I don't want anyone to hear anything or you'll be sorry," Robert whispered.

"Now Maria, you stand there, out of the way, Alex and I want to smoke a cigarette before I fuck you, isn't that right Alex? That's what they call it, fucking. I'm going to pull down your pants and fuck you. Then I'm going to fuck your brother, in his ass, and no one is ever going to know, are they? If you ever tell anyone I'll beat you up so bad no one will recognize you. And if you make a sound I'll beat you up right here. You understand don't you, not a word."

Maria was too terrified to do anything. She couldn't even look at her brother, but knew he was just standing there, perfectly still.

Alex had time to contemplate exactly what was going to happen. Robert was the oldest boy in the orphanage, the most developed, and at night, when Sr. Kostich thought all the kids were asleep, Robert would call some of the older boys over to his bed. He'd make them watch as he masturbated. Last night he smeared the stuff over Alex's face, laughing.

"Want more? I'm going to give you what that old janitor gave me; it will hurt at first then you'll like it, you'll beg me to do it, won't you?"

This was directed especially at Alex who was too terrified to answer. "Answer me," Robert said, "you'll like it, won't you, and no one will ever know, will they?" Alex shook his head up and down.

Alex had no idea what Robert was talking about but knew whatever it was he was not going to like it. He hated Robert. Why wasn't Robert nice to him? He never did anything to Robert. His cousins back at Aunt Margaret's house were sometimes mean to him, but never like this. What can I do? If I tell anyone how scared I am, Robert will kill me; or worse, he'll hurt Maria, he said so. Besides, who will believe me? And the rest of the kids, they aren't going to say anything; they'll do whatever Robert says.

"Okay, get back to your beds, the show is over, get going," Robert whispered as he slipped his underpants on again, then to Alex, "Tomorrow night, after church, I'm going to do it again, to you, and your sister, be ready."

5

Now, more than twenty years later, it is difficult to know what actually happened behind the church that night. Alex remembers little. Maria never ever uttered a word and by some implicit means they agreed to never discuss it among themselves—and kept their unspoken promise to each other.

What is known, and mostly forgotten, was that after that night Robert was never seen again. Not that anyone cared. The Steeters—Robert and his sister Maureen—were true orphans along with Nancy and Joan Norbert and also Albert Venden. The others were being boarded for various reasons.

As we've seen, Alex, Maria, and Dolores Fazio lost their mother; the Costella's parents just didn't want their kids Samuel and Estelle any longer and figured it was better to have someone else to take care of them. Kathleen Sprague was slow and awkward, so probably an embarrassment and a burden to her folks, seeing as how they never came to see her. Ryan Goodwin and Arlene Stern each had no father because their parents were divorced. Elizabeth St Ann and Peter Christian were abandoned on the church steps as newborns, and given names by the nuns who found them. In some ways they were the most fortunate of the miserable lot; the convent was the only life they had ever known.

Robert Steeter, being the oldest of all of them and already shaving his substantial moustache, was getting close to being kicked out. He was difficult to begin with and the nuns were becoming fearful with the idea of having a fourteen-year-old teenager under their roof who was maturing too quickly, so since that night he was never missed. Everyone thought he had run away...and good riddance!

The police were notified but they too figured he had merely run off; he was an orphan anyway so who was left to care? The officer doing the investigating however, thought it strange that he didn't take any of his meager supply of clothing; the nuns thought it even more strange that he didn't clean out his locker. They knew, since the kids had very little they could call their own, that a few of the things he left behind were among his prized possessions; especially his "Ruby Falls" pocketknife, but the policeman didn't know that and no one thought to volunteer the fact.

His sister Maureen, from outward appearances, did not seem to care very much; she seemed to take it in stride. She left the convent a few months later; taken in by a family from Brooklyn—after a while she too mostly disappeared from most people's consciousness.

No questions were asked of any of the other kids other than did Robert say anything about running away? Most kids figured "good riddance" as well, but were polite to the nuns, priests and police who were putting on a show of concern even though each inwardly believed he "just ran away."

Case closed.

Because the adults asking the probing questions figured they already had the answers, there was no reason to suspect that Alex and Maria had any knowledge that they weren't sharing, or more importantly, any idea as to what actually happened.

The only person who took more of an interest than the others, enough to prolong the investigation, was Father Mike Monahan. He called Alex into his office the next morning.

"So Alex, tell me exactly what happened last night. You and Robert often served Wednesday Devotions, didn't you? Did you both arrive at the sacristy at the same time?

"No Father, Robert was already there when I came in."

"What did he say to you?"

"He didn't say anything Father."

"He didn't say anything, not even *hello*?"

"No Father, he didn't say anything."

"Were you late, on time, early; what time did you get there?"

"It was ten to seven; I looked at the clock to make sure I wasn't late Father. Robert would yell at me if I was late."

"Then what did you do?"

"Yes Father, I started the incense pot and put on my cassock Father, that's all."

"What did Robert do?"

"He got your cassock out of the closet, put it on the bench and went out to light the altar candles Father."

"And all this while you never said anything to Robert and he didn't say anything to you?"

"No Father; I mean yes Father."

"Did anything unusual occur during the Benediction, during the service, that I don't know about; perhaps I didn't see?"

"No Father, I did everything right otherwise Robert would have yelled at me."

"Then what happened? Begin when we all left the altar after Benediction was over, what did you do?"

"Nothing Father, I went into the sacristy with you and Robert. Robert helped you off with your cassock, you left and he gave it to me to hang up in the closet."

"What did Robert do while you were hanging up the cassock?"

"Yes Father, he folded the alter cloth and put everything else away; on the shelf Father."

"And neither of you said anything...nothing...during all the time you were together in the sacristy, neither of you said anything?"

"Yes Father."

"That's hard to believe. Robert talks nonstop, he's always talking. If I hadn't been in a hurry to leave immediately after the service was over he'd still be talking to me. And you don't remember anything he said from the time you got to church until the time you left the church?"

"Yes Father."

"You told Sr. Kostich that you and Robert left the church at different times, don't the convent altar boys always walk back together?"

"Yes Father, I left first because my sister was waiting outside for me."

"Why was she waiting for you, doesn't she usually go across the street with the other girls?"

"Yes Father."

"Then what was different about Wednesday night?"

"Nothing Father."

"I don't understand, if she waited for you instead of walking across with the other girls, *why* was she waiting for you? And what was Robert doing; why did he stay in the sacristy after you did; don't you always finish up together and leave together, lock the door together...not only you and Robert but any of the altar boys?"

"Yes Father."

"I still don't understand something. If you left before Robert to meet your sister, what was Robert doing? What do you

27

think he was doing; was he waiting for someone and didn't want you to see them?"

"I don't know Father."

"Are you sure you are telling me everything, something does not sound right and I think you know something you are not telling me?"

"No Father."

"Was there anything unusual you saw; did Robert act strangely before, during or after the Benediction Service?"

"No Father."

"But you just told me that Robert didn't say one word from the time you arrived until the time you left the church, isn't that unusual?"

"Yes Father. I don't know Father."

"One of the girls said you and your sister didn't arrive back at the convent until almost eight thirty, yet the service was over a little before eight; what were you doing all that time?"

"Nothing Father, we were just walking slowly and stuff."

"Where did you walk for a half hour, and what did you talk about?"

"Yes Father. We just walked slowly Father, besides it wasn't a half hour; I had to put the vestments away; clean out the incense pot and stuff; put everything away, so it wasn't a half hour Father."

"Okay, run along but if you remember anything... anything...you come tell me right away, okay?"

"Yes Father."

6

In all, Alex and his sisters Dolores and Maria lived at the convent for a few months short of four years. The first year or so was spent getting used to the surroundings and routines. Because nuns ran it, everything was simple, with simple routines to keep it that way; you got up on time, ate meals on time, prayed on time and went to bed on time. There were times and places where you could make noise and times and places where you had to keep quiet.

It was a period of time when nuns and priests commanded respect: there were no threats, no punishments; it was the way it was. Oh, there was an occasional rap on the knuckles with a wooden spoon, made to stand in a corner for a half-hour or so, no piece of hard candy after the cod liver oil or, feared the most, a special trip to the confessional where you would have to tell the priest you disobeyed and he'd dispense your penance—three Hail Marys or, for more serious offences, the rosary—simple, but it worked.

On the other hand there were not many rules, only routines. And these were strictly followed; pretty much the same routines that the nuns kept. The kids, like the nuns, arose at the same time early in the morning, seven days a week. You knelt at your bed and said morning prayers; you washed your face and brushed your teeth; you filed into the chapel for mass; filed down to the dining room for breakfast, and either went to school or played in the great room; or if the weather wasn't miserable, went outside.

In the evening the routine was reversed, except for going to mass. Otherwise, play was mostly unsupervised and in order not to incur the wrath of the nuns, arguments, fights, brawls, in that order, and all other fooling around was adjudicated by the older and/or bigger kids—and all to the tune of "shush...sist-r's coming."

The convent building itself was rather old; smelled old—like old ladies—and creaked when you walked so that the kids spent an inordinate amount of effort figuring out and passing along to each other secret ways to sneak around unheard, and it was, on the whole, quite dark inside.

The main entrance, where Alex first noticed the name of the place, *Holy Ghost Convent* chiseled in the stone above the door, faced west and was in the center of the building, with the left side of the building—the actual convent—containing a small chapel for the nuns, their dining room, a common area for reading and relaxing and a few rooms where they could say their daily prayers in private. Upstairs each nun had her own room with three nuns sharing one of the bathrooms. There were also two more prayer rooms. The convent kids rarely went over to the nun's side; there was no reason to.

On the ground floor, as you walked through the main entry, there was a small, sparsely furnished room on the left, a waiting room, where parents or anyone making a call on the convent could wait. Directly across on the right side of the hall was another room, a reception room, this one had a few comfortable chairs and a small table in the center of the room. All too often, after spending fifteen minutes or a half hour in this room, many a kid's visitors, if they only came because they felt it was their duty, or to allay their sense of guilt, could pour out their excuse as to why they had to leave right away.

Under normal circumstances it is difficult enough for adults to have a conversation with kids, and when they don't see each other very often the topics become quite limited. After you ask: how is school, what games do you play, how are the other kids treating you, what did you have for breakfast? —both sides are anxious to get the torture over with.

If no one was using either of the reception rooms then kids expecting visitors were sometimes allowed to wait in one of them; otherwise they waited in the great room until called by Sr. Barbara—they were her rooms!

It was amazing how quickly those kids who had to put up with infrequent and or short visits became used to it. Visits to some of them, especially the two Costellos, who knew their parents didn't want to come anyway and when they did come the parents unashamedly showed it, was something Samuel and Estelle did not especially look forward to at all.

The Fazios were different. Alex, who doesn't remember much before his mother died, vividly remembers the times he was in that waiting room, nose against the glass, quietly thinking this was going to be that time he always dreaded: this time his dad would not come. Dolores would sit on one of the chairs reading a book and Maria, sitting close to her sister, quiet as well, would do her usual staring into space.

Out in the hall the main stairway was on the left side and went to the upper floor of the nun's quarters. If you walked down the hallway past these stairs, past the telephone table tucked under the stairs, and through the double doors you continued into the great room where the kids got to their upper floor via the staircase along the far wall. The great room was the largest room in the convent and was used by the kids for playtime, general horsing around and occasional studying.

The wall under the rear stairs was completely covered with cabinets that looked like gym lockers with no locks, except that they were made of cheap wood and painted dark brown. Each kid had his own; the lower section was used to store your winter coat, gloves, boots and so forth, and had a shelf on top referred to as your "cubbie."

It was the only space you could call your own. There was an unwritten rule, religiously followed, that no one would disturb another's cubbie. Oh, one might go into the lower portion of the locker to borrow a coat, or boots; but the top, the "cubbie" was sacredly one's own.

With few exceptions, each was set up as a scene or stage. One of the boys had his set up as a ranch. He had received a little horse figurine; he glued toothpicks together to make a fence in which to corral the horse; and drew a pasture of trees and mountains that covered the back wall.

Another had an altar set up: a few pieces of construction paper folded and glued into a rectangle was the altar itself; an ornate lace altar cloth was drawn on white paper, the lace carefully cut out with a scissor, and which hung down both sides of the altar; candle sticks and a crucifix carefully drawn on another piece of paper taped to the back wall served as the backdrop. Her prized religious medals were hung with straight-pins on the sidewalls.

Hours were spent kneeling on the floor in front of the cubbie carefully re-arranging the inside; each iteration of drawing and cut-and-paste designed to improve the scene. Apparently, it did not dawn on these children that their cubbie was their fantasy of being anyplace but where they actually were, or acting out someone they weren't.

It would be interesting to have been there during this time to interview the nuns who certainly knew about the various cubbies—the boys and girls were proud to show theirs off—and ask them if they ever gave thought to what was missing in reality, so that their charges spent so much time creating and caring for their fantasy. Since there were no organized activities to fill the days...who knows!

Robert's cubbie was essentially bare, yet orderly...perhaps so he could easily tell if someone disturbed anything. In it he kept his special leather gloves, an empty notebook, his "Ruby Falls" pocketknife, and a small box to keep his money. It had a dollar sign carefully drawn on the top. How much money? Nobody except Robert knew and perhaps nobody really cared. Certainly, nobody would dare to peek to find out. The nuns, of course, were oblivious.

In your cubbie you had to integrate into your scene enough space to store your "valuables." Guess what these were? Simple things—there was not much opportunity to garner anything of value—certainly your prayer book; a religious medal if you won a spelling bee or had outstanding penmanship in school; a post card or souvenir from a relative; and in Alex's case—and the focus of his cubbie— a small bank. It was made in Japan—you could see that it was born as a Campbell Soup can, was about four inches square and about three inches high. If you inserted a coin the amount being deposited showed up in the little window—twenty-five cents, ten cents, five cents or one cent. It was a gift for his birthday from his Aunt Catherine.

Alex had seen it in a toy store window several blocks from the convent—which is another story—and desperately wanted it. He must have mentioned it to Aunt Catherine because she surprised him by purchasing it from the local store, wrapping it up and giving it to him for his birthday. The few coins he also received and kept in this little bank were the beginning of a lifetime of saving things, especially little stuff, and especially little boxes!

Toys were shared. The nuns shared all of their things, so why not expect the same from the children? If a nun was given money for her birthday, for her anniversary, left an inheritance, given a donation by someone whose prayers were answered, it belonged to the convent, to the religious community. In the same manner, if one of the kids received a toy, a game, a piece of sports equipment, a book—with minor exceptions—it belonged to everyone, and all immediately shared it. And to their credit, the meager stash was generally well taken care of.

To the right after you entered the great room, was the dining/study room with its long tables and benches—some nuns called it the library—used for occasional studying. Occasional because each nun was busy doing her own thing, so monitoring homework periods was not something any of them did with any frequency. As long as the kids kept quiet enough, so they couldn't be heard on the other side, the nuns' side, they were left alone.

This was not a prep-boarding school. These kids were orphans, or in other cases not wanted by their parents so why should anyone care if they studied, got good grades, were accomplished in music, art, sports—as long as they didn't cause the nuns trouble no one cared what went on, from the time they were innocent little children until they matured into inquisitive, precocious adolescents.

Up the stairs were two dormitories: the girls at the top of the stairs and the boys toward the front of the building. Sr. Kostich had a room in the far left corner of the girls' dorm. Her walls were only three-quarters high, so she could readily hear what was going on—but really only on the girl's side—and she would occasionally yell out to "stop all that racket," "get into bed," "do you want me to come out?" The latter was an empty threat because the kids knew it had to be very serious before Sister would go through the trouble to put on her nun garb in order to cover herself completely before coming out of her room.

A corridor, also with three-quarter high walls, ran between the dorms separating the girls from the boys. Girls' and boys' bathrooms were in each of the far corners of the upper floor. Here too, the walls were only three-quarters high so Sr. Kostich, as she occasionally walked around while the kids got ready for bed, could monitor goings on without actually having to go in even though she never hesitated when she thought it was necessary; it never made any difference who was doing what in there when she felt she had to, she just walked in.

Privacy was unheard of. The stalls in the bathroom had no doors, three sinks were lined up against one wall, and the shower room had three faucets placed next to each other. Think about growing up here. Most little children at about the age of four begin to want their privacy. Here the youngest was five and the oldest, Robert—at the time he "ran away"—was fourteen. Only a little imagination is necessary to picture the horsing around that occurred. Quiet and not wasting water were the only constraints.

The dormitories were wide-open spaces with rows of metal beds, and next to each was a small two-foot square, yard-high, three-sided box with a shelf in the middle; used to keep your meager supply of socks and underwear. At the far end of each dorm was a closet for hanging "church clothes"—so called because as far as the nuns were concerned Sunday Mass was the only time you had to "dress up." The closets were covered by a heavy muslin drape so a good place to play in after Sr. Kostich shut off the ceiling lights and could be heard snoring.

The boys' dorm, which faced the street, had a little bit of light that came in from a street lamp. The girls' dorm was totally dark; not helped by the scarcity of windows, two small ones to be exact, and no outside lights at the rear of the building.

During the summer it could get very warm. If it was ninety-five degrees outside, it was probably one hundred on the upper floor of the convent. The kids would lie perfectly still in their beds, believing that the slightest movement would indeed add to their discomfort.

Strange how one remembers certain events—some good, some bad, some ugly. This night was good. Alex quietly got up from his bed and tiptoed to the open window. It was perfectly still outside; it looked like a photograph. The moon was to his back, beyond the building, and with its light showing brightly over the street, and with the city's glow at the horizon, it was extraordinarily peaceful.

Alex does not remember how long he stood at the window: elbows on the sill, his hands cupping his chin, every so often shifting his weight from one leg to the other, and occasionally standing on both at the same time, careful not to upset the quiet. His bare feet on the cool floor felt soothing.

It was an epiphanic event; perhaps merely Alex's first foray into an entering, a coming-of-age, a maturation, on to the next plateau of who he was, where he was, and what would become of him.

It went from the little boy who moments ago was fanning air into the dormitory with his cupped hand; believing wholeheartedly that if he coaxed enough cool air in, and did so for a long enough time, he could cool down the kids and Sister Kostich so they would sleep more comfortably; to the next moment beginning to understand that eventually he would be grown up; then daydreaming what it would be like when he was just a few years older—which in his mind was all grown up—and out in the world. He'd be with his dad; they'd do things together.

The week before when his dad visited he asked the three children, "Who wants to go to the park?' Alex definitely wanted to go; he agreed so quickly and in such a way, that one could easily claim that the girls didn't have any say in the decision at all; which, truth be known, didn't matter to them; they all wanted to go someplace, any place. So, they went to a park not far from the convent. They parked and the four of them just walked around, having a wonderful time, feeling good. Except...when they came back, his dad happened to look under the car and saw something leaking.

Alex was devastated. He immediately concluded that it was gas and he felt wretched. His poor dad—what was he going to do? Losing gas was wasting money that he had to work so hard to earn.

The little boy in him felt so sorry for his dad and he desperately wanted to hug him. He must have looked like he felt because his dad noticed.

"What's the matter son, are you worried about the car? It's okay; there is a little oil on the ground. I don't want you worrying on such a beautiful day. We are here to enjoy ourselves, aren't we?"

Sometimes exact words are imprinted on your mind forever, and this was one of those times. He was sure his dad was just saying what he did in order to make him feel better and to stop him from worrying. To Alex of course, it was evident that his dad too, was worried, but he didn't want Alex to see it; that's why he said what he did, about it being *only* oil.

Alex, the sheltered little boy, didn't know about oil. Gas, though, he equated with money that had to be earned through his dad's hard work. He blamed himself for being so enthusiastic about a ride to the park. What a selfish thing to do.

It had been little boy thinking—he didn't have enough experience to fully comprehend a drain plug and what was involved in removing the plug, draining the oil, and then replacing the plug...which in this case was not tight enough so it leaked, enough to notice but certainly not a costly amount. Besides, the mechanic who changed the oil would replace for nothing what was lost since it was his fault—losing gas however, which he knew from the times he watched his dad fill the gas-tank, was serious—aware of how much he had to pay only to have it leak on the ground would waste his dad's hard earned money.

Perhaps this night, standing at the window, vacillating between being a little boy and entering his coming-of-age, if Alex had thought of that scene in the park, which of course he didn't, he would now be able to recognize the problem for what it was...in the entire scheme of things, "no big deal." It would have been a clue that he was stepping into the world beyond the convent.

What he did think about while standing at that window was being out in the city. He had the strangest vision: he was standing on Fifth Avenue, in front of St. Patrick's Cathedral, but he was gigantic, in the neighborhood of ten feet tall; his legs apart firmly on the pavement; his arms folded across his chest; a smile on his face—he was no longer in the convent, he was out; he was grown up. He was so happy.

Until he almost fell down.

He began falling asleep just standing there. He tiptoed back to his bed, lay there looking up at the ceiling, realizing that before he knew it his dreams would come true. "I can't wait," he whispered to the air that now felt much cooler.

Getting ready for bed was a rackety affair that took about an hour. It was indistinguishable from playtime until Sr. Kostich came upstairs, clicking her little frog-shaped clicker a few times and signaling with "okay, that's enough, five minutes to prayers so no dilly-dallying."

Everyone kneeled down next to his or her bed and Sister led the prayers. She usually went directly to her room, leaving more time for fooling around, though the lights were off. Robert gave the impression he never slept and in what seemed like the middle of the night he'd wake up his audience and go through his antics. If Sister heard anything, she'd yell out, but would otherwise quickly fall back to sleep.

✦ ✦ ✦

On the first floor, to the right of the great room and in the center of the building was the kitchen. It was a large room with a curved wall on the far end; the curve extending up to the second floor to become the backdrop of the altar of the convent's main chapel. To the left of the kitchen was a smaller room with two deep, stainless steel sinks along one wall that were used for washing dishes, pots and pans.

To the right of the kitchen was the pantry, so the dishes, cups and glasses, after they were dried, were carted past the kitchen to the pantry where they were stacked on shelves. The knives, forks and spoons were put into wooden trays that were kept on a table against another wall. The kitchen proper had a big stove with an oven below, and next to it was a long, stainless work-counter with hooks above, where the few pots and pans were hung.

The kitchen also had a double-door refrigerator on one wall and along the other, on the floor, were wooden barrels of flour, sugar and cereals; and on the wall were cupboards with shelves of tin-cans containing vegetables and evaporated milk; and jars of jelly and jam; some of the latter made and donated by parish women.

The cook, a rather grumpy middle-aged woman, was hired from the town but only for lunch. Breakfast and supper consisted of "help yourself" corn flakes or puffed rice, or cereal cooked by the older girls—oatmeal, farina, or porridge (whatever that was!)

At the noon meal, after the boys cleared the tables, the girls washed the dishes. After that, Robert, Ryan and Roger did the pots and Arlene Stern dispensed the cod liver oil. Everyone got a large spoonful from the community pot, followed by one piece of hard candy. Sr. Claire, who doubled as the "nurse" made absolutely sure no one skipped this important routine.

"You better thank God in your prayers that you are fortunate enough to get this medicine; you'll notice that no one ever gets sick, do they? It is God's will, my prayers and the medicine," a constant exhortation.

The kids had many duties throughout the day and in doing so pretty much cared for themselves. Overseen from a distance by the nuns, they did the dusting, the sweeping, floor washing, window washing, yard work and their own laundry. Along one wall of the dishwashing room was a smaller, though just as deep sink where the kids took turns washing everyone's clothes at once; using a washboard and large dark-brown bars of laundry soap. Clothing was hung outside on rope lines both summer and winter.

Everyone had nametags sown into their underwear, their socks, their shirts, trousers, blouses and skirts. When you first arrived a three-by-five card was ordered for you that had a ribbon wrapped around the card with your name printed every inch and a half. Sr. Kostich kept the cards-cum-tags in a box in the pantry with strict orders not to touch. Curiously, some rules were strictly enforced, mostly those that none of the kids were eager to break anyway, like touching the cards. There were others, rules that is, that were not rigidly enforced—perhaps the nuns were not eager to create difficulties for themselves.

7

Each Saturday, a few boys were conscripted to polish the nuns' shoes—maybe ten pair of the Victorian-era kind; black ones that laced up above the ankle.

Sr. Josephine, the tall, lanky, drill-sergeant-one, took it upon herself to be in charge of the shoe polishing detail. One particular Saturday she announced to the boys, "When you have finished polishing the shoes I will inspect your work, and if you do an extra good job then one of you come up to me later in the day, after the noon meal, and say to me, *choc-a-lot-a-lazy-boom-boom*, and I will give you each a piece of chocolate. Only if you do an extra good job though...so get busy."

Later that afternoon, after a job well done, as confirmed by Sr. Josephine herself, Alex went to her and said, "Sist-r, *choc-a-lot-a-lazy-boom-boom*," at which time Sr. Josephine responded, "What do you want, what?"

"*Choc-a-lot-a-lazy-boom-boom*, Sist'r. You told me to say *choc-a-lot-a-lazy-boom-boom* to you and you'd give us each a piece of chocolate...the boys that did the sisters' shoes...this morning."

"What in the world are you talking about, don't you see I'm busy; take off now and stop talking baby talk."

Alex was devastated. Not only did he feel foolish, embarrassed and disconsolate, he'd been tricked. The lesson was learned and never forgotten. Alex doesn't remember that much about those days but a few things like *choc-a-lot-a-lazy-boom-*

boom continue to splash an indelible image. At the time it seemed to go along with the entire explanation of his life so far.

✦ ✦ ✦

Weekdays consisted of school—the building was across the street from the convent—homework, dishes, cod liver oil, prayers and bed. Weekends consisted of Saturday morning chores; and Sunday, aside from mass, just another day if no one came to visit. It was like Saturday without the chores. During summer school break, the only change in the routine was playtime substituting for school, and if the weather was nice it was outside; otherwise the boredom took place in the great room.

It is not that the kids were slow or dim-witted or just plain stupid, but there was little organized playtime; no checkers or chess; no getting together to put on plays or sing songs; no trying to learn to dance—perhaps an occasional game of hide-and-seek or stick-ball—but no card games; no pitching pennies; nothing competitive. And that was probably the thing—there was a hierarchy based on tougher, stronger and, in most cases, older, so competition was generally frowned upon between most of the kids, reserved for those at the top of the heap.

There was a large bricked-in-yard surrounding three sides of the convent. Over on the left side of the building, the nuns' side, there were fruit trees, a small grotto to the Blessed Virgin Mary, and some paths around the perimeter where the nuns walked while repeating their daily prayers.

On the "orphanage" side there was one large tree, a dirt ball-field, a swing that no one used, and a table with attached benches near the back steps around which most of the kids congregated throughout each and every day. There was no real place to play stickball and when you did play, you ran the risk of the ball going over the fence and forever lost.

Mostly the summer days consisted of doing nothing or fights—boys against boys, girls against girls, boys and girls against girls and boys, and of course, the ordinary one-on-one. There was lots of foul language, dirty talk and made-up stories about nuns, priests and townies.

If you drive past a school yard at a time when there is no "organized" play—for example at recess or before school starts, you see kids in groups; some running around yelling and screaming, seemingly without purpose; yet if you watch long enough you see that mostly there is a method to their activity: tag, catch-me-if-you-can, blind-man's-bluff; in any case, their activity is with purpose. Or you might see some children merely congregating in groups engaged in conversation.

This is not what you saw, save for episodes of screaming at each other or fighting, when you passed the convent yard or went inside to the great room.

These kids were relatively quiet and staid, usually sitting on and around the outside picnic table near the back door or at the long tables inside. You'd see quiet-talk with little to nothing of consequence being discussed about their background or history. They didn't talk about things, they didn't talk about ideas or how they felt about anything. No one had a history, or if they did, either they did not know it, did not want to discuss it, or no one was interested in hearing it. No one talked about the "outside" either; the world was the convent and since you couldn't see over the wall, beyond it was "out of sight; out of mind."

✦ ✦ ✦

Shortly after Robert's disappearance and Alex was now one of the older boys, he was given additional responsibilities. Instead of the Saturday morning chores mentioned above, on most weekends Alex was dispatched by Sr. Superior to the post office and the bank. One particular Saturday, Alex was given an envelope to mail and another to deposit in the bank.

It was enviable duty, getting outside the wall. For that short forty-five minutes, which was as long as he dared take, he was in another place; he was another person who didn't look the same, didn't walk the same, didn't feel the same.

Shoulders back, head up, he'd walk down the street to the corner, turn right on to Jericho Turnpike, the main road, and continue about three blocks to the post office. A little further down was the bank; but in-between were a few stores where Alex could pause to look in the windows. That is where he first saw the bank he eventually got from his Aunt Catherine. He would look at it each week and dream about owning it, always fearful that it would be sold to someone and he would never see it again.

He had no money to deposit in that bank so it is difficult now, years later, to determine what the fascination was, but he'd look anyway; dream of putting a coin in and watching the amount show up in the window.

Perhaps it was the mechanism, how did it work? How did it know the different amounts? Perhaps he related to how the little coins must have felt as they were being tucked securely into their secure space. All the things sensitive, inquisitive young boys think about, searching for answers.

48

On this particular Saturday, as he was turning on to Jericho Turnpike, his thoughts were on the bank. He deposited the letter in the post office then ran to the window to see *his* bank. Fortunately it was still there but he didn't have much time; Sister Hortense, the Mother Superior, specifically told Alex to hurry back. She was going out for the afternoon but had to have the receipt for the bank deposit before she left.

"If you keep me waiting I'll pass the job to someone else, someone more responsible than you are," as she often threatened.

When he got to the bank he handed the envelope to the teller. After a few seconds she looked at him inquisitively—he had put the bank deposit in the mail shoot—she was holding the letter.

First, he fought back the tears, took the letter from the teller who had no idea what could possibly have happened, and walked out the door. Passing the store with the toy bank, Alex made a point not to look in the window. He hated that bank; he never wanted to see it again, and when he got it for his birthday it was pushed to the rear of his cubbie and was never touched again.

He thought of all the alternatives he could think of to explain what happened. Of course he could lie and tell Sr. Hortense that there was no money in the envelope, better yet, some big kids stopped him on the street and took the envelope, anything but the truth, that he put the wrong envelope in the post office drop box.

Alex recalls the situation but not what happened as a result. Is it normal for unpleasant things to be totally forgotten: his mother; what happened the night Robert was last seen; the consequences of the bank fiasco; and more to come?

8

Robert Steeter and his sister Maureen were true orphans. As mentioned earlier, the convent kids didn't discuss their backgrounds. It wasn't that there was a determined effort to conceal the facts of one's background, but for some unexplainable reason where you came from, what your parents did for a living, what they were like, what circumstances found you at the convent; conversations like that were, by and large, absent. Some things however were general knowledge even though they weren't much talked about.

In Robert and Maureen's case, both parents died when they were toddlers—reason unknown to the rest of the kids and probably not much known by Robert and Maureen themselves. Whether it was bravado, or their need to maintain sanity, or a desire to fit in, or merely just the norm among a group of children who lived pretty much without guidance and had long ago figured out what worked best for themselves—it seemed, especially in the Steeter's case, to not make any difference whatsoever whether they had parents or not.

At the time Alex came to the convent Robert was the oldest boy; six-months older than Alex, and two years older than both Alex's younger sister Maria and Robert's own sister Maureen; the two girls being the same age to the month. Robert was a bright kid, rather rough and tumble looking, with mousy-colored straight hair, sharp eyes that you knew took in everything, tall for his age, and muscularly built. As a result he put himself "in charge," since there was no one to physically challenge him.

The oldest girl, Arlene Stern, was also tall; taller than Robert; yet lanky and, if she put her mind to it, could beat the crap out of Robert, but for some reason did so only on the rare occasion when he was causing a situation where it looked like one of the nuns would become involved in whatever altercation was taking place...an absolute no-no, to which everyone agreed.

Robert could be charming to the nuns; to anyone's parents when they visited; helpful to the priests; always first to volunteer; and fun to be around. He held court out in the playground or in the great room and mostly kept the days full with make-believe, roughhousing, dirty jokes and stories, and minor intrigues that at the time seemed bold and wildly dangerous.

The nuns had a closet on the first floor that the kids referred to as the nun's liquor closet. It was just inside and to the right of the door leading into their wing from the waiting room. True there were always a few bottles of rose-colored wine that were used for chapel mass, but mostly there were bottles of soda the nuns served to their infrequent visitors and occasionally had some themselves.

According to Robert however, it was the wicked liquor stash that added credence to his gripping stories of those secret sex parties between the priests and nuns. When Robert decreed, late at night, being careful not to step where the floor boards creaked, he would either lead a few boys down there to steal a few sips from any open bottles, or when in a more daring mood—because if they got caught, they'd kill the golden goose—he'd dispatch one or two of the younger boys to go in his stead and bring some back for him.

To the kids this was considered one of the most dangerous insubordinations, seeing as how, according to Robert, the liquor was for the nuns' wild parties and Robert said that those parties were top secret; no one on the outside was ever to find out what went on or all the convent kids would be severely punished by the nuns, then beat bloody by Robert himself.

His sister Maureen was a cute little redhead who the Irish side of Alex's family would have referred to as "wet behind the ears." She looked a lot older than she actually was, was dainty, always smiling, loquacious and looked and acted like a little angel. She was anything but. When no adults were around she was foul mouthed, always touching herself and in constant need to have any boy, including her brother, put his hand down there, eager to add that she didn't have on any underpants.

Many nights found her in Robert's bed, out of earshot of Sr. Kostich, under the covers playing with one another. It was incest but none of the others knew exactly what that word meant and if they did it would never dawn on them to consider applying it to Robert and Maureen.

There was a lot of stuff going on at night. Remember this was a closed world for these kids. Oh yes, right and wrong were taught in school and in church, but it was the catechism version; the version that nuns applied to each other: prayer, good deeds, obedience and respect for the word of God.

Right was memorizing the grade-school version of the catechism, wrong was not being able to answer a question like "what are the three requirements for a mortal sin?"

A big thing was made about the Examination of Conscience, the Six Commandments of the Church, the Sins Against the Holy Ghost, the Sins Crying to Heaven for Vengeance, Nine Ways of Being Accessory to Another's Sins, the Seven Deadly Sins, the Four Last Things to Be Remembered: Death, Judgment, Hell, Heaven. All of these had to be memorized...easy considering how often they were heard; as easy as learning the words to any popular song played constantly.

All the kids knew that thinking "dirty" thoughts was a sin that had to be confessed, but when it was, the priest glossed over it. There was no way he was going to probe any deeper. "Say three Hail Marys" was as far as he dared go. Actually the kids euphemized their sins with things like "I disobeyed my superiors," or "I told a lie." A good one was, "I sinned against the Holy Ghost," or "I was envious of another's spiritual good," or "I despaired against God." Despaired how or of what was never questioned, the priest did not want to go there; I suppose for them it was enough that you recognized that you, like all God's children, were a sinner and that you went to confession.

The convent kids grew up like little puppies, always together in every waking activity; privacy was not possible; and for several, especially the orphans, even though they had siblings, there was little familial relationship between them. Some boys selected other boys as their brothers, some girls selected other girls as their sisters—which could change at the slightest provocation—and other than that it was one homogenous group whose primary objective was to keep out of Sr. Kostich and the other nuns' radar.

It didn't take long before Maureen and Alex tried out their equipment together. It was one-night weeks after Robert's disappearance. Maureen remained curious, never seemed overly upset about his demise but she missed his company and Alex was about ripe.

The first time was rather late at night, warm so the windows were open to catch any slight breeze. Maureen tiptoed over to Alex's bed, he did not have any covers over him so she just lay down next to him and pulled the sheet over them both. He was easily awakened so she started kissing him; first on the mouth, then the ears, down his neck, over his chest and finally, after enough time to get him excited, slid him into her mouth. It only took a few seconds and she had to swallow.

They stayed wrapped up in each other for a little while before Maureen tiptoed back to her side of the dorm.

Incidentally, boys normally didn't go to the girls' side; too close to Sr. Kostich's room and too much possibility of waking her, resulting in her either yelling out or the next morning giving a few cracks with the wooden spoon on whomever she determined was the one who disturbed the nighttime quiet.

Thereafter it became a routine and it didn't take long before Maureen taught Alex what other tricks he wasn't aware that he could perform. The first few times he lost his erection as soon as she tried to put it in but finally, one night it worked. Alex didn't like it. He was embarrassed, shamed, he knew it wasn't right and wanted to forget it, like anything unpleasant, like his mother, like Robert, like the bank. He refused to look at her, talk to her, acknowledge her for several weeks thereafter.

However, it was not to be. Eventually he and Maureen developed a friendship. First it was knowing they had a shared secret, but then it got deeper, a strong relationship grew, they began more serious conversations, just the two of them, alone, sharing each other's feelings about the convent, their life in general, future plans, how each felt about the world—their world, each other—although her not going back to his bed for quite a while. Their friendship consisted of talking mostly, just enjoying being around and with each other.

As we will see, this relationship blossomed, became more intimate and lasted both of their lifetimes even though time, distance and others came between them.

9

Father Mike Monahan kept up his quest. Something just didn't fit and he wanted to know what it was. He didn't actually believe there was foul play, but all the same, he wanted to know what would prompt Robert to run away all of a sudden.

Father was de facto in charge of the orphans and he took his responsibility seriously. He was rather young compared to the other priests and nuns; one's guess would be thirty and, as a result, he seemed more in tune with how adolescents think and act than the two older priests and most of the nuns. For many of the boys he was their only source of male bonding; he sometimes played games with them; on occasion organized outings—to the beach in the summer, perhaps the zoo in the spring or fall. He heard confessions from the boys and girls; heard the euphemisms that substituted for what they were actually doing; occasionally probed; and was not deluded about what was going on.

His concern about Robert was that someone on the outside may have coerced him into doing something that may have seemed like a good idea at the time but then led to danger. He gave no thought to something untoward happening within the convent.

He mentioned his concerns on different occasions to the police but since Father wanted to be extra careful of what outsiders thought of the convent kids, he did not get far generating any excitement for re-opening the case. If any of his parishioners heard what he heard in the confessional they'd be shocked; they foot the parish bill, including the convent, and a few vocal ones questioned the wisdom of taking in orphans in the first place—and only needed some libidinous prattle to convert them to loudmouths on the campaign trail. He was on dicey ground, and besides, he only had a hunch.

Father Mike worked closely with Sister Kostich. He was officially responsible for all the kids but Sister Kostich was ostensibly in charge in all day-to-day matters. She felt comfortable working with the girls on certain difficult occasions and similarly, she left the boys to Father Mike. Unfortunately he was used too often as the disciplinarian, which he didn't relish but had to admit that with most of the boys they respected him for it and were not afraid to show it in numerous little ways.

When no adults were in earshot, he knew, whereas the nuns were sometimes referred to as Kostich or Hortense, it was always Father, never Mike or Monahan.

Two days after the disappearance and after Morning Mass, he walked over to the convent and he and Sister Kostich sat in the reception room. The two of them had not the opportunity to privately discuss the "runaway" in any detail and Father looked forward to doing so.

"I thought I knew the boy," he began, "it should be a lesson—you can't know what goes on inside a person as much as you'd like to think you do. Yes, there are times you can 'read' what someone is thinking but if they do not want to let you into their head you will not get in, don't you think so Sister?"

"I do," she replied. "Robert is an intelligent boy. He is street smart, he can connive, he can sweet talk you even when he knows you know he is doing it, and he has a magic touch for getting his own way. Father, I am loath to admit, all too often he has gotten what he wanted from me, too."

"Oh, I am absolutely sure Sister, that if you did not want to give in to him you would not have given in, no question."

"Perhaps. My point is that he is exceptionally advanced for his age and I only hope it has not gotten him into trouble. You knew him too Father, as well as anyone...including, I think, his sister Maureen, another strange one don't you think?"

"All indications point to his having run away." Father answered then stroked his chin a moment while he thought about what he just said. "The reason I am here though Sister...my wanting to talk to you...is because I also have a feeling that there is something I don't know. There are too many loose ends, too many unanswered questions."

"Yes Father, the one that I find most troublesome is that he did not take any clothing with him. I can only explain this to myself in that he planned it; he knew wherever he would end up he would have a roof over his head, he would have food when he got hungry, and he'd have clothing. How else can you explain it?"

"Yes," Father answered, "Robert is not a scatter-brain, he is practical. He thinks things through and I wrestle trying to find an example of where he acted completely spur of the moment. I can't find one. He isn't a saint Sister, not by a long stretch, but he isn't foolish either."

Sister Kostich answered, "I am troubled by the other two Father, the boy Alex and his sister Maria. I have asked them separately and I have asked them when they were both together—

yesterday afternoon in fact—where they were after Benediction, and got nowhere. The little girl said she wanted to wait for her brother. The brother, he's another story.

"You mentioned earlier," she continued, "how you cannot get inside someone's head if they are adamant that you don't? Well I got the feeling they were adamant. The little girl uses her crying to disarm you; the boy answers 'yes' no matter what you ask him. 'What took you so long to get back from church Alex?' and his answer was, 'Yes Sister, we walked slowly Sister.' What kind of answer is that? I ask you, isn't he trying to hide something?"

"But what?" Father Mike shifted a little forward in his chair. "I've tried to put scenarios together and only come up with the fact that either both Alex and Maria, or more likely, only Alex at first, then he told Maria, knew Robert was never going to come back to the convent that night. They served Benediction together and I would not put it past Robert to make Alex his accomplice. Afterwards, while they were walking back to the convent, Alex told his sister all about what happened. It could explain why they didn't arrive back here until thirty minutes after the Benediction was over."

"I've thought of that too Father," Sister Kostich responded.

"But there is only one thing Sister," Father Mike continued as if he hadn't been interrupted. "You said Maria told you she was waiting for Alex. Why did Maria wait for Alex instead of coming back here with the other girls? Isn't that what the girls usually do?"

"Yes, for her to wait for her brother, and more importantly, to not be able to tell me why she wanted to wait for him; it is suspicious, I agree Father. Perhaps you should talk to them, hopefully you will get more out of them than I did."

"I've talked to Alex," Father Mike added, "and I walked away realizing there is more to the story. I will talk to Maria, and let's hope—since a few days have now passed—let's hope she can offer some insight."

Father Mike got up to leave and was walking toward the door. "Just a moment," Sister Kostich gently held his upper arm, "I've just thought of something. When I was talking to Maria I told her to stop that crying; then I got a little harsh with her, 'if you don't stop that crying and answer my questions I am going to get angry and you know what that means?' She stopped crying and only sniffled, so I said to her, 'you were waiting for Robert, weren't you, and you don't want to tell me the truth? If you were...' " Sister Kostich stopped talking and looked directly at Father Mike.

"Here is what I just realized: she gave a shiver; the girl just gave a shiver...you know, like when someone is terrified. I thought it was because I was being harsh with her but now I'm not so sure. I think it was my question; I think the question is what scared her." She thought for a moment then continued, "However, I don't know what to make of it."

"I see what you mean Sister, but if she knew Robert was going to run away why would she wait outside the church, and if she didn't know he was going to run away...." Father Mike's voice just trailed away.

"Perhaps I am reading too much into it," said Sister, "let's see what you get out of your talk with her."

✤ ✤ ✤

A few days after he spoke to Sister Kostich, Father Mike asked Maria to come to his office. She was naturally timid, cried easily, scared of her own shadow and trembled at the slightest provocation. She and Alex were very close, closer than any other siblings in the convent and seemed to think as one.

"Nothing to be alarmed at Maria, I would like to ask you a few questions, that's all. Would you mind sitting over here?" Father Mike chose a spot where he hoped she would feel more comfortable and not so threatened.

"I have some soda, would you like some?"

"No Father, thank you."

"Well, I'm going to have some; I'll pour an extra cup and leave it over here by you; so if you want, just help yourself, okay?"

"Yes Father."

"Maria, I'm just following up on Robert. First of all, were you surprised when you learned that he ran away? Do you find it curious that he disappeared so suddenly, or weren't you surprised?"

"I don't know anything about it Father."

"But were you surprised Maria?"

"I don't know Father."

"Did you like Robert; I mean did you and he get along okay?"

"Yes Father, he hung out with the boys and with Arlene Stern, so I didn't spend much time with him Father."

"Do you remember the last time you talked to him?"

"No Father, he hung out with the boys and with Arlene Stern, he didn't hang out with the younger girls. Father, can I go now? I'm scared and I don't feel well and I want my brother." She started to cry; a few sobs at first then real tears.

"Maria, I don't mean to upset you, I just want to know what happened to Robert. You are all my children and I love all of you. I'm responsible for you and don't want you to be sad or unhappy, that's all; please don't cry. Can you just take a deep breath and look at me? Here, here is a little sip of soda, you'll feel better."

Father handed her the cup of soda; Maria took it but didn't drink any, and reduced the crying to a few sobs.

"Maria, I have to ask you, when you waited outside the church for Alex, did you see anyone else around; any grownups, townies; anything strange?"

Sob, "No Father, I didn't see anyone. I was waiting for my brother so we could walk home together, I didn't see anyone."

"Did you see Robert...after the Benediction, that is?"

"No Father, I didn't see anyone. Please can I go now?"

"Sure Maria, but you said you were scared, can you tell me what you are scared of?"

A few more sobs were Maria's answer.

"Did Robert scare you?"

Maria shook her head very slightly, "no" all the while looking down.

"Okay Maria, thank you for coming in to talk to me. Perhaps, if you think of something unusual about that night could you come and see me again, bring your brother if that makes you feel more comfortable?"

"Yes Father."

"Maria, one more thing, we can keep this little conversation to ourselves, can't we? There is no need for anyone to know we talked...except Alex, of course. It that okay?"

"Yes Father."

✢ ✢ ✢

Father Mike had this strange feeling that something was not right. Maria said she saw no one when she came out of church; almost an impossibility considering how many people attended evening services, unless something caused her to be totally oblivious to what was going on around her that night.

For as many times that Alex and Robert served as altar boys together yet not to have said one word to each other meant one of two things. Either they had an argument about something and weren't talking to each other as a result, or there was something else between them. In either case, Father knew he had to get to the bottom of it.

He'd heard Maureen's and Robert's confession many times, as he did most of the kids, so it didn't take a Sherlock Holmes to put two and two together about what was going on. He had to be careful however, he was on dangerous ground not only as a priest but also as a guardian of these kids. He had to consider how Maureen would view any information he used. He could ruin her relationship with her God and her religion forever if she believed he had compromised her trust in confession. Similarly it could ruin her trust in him; in which case, he believed, she would truly be alone.

A few days after he spoke to Maria, Father Mike called Maureen into his office.

"Good morning Maureen, thank you for coming to see me. Here, have a seat, this will only take a few moments, I just want to talk to you a little, is that okay?

"Yes Father, it's okay."

"Maureen, I am concerned about you; I'd like to know how you are getting along, you know, without Robert. Sometimes it is hard all of a sudden to not have your brother around all the time. I was hoping that together we might piece together what happened; what made him want to run away and if he is in any sort of trouble we'd want to help him, wouldn't we?"

"Yes Father."

"Tell me Maureen, now that you've had some time to think about it, do you have any idea where he may have gone? You don't have to tell me if you don't want to...exactly where he may have gone, that is, I'm only interested in if you think you might know where he went. Do you Maureen, do you have any idea what happened to him?"

"No Father, I don't. It was just as sudden to me as it was to everyone else."

"Would you say Maureen, that you were very close, that he confided things to you that he might not tell one of the other boys or girls?"

"Not really Father, he was just my brother, that's all he was."

"Sr. Kostich told me that Robert didn't take anything with him, as far as she could tell, just the clothing he was wearing when he went to church that night. Have you been through his things, was there anything he might have taken other than the clothes he was wearing?"

"No Father, he didn't take anything; there was a shirt and some socks and some underwear in the cabinet next to his bed. His school books were in his cubbie; his tennis ball. There were two medals from school in his cubbie, too."

"Sr. Kostich told me she was most surprised he left his pocketknife on the cabinet next to his bed. Have you seen it?"

"Yes Father."

"I asked Sr. Kostich where he got it but she said she wasn't sure enough to say with certainty. Do you know were he got it, I understand it had 'Ruby Falls' printed on the side, am I correct?"

"Yes Father."

"Do you know where he got it Maureen?"

"Not for sure I don't Father."

"Please help me out Maureen, Sr. Kostich told me she thinks Robert got it from the janitor that used to work around the school yard; did Robert tell you that's who gave it to him?"

"Oh maybe he did Father, maybe he said he'd gotten it from the janitor, but I don't remember."

"Did Robert tell you anything about the janitor; why the janitor would give him that little pocketknife?"

"No Father."

"Maureen, I want you to be honest with me. You will not get in any trouble and whatever you say to me is like in confession, I am forbidden to tell anyone, but I must find out what happened to Robert; I don't want him to be hurt, you must help me, please.

"I know some of the things that go on, Maureen. When I walk by sometimes I see things but the kids don't see me. It's not that I sneak around, I am very quiet, that's all. I've seen boys putting their hands up girl's skirts and laughing and I've seen boys touching other boys in private parts. Do you think that janitor was playing around with Robert and in order to keep Robert from telling anyone he gave him that pocketknife?"

"I don't know Father. Robert told me he didn't like that janitor, he was mean and selfish. Robert told me that he told the janitor that if he didn't quit his job Robert would get him in trouble, big trouble. Then he quit. That's all I know Father."

"Do you remember when Robert told you all this Maureen? Was it recently? I know the janitor has been gone for a while now, but did Robert tell you while the janitor was still here or after he left?"

"I don't remember Father, it was before now but I don't remember when."

"And what did you say to Robert, Maureen, when he told you?"

"I didn't say anything Father. Robert showed me the pocketknife and told me the janitor gave it to him...for helping him or something. I don't remember."

"Okay Maureen, thank you for telling me. This is between you and me, isn't it? I won't tell anyone what we talked about if you don't want me to, okay?"

"Yes Father, thank you Father, can I go now Father?"

"Sure Maureen, and God bless you."

10

Mrs. Jean Reilly, whose husband Patrick was a judge, was Maria's teacher. Her best friend was Mrs. Rose McGinty. The Saturday after the disappearance, the two women were having a cup of coffee in the little bakery next to the butcher where they would go next to pick up meat for dinner.

They weren't really gossips but did find it necessary to let each other know what transpired during the week. Mrs. McGinty worked in City Hall and was full of local news. Mrs. Reilly was just telling Mrs. McGinty what she knew of the disappearance of the local boy—she was sure he didn't run away and was about the tell Mrs. McGinty exactly what happened.

"I know there is something more to this story than meets the eye Rose. You know that little orphan girl in my class I told you about, the crier who several months back said something that made me suspicious of what that janitor and the boy who disappeared might have been doing, and who got fired when I told my Patrick about it, and he brought it up to Father Mike?"

"Certainly I remember. It was all over City Hall; I don't know why they hired him in the first place. It wasn't the first time he was in trouble you know, he was caught peeking into windows by the police when someone called them. I don't remember his name though, but you'd think they would be more careful before they hire someone."

"Well I thought there was something fishy. That night when the boy disappeared I saw the three of them, the little girl

Maria, her older brother, and the boy himself, Robert Steeter his name is, standing outside the front of the church after service. Gladys and I were waiting for my Patrick to pick us up in his car. You know we usually walk home, Gladys and me...but he was at a meeting and said that since I have a key for the school door we should wait for him just inside the main entrance. He never wants me to get chilled. He was a few minutes late and we waited inside like he told me; we saw the three kids through the door of the school."

"What were they doing?"

"They weren't doing anything, just standing there, and the next minute they were gone. Then a car came down the street, I couldn't immediately tell that it was my Patrick because the headlights were in my eyes; but it was; he was driving real slowly. After I got into the car I looked toward the church again and I could swear that now there was only one of them. The other two were not there. It may have been Maria...it would have to have been Maria, wouldn't it? Anyway, I can't be absolutely sure which one it was; the headlights, you know how they affect your vision.

"It was very strange, but I didn't think anymore about it until after I heard that one of the boys had run away. Don't you think it is strange?"

"Have you told anyone? But, if he just ran away I suppose there is nothing to tell, is there?"

"There is more. For the past two days, since the *supposed disappearance,* the little girl Maria, the crier I call her, every time I even look at her in class she starts to cry, won't answer any questions that I ask the class; I think she is scared. After class I asked her what's the matter and I brought up what she had told me several months before about the janitor and that boy. She started crying even harder so I asked her if there was something more she wanted to tell me; asked her if she was afraid of something, but I couldn't get anything out of her."

"Did you bring up that you had seen them; seen them standing in front of the church?"

"No, I didn't. First of all I didn't think of it right away, then I didn't make any connection about the boy's disappearance—everyone was talking about him running away, so that's what I thought about it too."

"So now you are wondering? Right? What do you think is making the little girl, Maria you said her name is, so scared? Do you think there is a connection?"

"I sure do, I told Father Mike on Friday afternoon. I told him that I think he should call the police and tell them to arrest that janitor. He told me he couldn't ask the police to arrest him; there is no evidence that the janitor had anything to do with the disappearance; there was no evidence the janitor was even near the church on Wednesday night; that's what he said."

"Really!"

"Yes, I told him that I was suspicious and I would bring it up to my husband."

"Then what did Father say?"

"He told me to be careful about trying to make connections that may not be there. I think, Rose, he did not believe me about the janitor. You believe me, don't you?"

"Of course I believe you. Then did you tell Patrick and what did he say?"

"He repeated the same thing that I told him Father Mike had said when I told *him*. He told me to keep it to myself until any further evidence of foul play, that's how my Patrick put it, any 'evidence of foul play' shows up."

"Well, Mrs. Jean Reilly, I think you are on to something! I'll keep my eyes and ears open at City Hall and if I hear anything I'll let you know. Meanwhile, what are you going to do?"

"Strange, Patrick asked me the same thing. 'Keep it under your hat, in case something turns up,' he said, 'don't be accusing anyone of something that you are not sure of.' That's what he said, so I'd better do as he says. But, I thought you'd want to know, being in a position to hear things, you know, like where that janitor is now and stuff like that."

"Like I said, I'll keep my eyes and ears open. Are you finished with your coffee? We'd better get on with the shopping, I've got a lot to do today."

11

Eventually Alex and Maria, although they probably did not realize that their behavior changed, began keeping more and more to themselves. None of the others seemed to notice either; except of course Maureen. She liked Alex, liked being around him and was jealous that he spent so much time with his little sister. Finally, she decided to do something about it. She tiptoed to his bed and carefully slipped under the covers.

"Alex, it's me, Maureen. I need to talk to you, it's important," she whispered. It was an unusually dark night and rather late so no one was awake.

"What is it, make it quick, I don't want to get into any trouble with Sister."

"Are you mad at me, are you angry about something I did or what? What's the matter? It seems like you're mad; you never talk to me anymore, are you avoiding me? All of a sudden it seems you are spending all your time with your sister. Did I do something wrong?"

"No, of course not. I just want to be alone, that's all. There's nothing wrong. I just suppose…" and he trailed off in mid-sentence. "I've become very sad. I hate being here and I think about my mother and I miss her, that's all. Don't you miss your mother? Don't you miss your brother? Don't you think of what it would be like if you weren't in this place? No wonder your brother ran away. I wish I could run away but I don't have anyplace to go. I just want to be left alone, can't you understand that?"

"Do you think he ran away Alex, do you really? Where would he go, I don't know of anyplace he'd go? He can't just be wandering around; where would he sleep; where would he get food? I think of things like that and I don't have any answers. Father Mike thinks that janitor who worked here may have done something bad to Robert but he told me not to tell anyone. I'm telling you because I know you'll keep it to yourself and because I like you. You're my best friend. Do you think the janitor did something bad to Robert?"

"Why ask me? How should I know? I was just as surprised as everyone else that Robert ran away. But he was always cooking up something; maybe he cooked up running away, getting away from here, figured out where to go. That's probably what happened, you know how he was, he made up a plan and just ran away. Someday he will show up and let you know that he's all right, tell you all about it, that's what will happen."

"I'm not so sure. Don't you think he would have told me? Besides, he left his pocketknife here; he would never go anywhere without that pocketknife. You know how Robert always talked about it, how he told everyone that he got it from that janitor?"

"Did he tell you why the janitor gave it to him?

"No, he never said anything. Well, it isn't like he never said anything, he talked about him like he was his best friend or something, maybe even like a dad; told me a couple of things but that's all. I know Robert was weird but still, any time I asked him why the janitor gave him that pocketknife he would get mad and tell me to shut up and keep out of his business. That's being weird, isn't it?"

"Like I said, I don't know anything about it. He ran away, that's all. One of these days he may even come back, who knows? Now you better go, I don't want to get into any trouble, okay?"

"Sure, will you talk to me from now on?"

"Sure, just go now."

It took a few weeks, but gradually Alex and Maureen became fast friends again, spending a lot of their time together. The subject of Robert's disappearance rarely came up and if it did it was more in reference to something he had said or done before he "ran away." However, when the subject of Robert came up, Alex was forever on his guard, fearful he would slip and say something he would later regret.

Father Mike Monahan put Robert in the back of his mind too—at least from all outward appearances he did. Some of the kids, and in particular Alex and his sister Dolores, Kathleen Sprague and Arlene Stern were getting older and would soon have to find other accommodations. In the convent it did not work to have teen-agers; first of all with nuns and second without the guidance that comes from parents, real or foster.

It was difficult to tell who had it harder, the boys or the girls. For the boys, it seemed that what ever they were doing they got on the nerves of one or more nuns.

If they were outside playing, when they came in it was, "Go upstairs and wash up, I don't want to be smelling you all the time," or if put more nicely (???) "Cleanliness is next to Godliness, God does not want you praying to him when you smell and are dirty, and that means on the outside as well as on the inside, so go wash up and say a prayer that God will forgive you for all the sins you've committed today."

When the boys were inside they were too noisy, did not sit still, too much fighting, and if sitting together in a corner, it was, "God knows what you boys are talking about and if it is not to his liking he will punish you. Each of you, go say a prayer of forgiveness, right now or I'll get the stick."

Dolores and Maria were the easy ones to place. After a conversation between Father Mike and their dad, it was agreed when and where they would go. Maureen was also rather easy. Friends of Father Mike's parents were interested in being foster parents to Maureen. She was a pretty child, had nice manners and seemed quite bright. They figured it would be pleasant for everyone if she would live with them.

They lived in a small parish in Brooklyn, you could see lower Manhattan from their window, didn't have any children and the wife did not work so she was home during the day to devote full attention to Maureen. It seemed perfect and Maureen, after spending several weekends with them, confided to Alex that she was quite excited.

She told Alex details about her new *parents,* "—A little strange, but who isn't, especially compared to the inmates in this place," is how she put it to Alex. She was most excited about the accommodations: an apartment on the second floor on a street with a lot of trees; near a park; she saw many other boys and girls her age playing, and the best part of all was they had a little dog named Cozy, who loved Maureen as much as Maureen loved Cozy. She couldn't wait for the day she would leave the convent forever. And, she told Alex, "I can see all the tall buildings from my bedroom window, isn't that the best?"

It all happened rather quickly so it was agreed that Maureen and Alex would write to each other. There was no problem with this arrangement; never a thought that anyone would open another's mail, so they could converse with impunity.

In Maria's case, she was scheduled to leave a few months after Maureen. She would go live with her dad's sister, Aunt Catherine. I don't know about this arrangement. Although Aunt Catherine deeply loved her two nieces and young Alex, she was a spinster—had been now going on twenty-five years—and was rather set in her ways. To have a nine year old under the roof full time would be a challenge. However, it was agreed that Aunt Catherine would give it her best.

✦ ✦ ✦

Their uncle, Father John, was the Pastor at Saint Michael's Parish in Queens. It was a large parish, active and with many families. In this regard, there are two kinds of priest: the first is outgoing; deeply involved in his parishioners' lives as evidenced by being invited—and attending—their celebrations as well as their tribulations: significant birthdays such as twenty-one or sixty; fiftieth wedding anniversaries; baptisms...and the annual problem dates because he was invited to just about every house on the same day: First Communion and again for Confirmation.

Of course a priest who celebrates a Funeral Mass is always invited to the funeral breakfast that follows. Father John was a priest like this.

The second kind is more reserved than the first—he is there when needed or summoned; attends the sick either at home or in the hospital; comes if called during a family crisis—often to adjudicate an internal squabble; is invited to significant family occasions, but more to give his blessing than to participate in songs and laughter. There is a need for both kinds. Father Mike Monahan was more like the second kind.

Father John knew of a family, the Tully's. Rose and Joe had three girls; the oldest at this time was Katie, age seventeen; Linda, at fourteen one year younger than Alex's sister Dolores; and Patti, the youngest at twelve. Joe passed away about a year before and Rose was amenable to taking Dolores in as a foster child.

Dolores was a pretty, though serious child. She had very Irish features: big blue eyes and long eyelashes; smooth ivory colored skin; and wavy, auburn hair. She was alert, inquisitive and, for what Rose Tully needed—someone to help her with her girls—Dolores was mature for her age. Father John knew she would exert an authoritarian influence on the more rambunctious younger Tully girls. Katie, being older than Dolores by three years, had a job in a pet hospital after school and would soon be going away to college. Dolores seemed like a perfect solution and moved in. It worked well, and Dolores stayed until the time that all the girls married: Katie, Linda, Patty and, soon after Patty, Dolores herself.

The interesting case was Alex. His dad had a woman friend who lived in Manhattan on Sixty-Second Street and Second Avenue on the Upper East Side. It was an *elevator* building with a *doorman,* a far cry from the accommodations of the convent.

The three Fazio kids had been to the apartment on many occasions and always looked forward to their next time. You walked into a large room, and at the far end was a bay window with a seat underneath. This area was a step up from the main room, and contained the dining table that could easily fit the three kids as well as their dad and Rosita. Wow, what a change from the dreary convent—Alex and his sisters agreed! It was like a dream, and with the walls a trendy dark green it had the feeling of being on the cutting edge.

On the left side of the apartment was a doorway leading to a narrow hallway with a bedroom to the right and a bathroom to the left. On the right side was a narrow, yet very long kitchen.

On the weekends when the kids slept over, the cushions were taken off the sofa bed, put on the floor for Alex, while his two sisters slept on the foldout part.

What a pleasant time they all had! Rosita would cook a huge breakfast for everyone, they'd take baths and dress up so they could spend the day doing stuff: museums, walking along the East River, visiting Times Square, trips to the Statue of Liberty, the top of the Empire State Building and Alex's two favorites: St Patrick's Cathedral and the lobby of the News Building. The only bad part was that too often their dad was in Cleveland, working. It seemed the more different things they did in the city, the more they missed him.

Considering that Alex spent a good part of his life to date around the trappings of religion, it seemed strange that whenever they visited the Cathedral he got goose-bumps. Perhaps it was the height of the ceiling with the departed bishops' red hats hanging there. Perhaps it was, on a few rare occasions, usually Sunday

Mass, seeing Cardinal Spellman, one of the most famous persons in New York if not the world. Alex's father was just as exuberant when he was home and they visited St Patrick's; Alex being a young boy trying so hard to be a grown, up it all had a terrific impact on him.

The News Building was an entirely different matter. In the lobby was a huge globe sunk into the floor, and around it a myriad of clocks showing the time in different cities of the world. To a sheltered kid pretty much confined to Long Island, it—Manhattan—seemed like it was the entire world and Alex could not get enough of it.

Rosita must have been a saint! Alex's recollection of what she looked like is quite vivid. She was shorter, came up to his dad's shoulder, not heavy but not real skinny either. Alex thought she was one of the most beautiful women he had ever seen—not surprising after the recent women in his life. She *was* beautiful. Her striking face was surrounded by dark hair that was always perfectly groomed; and she was always dressed like she was ready to go to a party or, as he remembers his dad saying, "To visit Buckingham Palace." When she walked she took shorter, elegant, deliberate steps that accentuated her perfectly erect posture.

But she didn't work and that preyed on Alex. When he finally moved in, he first wondered why she didn't work—because everyone he knew worked—he couldn't explain why, but it made him nervous, bordering on scared. Perhaps he was afraid if anything happened to her his world would end, and he'd be off again, somewhere unknown, not be by his dad. He wondered where she went for a good part of every day and if she would return.

To make matters worse, during this time, his father traveled a lot for his job, spending several days a week, often over a weekend, away in Cleveland; so for much of the time Alex and Rosita were alone together. Alex loved Rosita, probably because she was like a mom; she was the nearest thing to his mother; she seemed to love him as well, like his mom would have. But she wasn't his mom; yet he never hesitated to do whatever she asked of him: neatly hang up his clothes, take out the garbage—actually a treat throwing it down the "incinerator" listening to it crash at the bottom—take the dishes from the table to the kitchen.

He watched her for long periods of time; he couldn't get enough. One day he asked Rosita about work. It was difficult to understand her explanation, but here is how it went...

"Rosita, how come you don't work? How can you have money if you don't work?" It confused him and it worried him.

"Well, Alex, I do work, sort of. My family has a department store back in Santiago, in Chile, and when the store makes money the people who work there send some of it to me."

"But I don't understand Rosita, why would they send you money if you don't work there? Why wouldn't they just keep it themselves?"

"That is just how it is. The people work for my family, which includes me, even when I am here in the United States. They are good people who work hard for the store so the store can make money. After my family pays them for working I get the rest. I am saying 'I', but really it is my family, my mother, my sister and my two brothers who all work there but also own the store which our father left to us when he died."

"I think I understand, but not exactly. The nuns would say you are taking advantage of people and they would say that's a sin." Alex was through and through a "convent" kid, brought up on parables of selfish Philistines!

"I know you are a good Christian; I certainly want you to go to heaven—my mom would like you; you'd be good friends," Alex said with a serious smile, "I'd be with you too; I'm going to heaven; I'll be with my mom and my dad—and my sisters are going to heaven too. We'd all be together, forever." Alex looked lovingly at Rosita.

Sometimes he wasn't as grown up as he might have thought.

"Alex, I love you too, but do not worry, Rosita is a good person and will not go to hell."

"How about you and my dad getting married? What will happen? Will we all live together, not here because it is too small, but maybe in a bigger apartment, after my dad is finished traveling...to Cleveland?"

"Well, we'll see. Your dad and I love each other like I love you, so we'll see won't we? But you don't have to worry, I will always take care of you, won't I?"

That night Alex thought about it and concluded to himself, "How could I be so lucky, God has been so good to me!" He felt comfort in these times when the three of them were together. It made him love his dad so much, even if he did miss his being away so often.

It occurred to Alex some time later, that Rosita and her family did indeed own a large department store in Santiago, and she was in New York as its buyer. That was where she went during the day; it was the reason for the catalogues of clothing, furniture, shoes, lamps, tools, pots and pans, that were strewn around the apartment.

His dad and Rosita never did get married. She just vanished out of sight. Alex has forgotten the detail about that event too. One day she announced she was going back to Chile, but never said anything about not returning. It quickly became evident that she was not.

Again, years later when Alex was old enough to put bits and pieces together, he figured that she was probably not able to get another visa. Perhaps her family rebelled at her enjoying New York. More important for Alex, there was never any suggestion of any disagreements between Rosita and his father, and the subject, if it did come up, his father adamantly refused to discuss it. No question, his father missed Rosita, but like father like son; he just put it out of his mind. Rosita was his father's "little toy bank."

12

During the time he stayed with Rosita, Alex went to the Catholic school a few blocks from the apartment and a few blocks from the East River. He quickly found that he could very easily play hooky from class. He would arrange for Maureen to skip classes as well; she'd take the train into Manhattan and together they'd wander about the Island.

Money wasn't a concern, since Rosita always made sure Alex had a few dollars—one wonders if she knew he was playing hooky. Early on, Alex had introduced her to Maureen—so he and Maureen would see movies, go to the Horn & Hardart Automat for a sandwich and still have enough to give her for the trip home and for the next visit. For Maureen, coins were a little harder to come by.

On days when Rosita was off on her buying trips, Alex would bring Maureen up to the apartment and before long they were at it. Though young, they added to what they already knew about life and put more to the test with what they saw when they passed the book stores on 7th Avenue. Though they were technically not permitted in the dirty bookstores, no one seemed to give them any notice. They were not allowed to purchase but they could certainly page through with impunity. Alex prepared himself for the inevitability of being caught by Rosita in the apartment, but it never happened—all the way through high school.

✦ ✦ ✦

Meanwhile, returning back to the time when Robert disappeared, and almost a year since, Mrs. Rose McGinty did not put it out of her mind. Almost daily, as she was working at City Hall, she kept her ears alerted to anything that would shed light on what her friend Mrs. Jean Reilly told her she saw that night, and how she was so sure the old janitor had something to do with the mystery.

In Rose's mind it was not if, but when, the case was broken wide open. City Hall housed the mayor's office, city clerks, the city engineer's office and the police department. The City Jail, referred to as "the lockup," was in a separate building just behind City Hall. Sure enough, it wasn't long and the old janitor was brought in to the lockup. He wasn't old at all, forty-two but looked a lot older. Rose felt it her duty to find an excuse to go "see" him. She wanted to find out for herself if he was the party behind the young boy's disappearance. She had no hesitation whatsoever in her ability to make that determination.

She had worked at City Hall for a good many years, so it was not considered unusual for her to walk over to the lockup—it only took having a few important looking papers in her hand—and there was her excuse! Normally she would spend a good portion of her day prattling anyway; kibitzing with other clerks, so it was no different when she found a reason to go to the lockup to gab with whomever was working the policeman's desk. She knew almost everyone who worked for the city, so not a problem to get a look at the janitor.

"What do you think?" she asked the policewoman who was at the desk this day, "is he the one who is responsible for that Holy Ghost boy, the one they say disappeared but my friend, you know Jean Reilly, don't you, Judge Reilly's wife, she thinks the man you have in lockup is responsible. There is a lot to the story you know, the young boy, Robert his name was..." and Rose looked around before she uttered the next words, "was 'abused' by that man, gave the boy a pocketknife to keep quiet, but then probably did away with him when the boy said he was going to tell Father Monahan. That's what Jean Reilly believes happened, and I think she is right, don't you think so?"

"Well, keep this to yourself," the policewoman whispered, "but he has been locked up before. This isn't the first time he was caught peeping into someone's window; and they've assigned Sergeant Arrondondo to his case; and of course you know, *he* is very, very good; nothing gets by him. You know who he is, of course, don't you?" The policewoman looked around to make sure no one else was in earshot before divulging this secret: "he was telling me that he is going to look into the Holy Ghost boy's case; maybe reopen it. He told me he was going to see Father Monahan and is probably there right now. 'We'll get to the bottom of this, don't you worry.' That's exactly what Sergeant Arrondondo said; and like I said, he's good."

✦ ✦ ✦

"I don't know what to make of it," Father Monahan was telling Sergeant Arrondondo. They were in the rectory, a nice, not very large, older house, located south of the church with the school in-between. The housekeeper poured a fresh cup of coffee for the two men who sat opposite each other. It was a little after noon and the sergeant had brought Father Monahan up to date with the arrest of the janitor—the visit was to try and get some additional information.

The sergeant re-opened the disappearance case mostly because Mrs. McGinty considered it her duty to bring up the connection to the chief of police who then passed the concern on to Arrondondo. She was on a mission, she admitted to anyone who asked. If her friend Mrs. Reilly thought there was foul play then there was definitely foul play. Period.

"But," Father Monahan was continuing to the sergeant, "somehow the idea that the boy just disappeared doesn't quite fit. He may have run away, that is not an impossibility, I could see how it could happen, but wouldn't his sister at least have heard something by now? Robert was clever, more clever than his age and a charmer; could easily have charmed his way into getting a ride somewhere: the city, upstate, get a job...with room and board, change his name. If you knew the boy you'd understand. It doesn't quite make sense in my mind though. Possible, but it doesn't make sense, if you know what I mean."

"Yes, I do," answered Sergeant Arrondondo, "you get that feeling that something doesn't quite fit. Let me ask you though, what do *you* think happened Father? Do you think the former janitor was involved in any way?"

"My first inkling that something didn't fit was that the boy Alex—he was also an altar boy—he and Robert served devotions the night Robert disappeared or ran away; whatever it was. I asked Alex if Robert said anything unusual to him during the evening, and Alex said that Robert didn't say anything. Didn't say anything is almost an impossibility, Robert never shut up; was always saying something; a nice kid and all; courteous to adults; you know the type; outgoing; sure of himself. It doesn't fit together. Do you know what I mean?"

"I think I know what you mean, I know the type of boy you are talking about too...but, you know, they can also be sneaky. Sometimes you find out they are trying to pull the wool over your eyes as they say, the charming ones; I don't know if they do it on purpose but they can mislead you so you don't know exactly what they are thinking. What did the other children say that you spoke to; was there anything enlightening from them?"

"Like I said Sergeant, it is difficult to make heads or tails out of what any of them said. The boy Alex is the most disturbing. I got the impression when talking to him that he was keeping something back. Also, you know, the timing has me worried."

"The timing, what do you mean by the timing?"

"The Benediction, where the two boys were serving that night and the little girl was in the congregation, it was over at about seven-forty-five, that is the usual time. I can't be absolutely sure because I did not look at my watch and if I glanced at the clock in the sacristy it didn't sink in, if you know what I mean. I may have looked at it but it didn't register. In any case, I am putting the time at seven forty-five. Let's say it took at most fifteen minutes for the two altar boys to put everything away—my guess is *that* is about what it *always* takes—that would make it eight o'clock.

"If the past is a guide you know, the boys are usually anxious to get out of there, back across the street to the convent; they tell me there was usually a bowl of cereal or some little treat the sisters put out for them, the altar boys and anyone who went to the church service. As you know, the church is right across the street from the convent, yet Alex and his sister did not arrive back at the convent until a little after eight-thirty, or so Sr. Kostich told me, and she is known for keeping tabs on who is in and who is out. The convent kids are her responsibility and she takes it all quite seriously."

"Did the boy Alex or his sister tell you where they were or what took them so long to walk across the street; I am assuming you also talked to the altar boy's sister, right?"

"Yes, I did. Well, that's the strange part. I couldn't get anything out of either of them. It was just, 'we walked slowly Father' or, 'I don't know Father.'"

"Would it help if I talked to them? As you know, a policeman can sometimes get things out of folks; the uniform, I think, has a lot to do with it."

"I think you should Sergeant. They don't live at the convent any longer, but I'm sure you already know that. I am correct, am I not?"

"Yes," the sergeant murmured, nodded, took another sip of his coffee. He was listening intently.

"Gone about a year now," the priest continued, "but I want to get to the bottom of this too, as I know you do. Somehow I feel the boy did not run away. Perhaps enticed to go with someone, somehow fooled into going with somebody, I don't know exactly what I am trying to say but I just don't feel like this picture is in focus. Know what I mean?"

"Yes," answered Sergeant Arrondondo, "I'm glad you agree that I should talk to them. I *had* planned to talk to Sr. Kostich also; to clear it with her, but first I wanted to make sure you agree. With Sister's help I'll get in touch with the children's guardians and arrange a time and a place to talk to the two of them. I am thinking separately at first and then together. I have one more thing Father, two actually. The first is the boy Robert's sister, the name is Maureen, right"

"Yes, Maureen," Father reacted, "as you may know, she is no longer at the convent either...in a foster home, but it will be no problem. If you want to see her, I think it best if you work with Sr. Kostich on that one as well; it is more her responsibility than mine and I am sure she will be absolutely willing to do anything you need. She'll put you in contact with her, if that is okay? What is the second thing?"

"Yes of course, the second thing. But first," Sergeant Arrondondo said, "I have another question about Maureen. You talked to her right after her brother disappeared I'm sure, was there anything she may have said? Often, as time goes by you recollect something that you didn't think important at the time. That's what I'd like to know, that's what I'm wondering. Is there anything she said, maybe the way she said it or the way she acted...now that you've had time to think more about it?

"You know," the sergeant continued to try to explain what it was he wanted to know, "it takes a while for it to sink in that your brother is no longer around, it must have affected her somehow, isn't that right? Perhaps something as simple as a slight movement of her eyes, her head...at a particular time when his name came up...that after a while you recall, '*yes, that gave me an insight into what she knows or how she feels'* —a clue that she knows something she does not want to talk about—something of that nature?"

91

"Well Sergeant, we did talk. I am not sure what to think. They were an interesting two kids, Maureen and Robert; they are orphans; both parents are deceased, orphaned as infants, but they never seemed to be affected by it in any way. They are like free spirits, if you know what I mean, brother and sister but not brother and sister, almost more like acquaintances or casual friends.

"It *is* hard to explain. And who's to know what goes on in the heads of youngsters who have no parents. Both parents are dead; they probably do not remember anything about them. The only thing they know is the orphanage; the nuns who take care of them, and they do a good job; try hard; but they are not parents.

"But to answer your question Sergeant, the sister Maureen never showed any emotion whatsoever; it is like she didn't care that he was gone. Well, didn't care may be too strong, perhaps not outwardly concerned may be more like what I mean. I find it difficult to explain and I don't understand her behavior myself. I found it very strange, I still do.

"The nuns love all the kids they take care of," Father continued to clarify, "but it is, frankly, no substitute for parents. Perhaps that explains her behavior—or lack of it, emotion that is. Can you understand what I am trying to tell you?"

"I think I understand Father, but how can any of us really know what goes on in youngsters—needless to say, youngsters who have lost their parents. I suppose they quickly learn that they themselves are the only thing that they have and, I suppose, become vulnerable to anyone who shows them attention. That is, I think, the problem I am wrestling with. Getting back to the janitor, did he show the boy any attention, was he susceptible or easily influenced by him?"

"Sergeant Arrondondo," Father Monahan said with earnest, "I don't know. Alex and Maria were afraid of something, holding something back, of that I am certain.

"I think that if anyone will get to the bottom of this, you will. I commend you on your understanding of children and of the darker side of life itself. We as priests also see, I mean mostly hear about, the trials people have in life, but we don't have to make decisions based on it. We only have to be compassionate, give comfort and, in some ways foster forgiveness along with the penance we prescribe; and I suppose that is useful too. What you do may have more dire consequences. Sergeant, you said you had a second point?"

"Yes Father, I wanted to ask you," the sergeant wiped his forehead with his forearm, more to indicate he was thinking than that he was sweating, "you know Judge Reilly and his wife Rose I am sure, well she was at the Benediction and as a matter of fact supports your time frame. She waited inside the main door of the school for Judge Reilly to pick her up in his car. I'm not telling you something you already know, am I Father?"

"Go on Sergeant, I did hear something but I'd like to hear what you've got."

"She said at a little before eight o'clock, Rose Reilly that is, she said she saw three kids in front of the church. She has the little girl in her class, says she has been acting strangely, but she saw them, turned her attention to see if the car coming down the street was the judge's, and when she looked back the kids were gone; 'disappeared' is how she put it.

"She said she didn't think much about it, thought it was strange at the time, but when she got into the car she began talking to the judge and never thought of it again, not until she heard that the boy ran away. 'Next day'—I think she said next day—'he might have been one of the kids I saw, just before he ran away...with the other two,' is how she put it to me yesterday when I talked to her."

"Well Sergeant, I had heard that Mrs. Reilly said she saw three children but her story doesn't fit with what Alex and Maria both told me. Alex told me he left the sacristy before Robert who, he said, stayed behind to finish putting things away. I remember very clearly that he said he and his sister then walked to the convent together, just the two of them. Sister Kostich confirmed that just the two of them came back together."

"So," Sergeant Arrondondo took over, "either Mrs. Reilly is mistaken about whom she saw or perhaps she saw Alex and Maria together and a third, not involved, who also happened to be standing nearby...and who could that have been? Otherwise, why would Alex say it was just the two of them if Robert wasn't still in the church? Someone is mistaken. Alex wouldn't lie, would he? What reason would he have to lie?"

Father Monahan screwed up his face in thought before answering this question. "Not a lie perhaps; it could be they knew Robert was going to run away, and were afraid if they told they would get into trouble, or perhaps something with the janitor."

Father Mike became disconcerted, deep in thought, trying to work out an explanation for all that the sergeant just told him.

"There is something very wrong here," he continued. "I don't understand; Mrs. Reilly must be mistaken; perhaps she saw some other kid and mistook him for Robert. Sure, I'll bet that is the explanation.

"Well Sergeant, if the boy Alex and his sister didn't get back to the convent until after eight-thirty, that leaves a question; two questions, I might add. How could they just vanish as Mrs. Reilly's maintains, and where did the brother and sister spend a half hour or so before returning to the convent?"

"Yes Father, there are some questions and I agree, there is something strange in this case. Don't worry though, we'll get to the bottom of it before you know it. Thanks for your time," Sergeant Arrondondo said as he shook Father Monahan's hand and left.

13

The old janitor was sentenced to prison for two years and six months. Judge Reilly found him guilty of being a peeping tom; it was his second offense and although Judge Reilly was a good man, he was human and if Rose, who was a good woman, thought the old janitor had something to do with the orphan boy's disappearance, then the maximum sentence would keep another dangerous person off the streets, wouldn't it?

There was more confirmation other than just Rose's hunch. Sergeant Arrondondo interrogated the old janitor who admitted he worked at Holy Ghost Parish as a janitor, admitted he knew the boy Robert, admitted he gave him the pocketknife, but was adamant that there was nothing erotic between them.

Sergeant Arrondondo later told his chief that he was sure the old janitor was lying because he was clever and way too familiar with the penalty for such activity with a minor—that was clear from the interrogation—and furthermore, he told the chief, it came out that the old janitor knew a whole lot, way too much, about the boy's personal life and his habits: that he was an altar boy, that he had a sister Maureen (even knew her name) and, most important, about the goings-on, "if you know what I mean," is how the sergeant put it, "between the boy Robert, his sister, and the other kids at the orphanage."

Unfortunately for the sergeant however, he couldn't get even a trace of a confession, so the only thing left to establish any guilt for something "troubling" was the fact that the old janitor, (remember, he was only forty-two years old but his moniker stuck like dried egg) could not remember where he was the night of the disappearance; he couldn't even remember where he was living, or working, or even if he *was* working.

All in all he convinced Sergeant Arrondondo, the chief of police and, as a result, Judge Reilly that guilt was written all over him, and conveniently the peeping tom offense would get him off the street and where everyone could keep and eye on him while the investigation continued.

There was one more thing however, that Sergeant Arrondondo could not get out of his mind. The old janitor seemed to know—alluding to actually—the fact that Robert had plans to do something naughty to both Alex and his little sister. As much as he tried though, Sergeant Arrondondo could not get anything specific. The old janitor was very cautious and it was only because the interrogation took many hours that there were several tiny slips that resulted in only the hint.

More specifically, it came out that he knew that both Robert and Alex were the altar boys serving the Benediction Service the night in question, but then again he could have read about that in the newspapers, heard it in the course of the gossip about the disappearance, could have known about it in any number of ways. But the fact that the old janitor couldn't remember if he was even in the same town, yet remembered who served at devotions, made it another note on the suspicion scale. Arrondondo's strategy was to let it all percolate and pick up on it at a later date.

In any case, for the time being the janitor was safely in the county jail.

There was one more clue in the case, but at the time it didn't seem like much of a clue. When Arrondondo squeezed through the space between the church and wall which bordered the street, he saw all the junk as well as the doorstep but saw no reason, other than his large bulk, to go further—beyond the very narrow space into the left quadrant formed by the curved wall, so he didn't spot the entrance to underneath the sacristy which was on the far side of the second doorstep, and which, from where he was peering over the two-foot high barrier, was not visible.

What did perk up the sergeant's curiosity however was the presence of eight or so cigarette filters; the ones made of a cotton-type material that did not disintegrate very quickly and looked to have been there a long time. They could just as easily have been thrown over the wall by town-kids sneaking a smoke behind the bushes, but what struck the sergeant as strange was the lack of any fresh ones.

"That doesn't fit," he spoke out loud to no one in particular as he shrugged and wrote in his ever-present book.

He was a professional and told himself frequently that it was only a question of time and he would solve this disappearance. He figured he'd even find the boy, maybe the worse for wear, but he'd find him.

"I hope," he murmured to no one in particular.

.

BOOK TWO

Nineteen Seventy-four

14

"Alex, what time do you think you'll be home on Thursday?" Sara called into the bedroom where Alex was packing for his next trip. This one was to NYC...again. He worked for an Illinois software engineering firm; now a senior executive with responsibility for larger accounts such as banks, financial institutions, and government installations. His job took him out-of-town easily three times a month.

Though he, Sara, and their two kids lived just outside of Chicago, he had to visit New York City frequently. He liked going to NY, it was a chance to see Maureen again.

Maureen was married to a nice enough man: Tom. They also had two kids, two girls to go with Alex and Sara's two boys. The four kids paired up in age and often, lying in bed, Alex and Maureen would fantasize about how their kids would eventually marry each other. It was definitely a fantasy because there seemed no conceivable way they would ever meet, unless by a long-shot chance. The boys would more than likely want to go to college in the Midwest, the girls out East. The four of them were homebodies.

You'd think it strange that Alex and Maureen would discuss things like their kids meeting and their marrying each other all the while they were fornicating their brains out under a canopy built of adultery. They'd been at it for years: in the convent; at high school; during Christmas and college spring breaks; while Alex was on leave from his stint in the army; during each of their engagements; the day before each of them got married—they went to each other's weddings and knew, or more accurately met, each other's spouse—and as much as they could while working, raising kids and getting older, a little more hefty, and beginning to turn gray.

What did they talk about? One evening in particular would act like the stage-set of the typical conversational scene.

Tonight they were at one of their favorite restaurants in the big city: Il Vagabondo, noted for their Italian food and their unique bocce ball court inside the restaurant.

The waiters were one-of-a-kind too. After looking through the menu, you would of course order; but if the waiter didn't think you ordered the right thing he would tell you matter-of-factly, "No. No. No, you are having the veal piccata because it is outstanding and I know what you want," and you'd get the veal. The waiters knew Alex and Maureen as frequent patrons and thought they were another "ideal couple," vicariously enjoying them being very much in amore.

They weren't in love, not as we think of it; they were joined to each other by history, experience, circumstance, individual needs, secrets, and an unexplainable bond built during their life up to this point. No, there was no question about it, they weren't in love.

"Sometimes I get a kick when I talk with you about our past," began Alex, "the convent, the nuns, the crazy kids, the stupid things we did—alone and together—I think we were *good* kids, don't you? I wouldn't change a thing in my life. Sure, my mother died and you had no parents, but life was an event, wasn't it? I know you agree because this isn't the first time we've discussed it. We grew up quickly; did we miss a lot? I don't know, but then again we experienced a lot that many kids don't have a chance to."

"Of course I agree Alex. Every time I think of the silly little things we did I get either a huge grin or a big frown or a pissy face. I even remember our first time. You were such a little boy. I'd been doing it with Robert for a long time. It wasn't that I liked you or you stimulated me or anything, I just figured you had equipment that worked. None of the other boys were tempting at all. I even thought about doing it with a girl but I didn't like any of them. Kathleen Sprague perhaps, because she was a little slow and wouldn't know what was going on anyway. That would have been exciting. But in the end I liked boys, you. I still like you, self-interestedly, of course. Do you think you will always want me around? Should I be worried?"

"Sure. I am going to dump you for my wife! Wouldn't that be a hoot!

"Maurie," Alex's oft used nickname for Maureen, which of course she hated and told him so whenever he used it, but he persisted, he liked it when she pursed her lips in an *I'll get even look*—"you are a part of me, like taking a shower, or my deodorant; we need each other. Do you ever feel guilty? You know don't you, they call what we are doing adultery—something I am sure you are familiar with. You are, aren't you?"

"Adultery, smart-ass? Did my brother and I commit incest? Don't you think it depends on whose viewpoint? We didn't have parents—so were we really brother and sister just because we were produced at the same factory? You and I—is it adultery just because we have always fucked; like we've been doing since little kids; not having the slightest idea which way was up?

105

"It depends on how you see it, right? The entire convent thing was to get by. Robert knew that, he and I talked about it...not in adult talk but in kid talk. He had dreams, probably different than yours. You probably dreamed of the day you'd get out; expelled more likely, be with your dad, your sisters, live in a little flat in the city, maybe a little house out on the Island.

"Robert didn't think like that," she continued. "He thought of the moment. He didn't like being in the convent or not being in the convent. He was there, that's all...he lived for the moment, just like the Italian expression says: *Vivere per il momento*. He did like older people though, and wanted to please them. He liked being with older people. He'd do anything an older person wanted. He really liked the old janitor, I know—one day he told me that he wished he was his dad."

"Did Robert ever tell you any more; go into detail about anything they did, you know, have sex or stuff?"

"No, not in detail, that was not how Robert was. He was for the moment, like I said. Even when he and I were doing it, it didn't mean anything to him. He told me it made no difference, boy or girl, young, old, made no difference. 'What does it matter,' he'd say. I don't think that was strange...for him I mean. For you, for my husband Tom, very strange, weird and kind of like incestuous!" Maureen gave a slight chuckle and lightly slapped Alex's hand, which was resting near the middle of the table.

"Do you miss him?" Alex asked, "Where do you think he went?"

"I'm not sure—to either question. Sometimes I think he was such a self-possessed individual that it made no difference to him where he was or what anyone thought. I suspect he never gave the slightest thought that anyone would even miss him. Why would they? That's what he'd think, why would they?

"Like I said, he didn't think of me as his sister and I didn't think of him as my brother so why would he tell me where he was going? Sometimes, because of how he talked about that old janitor, I think he went off with him. Then sometimes I don't think so. Maybe the janitor was afraid Robert would tell on him and did him in!"

"I know the old guy got fired from the church," Alex added, "because someone told one of the teachers that Robert and the janitor were doing sex stuff. Did he ever tell you who snitched?"

"Robert would maybe have told me if he knew who it was, but I don't know..." Maureen looked at Alex, "or maybe he would have beat the crap out of whoever it was...if he knew, but he didn't."

"But he took off so suddenly," Alex interjected, "I always wonder about that. It doesn't seem like he'd just take off. On the other hand, like you said, he wouldn't announce it, would he? He wouldn't leave a note to Sister Kostich or anything, so maybe that's the way it was. Off!"

At this point this particular night, the waiter delivered their dinner and a quiet time followed with Maureen and Alex deep in thought. Alex however, was always carefully guarded to not divulge what happened on the night of the disappearance. He and his younger sister Maria made a pact, unspoken as it was, but it was never broken.

15

Maureen and Tom lived just a few blocks from where Maureen had grown up with her foster parents. Tom worked for the Borough of Brooklyn: streets and sanitation chief engineer. They met at NYU and Tom fell in love with Maureen. If truth be told, Maureen didn't love Tom; she didn't love anyone. Love was not a part of her makeup.

She and Tom were happy. Maureen didn't 'not' love him—they were best friends; had their two girls that were the delight of Maureen's life but they could have been her sisters, her girlfriends, other folk's kids that Maureen happened to like a lot...love was not in Maureen. She didn't love Alex, either.

Maureen had an inkling that Tom knew about Alex, his name never came up and only once did Tom touch on the subject. They were on vacation. Each summer they looked for a little cottage to rent for a week somewhere on the ocean and this year it was the Jersey shore. The girls were around six years old and off playing at the ocean's edge while Tom and Maureen sat under an umbrella having the typical lazy, sunny day at the beach.

Alex had been in town the previous week and Maureen gave her usual excuse that she would go shopping in Manhattan, go to the theater that night, and stay over. And why not, Tom didn't like to go shopping in Manhattan, didn't like going to the theater, and wasn't particularly excited about staying at a New York hotel, no matter how nice Maureen said they were. Besides, he enjoyed the special time this gave him to be alone with his girls—which he didn't often get a chance to do.

While sitting on the beach Tom asked about the trip. With nothing but time while sitting under the umbrella he asked a lot of detail, which he didn't usually get into. He'd usually dismiss the details of her "shopping trip"—by asking a general question, how was your trip? —which left Maureen a wide swatch, six lanes wide, from which to choose. This time however, Tom wanted to know: what stores did you shop at, visit any museums, was the play a drama or a musical, what was the hotel like, what time did you get home from the theater, where did you have dinner, what did you have, don't you mind eating by yourself, did you have wine and how was it, did you buy anything?

It went on and on. Of course it was Tom's innocent, idle chatter, sitting on the beach, nothing else to do or talk about; watch the girls play in the sand. The only problem was that Maureen found it difficult to make up a whole bunch of lies and carefully keep them in order. Besides, she usually bought him a little gift, but this time she forgot.

Finally she got, as she was fond to say of herself, pissy. Tom of course couldn't understand why all of a sudden she didn't want to talk about it any more. To him Manhattan was her day out, her vacation from him, the kids, the house. Maureen didn't work so Tom looked at her little trips to the city once or twice a month as her way of maintaining sanity. He didn't mind, and actually rather liked the idea that she could get away from her daily routine catering to husband, kids and dog; stimulate her mind and get a little time to herself.

Their neighbors were nice enough. Separately and together they saw a few of them frequently but, as Tom saw it, spending time with them wasn't the same as going to the Big Apple; in the midst of where everything important was happening; a chance for Maureen to refresh herself. He liked that she was informed about what was going on in the world. He liked that she had a range of interests which, he believed, was good for the kids, too. Tom had his personal time as well; liked playing golf in the warmer weather and when there was snow, liked to go up to Vermont for a weekend of skiing with a few of his guy friends. Even-steven he called it.

"Am I asking too many questions?" he gave a bewildered look at Maureen and asked in what he thought was a kidding tone. "Did you go to meet your boyfriend and you are keeping him from me," he added, but Maureen was not amused. Tom noticed the look he got, her almost imperceptible freeze, and he immediately returned a look—a look without blinking—that lasted only two seconds.

Two seconds staring into someone's eyes however, is a long, long time. It is enough to penetrate their inner most thoughts and even if you can't completely decipher them you can get the sense of them. And, in this two seconds Tom knew he had stumbled on something he would be sorry that he did.

To confirm his chariness all conversation ended. Maureen picked up her book and resumed reading some mystery novel. Tom watched the girls and tried hopelessly to think of something else, anything: work, his gaining weight, jerking off, sea turtles, anything. But he knew—not who, but whom.

Tom desperately tried to put that afternoon out of his mind and he did. Actually he came to terms with it and eventually believed, rightfully so, that whomever Maureen was seeing, "if it is the same person each time," Tom wondered out loud at one point while driving out to Montauk Point for a meeting, "which would be better," he asked himself, "the same guy or any Joe she picks up?

"She's still attractive," he knew, "she's pretty sexy; likes to get it on. She was obviously experienced when I met her; I had no idea people did the things she did as easily and naturally as holding hands. Guys talk about their sex fantasies but Maureen could give them a lesson or two."

Although he did not really want to find out any details of what he knew was fact, it was impossible to not analyze whatever Maureen said, how she said it and how she looked; and eventually he begin to see the full picture. He did not remember the first time he found out the name: Alex. Soon after he learned where he was from: Chicago. Then that he was married and had two kids: boys. Then that his wife did not suspect anything: okay...?

"And if I do go to the city to meet someone," Maureen confirmed one day as the full picture unfolded, "so what? We aren't in love. We are different than that. I don't know if and how many other people are like Alex and me and I don't care. At the convent we were infused with needs; perhaps we were born with them but I don't think so. Unless you are an orphan, or put into the kind of institution we were in I don't know if you can understand, so don't try.

"Do we feel like we're unique or do we feel sorry for ourselves," Maureen continued, "Do I feel a need to go to confession, of course not. Things are the way they are. Let's leave it at that."

Afterwards there were no more secrets that Tom was interested in knowing. He became resigned to the situation, perhaps even began to understand it. At first he was jealous, then pissed off, and finally he understood...at least so that things returned to normal. He loved Maureen and she did not change one iota in her relationship to him. In some ways, Tom began to appreciate the mysterious Alex. It was all like a transcendental bond between the three of them. Strangely enough, it was several years later that it came out that Tom had actually met Alex. He had been to their wedding and Alex was introduced to Tom along with some others as one of Maureen's friends.

16

Alex had no such problem with Sara. Sara was born in Chicago, and like her husband, came from a very close Italian/Irish family. Sara's mother was Italian and her father was Irish, just the reverse of Alex's parents, and had none of the friction that Alex's dad shared with his Irish sister-in-law Anna.

Neither side of Sara's family was large; each parent had one sibling so perhaps there were not enough of them to get deeply into the Northern versus Southern European heritage issues. Her father had a brother and her mother had a sister and now they all lived within a few miles of each other out in the suburbs west of Chicago.

Sara, however, was the youngest of three children and took it upon herself to care for her father who was older but still quite spry; wanting to go to any event that was free—both he and Sara enjoyed their outings together.

Her boys were in grade school, which gave Gramps and Sara the morning and early afternoon to enjoy their outing. If it wasn't an outing, Sara was visiting her sister or sister-in-law. Sara had a cleaning lady twice a week who would double as sitter if she and Gramps were not going to be home by the time the boys got out of school.

Frankly, she didn't have that much time for Alex. Since he traveled so often, and they both agreed that there was nothing interesting about his work to talk about—she saw it as technical stuff that made her mind wander—the only things left were the kids, what her sister and sister-in-law were up to, so an automatic "how was your trip," was all that was said, neither one looking for a response other than "fine."

If you saw Sara walking down the street, chances are you would take a second look—women as well as men did so.

Women looked at Sara because she had a certain knack for dressing well. It wasn't that she bought expensive clothing; she inherited the propensity often attributed to Italian ancestry to be able to put pieces of clothing together with "style."

She tended to purchase clothing for herself and her boys that was good quality; they didn't have a lot of clothing but what they did have could be mixed and matched with the end result of always looking smart.

Her looks accentuated her sense of style and fit the rest of her to perfection. Her face was round and if you looked closely she had faint freckles that gave her skin a smooth and girlish texture. She would never be a "cover girl" in terms of beauty, but was easy to look at and had a magnetism that helped her features noticeably stand out. She was more on the taller side by just a little so that when she stood next to most of her girlfriends she was usually the tallest, but was shorter than all but the shortest men.

Her hair was cut short and was a satiny blond: natural. Perhaps the thing you noticed most were her eyeglasses that perfectly matched the color of her eyes and the shape of her face, so that you immediately got a sense of her personality. They were black, and fortunately the lenses were not so strong that there was the distortion of the eyes you sometimes see in people who have to wear glasses.

More than one of her acquaintances, when describing Sara, mentioned that she was one of a handful of people who looked better in glasses than without. There was no question—they described her correctly.

Also, Sara favored darker clothing, which gave her a sexy appearance but at the same time there was no difficulty sensing that here was a woman who was no-nonsense; if one thought she might be "easy" they'd be greatly mistaken. When she talked she did not shy away from sounding earthy—she did not hesitate to tell it like it was in earthy tones, but that was probably more from her Chicago up-bringing and words learned from her deceased mother, who used them with impunity, because she was born in Italy and never really got the English definition of the colorful words that slipped off her tongue.

Sara traveled to New York for college and that's where she met Alex. She wanted to be a physical therapist and got a job right after graduation while Alex went into the army for two years. They moved back to Illinois, she got pregnant and Alex was lucky to have a nice-paying job so she could "retire" and raise her all-important kids. So, to repeat, she had no time left for Alex and didn't give any thought whatsoever to what he did when he was away.

Alex, on the other hand, was always on guard and became adept at rapidly and subtly changing the subject if—when they were with friends—the subject of his trips came up. He formulated the same repertoire of responses: "It is always nice to get to NYC; my clients take me to nice restaurants and my company puts me up in nice hotels so I don't mind the trip. Also, my secretary sets up one meeting after another so by the time I get back to my room after working all day I am exhausted." End of story.

Or...

"The strangest thing happened while I was in Manhattan one time. I ran into an old buddy of mine that I went to college with, staying at the same hotel. He now lives in Phoenix and was, like me, in New York on business. Sara knows him too, (it happened once and Alex kept repeating the basic story as the need arose) and we did such and such. We renewed our acquaintance and now talk a few times a month by phone, and he has since invited Sara and me to visit Phoenix, says we'll love it. Funny isn't it, how you renew your old acquaintances just by happenstance; literally bumping into someone you went to college with...."

Boring!

In the final analysis, Sara didn't care. She didn't care because she didn't consider the possibility that Alex was and had been seeing someone else for most of his lifetime. It was always in the back of Alex's mind though, that she'd find out. If the truth ever came out, regardless of how it came out, neither Alex nor anyone else for that matter would ever be able to explain it to her—she would be devastated.

Sara lived in a sheltered world, didn't read trashy novels, hardly watched T.V., her world was home, children, sister, relatives and mostly Gramps. Even visiting her brother, Sara didn't have much in common with him. Guy talk was just not in her with him or with Alex.

She thought about this on occasion and wondered when the boys grew to young adults how she would handle it; "I'll just cut the cord until they come begging me for advice," she'd murmur if she thought about it while brushing her hair or cooking dinner.

Alex could not remember any specific, extended conversation with Sara about his youth; either his time right after his mother's death when he lived with his Aunt Margaret, anything leading up to his being sent to the convent; or his time living with Rosita in New York. Between Sara and him time began in college.

It wasn't that she was self-centered, shallow or would not be interested; it never seemed to matter between them. And, you could say, why should it. They, especially Sara, lived now and in the future, as she would maintain: what is over is over. Right! Except...Alex knew...if she ever found out about Maureen.

17

Sara was looking through a magazine when the phone rang. She looked at the clock on the mantelpiece: ten after nine. She was waiting for her sister Beth who just called to say she was just leaving to pick her up and would be there in a few minutes. They planned to spend the morning shopping, lunch, then hopefully, back before the boys got home from school.

"Now who could that be?" as she went into the kitchen to answer the phone.

"Hello," Sara said into the mouthpiece.

"Good morning, this is Sergeant Arrondondo calling from New York, may I speak to Alex Fazio, please?"

"He's not here right now, he's at his office. This is his wife. Is there something I can help you with?"

"I just have a few questions to ask about something that happened a long time ago. Can you give me the number where he can be reached?"

"Sure, do you have your pencil ready?" and Sara gave the sergeant Alex's office number.

The sergeant took notice. It was unusual for a wife to not get apprehensive whenever he called their home asking for their husband...the first thing they asked was, "Is there something wrong?" or something similar. Sara seemed totally un-concerned.

"Strange," he thought.

Sergeant Arrondondo called the number Sara gave him; a receptionist answered; she transferred the call and after a short wait Alex answered. Arrondondo told him why he wanted to meet.

"We have arrested a person of interest in the disappearance of Robert Steeter back when you were in boarding school, and would like to have you review some evidence that has surfaced."

"What kind of evidence, and why me?" Alex answered.

"I don't want to go into it over the phone; we need to meet in person. I am prepared to come to Chicago if you will schedule a convenient time within the next few weeks," the sergeant answered.

Alex noticed the absence of "please," so it had to be serious.

"Well," he told the sergeant, "I will be in New York at the beginning of next week; I'm leaving here Tuesday evening and could meet you early Wednesday morning. I have an appointment at ten-thirty in mid-town. Does that work for you?"

"Yes, that is perfect. I will meet you at your hotel at eight in the morning and it should not take more than a half hour. Is that too early?"

"No, that's perfect." Alex gave Sergeant Arrondondo the name of the hotel and arranged to phone him Tuesday afternoon to confirm, just before boarding the airplane.

✦ ✦ ✦

Sara's first thought was that since the policeman was from New York he was calling about something to do with Maria...or with Maria and her husband Eric; after all, they lived in New York and she didn't. They talked by phone, but did not see each other that much. Actually, Sara mused with a mumble, "He said a long time ago and come to think of it, I really don't know Eric *that* well, perhaps he's in some sort of trouble from his past. Oh well, we'll see." She dismissed it from her mind.

As far as anything that had to do with the convent, Sara was clueless. When their oldest boy was four they took a vacation out east and on the way to the tip of Long Island they went past Holy Ghost Parish and Convent. They parked the car and got out and Alex told her, as he pointed out the various landmarks, about some of the kids, and that he had no idea where any of them were but certainly nothing about the disappearance of Robert.

Afterwards, they visited Maria and Eric who lived on the northern side of Long Island. Of course Alex and Maria talked frequently on the phone, and each time he traveled to New York. Furthermore, there were several occasions when Maria and Eric found themselves in Chicago for one reason or another; then the two couples would have dinner downtown—where the out-of-towners preferred to stay. So...although they were all related, and got along well enough, they were not necessarily best friends.

Because Maria lived in New York and Sara in Chicago there was not a lot they had in common with each other. Maria and Eric had no children so her outlook could not have been more different than Sara's. They liked to travel outside the United States, Sara didn't. Eric's hobby was restoring old cars which Sara

123

could not understand sinking all that money then not wanting to drive it, and Maria liked acting in the local theater and serving on the village council which Sara found commendable but it wouldn't be for her.

For Maria and Eric it is twenty miles from Huntington to Holy Ghost Parish and only once did they have the occasion to be near enough to visit; they drove around the block, that's all. Maria did not want to stop and get out of the car and did not want to talk much about her time there.

She felt she had a problem with the past but it was her problem, and she never talked to anyone about it, not Eric, no one, and only occasionally with Alex. She never got over the night when Robert disappeared though she thought of it often. It was the reason she didn't want to have any children, though no one in the entire world knew that...she guarded it as her very own and very personal secret.

She feared that someday it would become known what happened and she feared if she had children, how they would react. It was easier to spare them.

Maria was a realist and knew she was not being completely rational, but figured it was not worth the devastation if her worst fears became a reality.

18

It was a miserable day in Manhattan. Alex decided to travel Monday night, a day earlier than he had told the sergeant, so he could see Maria. It was teeming, which is indigenous to the east coast, or so the inhabitants believe. Teeming is not raining because real drops don't fall. Teeming is more like a heavy mist of miniature droplets. If you are walking, your clothes will get damp, almost wet depending how long you are in it, but there won't be drops on your face or if you use an umbrella, no drops, just a heavy dew.

Yes of course, New Yorkers will argue, it doesn't teem anywhere except New York; well, maybe the jungle. In any case it makes for a dreary day especially when, like this particular day, it was extremely overcast, dark and the city looked dismal.

It is the way Alex felt and had been feeling, regardless of the weather, for more than a month, and lately even worse—since the sergeant's call. He knew the reasons for the way he felt but was loathe to do anything about it.

Actually, there were three things bothering him. First, he was beginning to suspect that Sara was becoming suspicious of his trips to New York. She hadn't said anything, but as is often repeated, *silence can be deafening*. She had never taken much of an interest in his trips, but lately she stopped asking altogether; she didn't seem interested if he mentioned anything that happened, and in general she seemed to lose interest in anything he had to say, whatever the subject; nor did she seem anxious to tell him about what was going on in her life.

The second thing that was preying on him was Maureen. Lately it was bothering him—a lot, that he was keeping something from her; his whole life with her was based on lies; like recently when he pretended he didn't know that it was his sister who snitched on Robert and the janitor. He was uneasy whenever the subject of Robert came up which, when they were together the subject came up more and more frequently.

To add to this confusing issue, he readily admitted to himself that he was the one who always initiated the conversation—and the question he wrestled with was why.

"Why?" he'd reflect. "Why do I feel the need to have her talk about what she knows or doesn't know; it's crazy." He was also aware that whenever they discussed the disappearance he broke into a slight sweat. He felt, like with Sara, that Maureen was beginning to notice his discomfort but was not letting it show.

Thirdly, Sergeant Arrondondo's upcoming appointment was popping up in his mind throughout the day and night. Almost every night since the call he would wake up from having dreamed of their past encounter. The sergeant had interviewed Alex, Maria and Maureen many years ago. It seemed harmless at the time but Alex found himself reading more into that one interview than he probably should have.

"Why am I working myself up?" he'd ask himself, "I will wait until the sergeant and I meet; I'll find out what he wants...he said it was new evidence...I'll claim I've forgotten because it was so long ago, and tell him I'll have to think about it—whatever 'it' is."

This talking to himself didn't really solve the problem. He was disturbed that it popped into his mind at random times: in the middle of a meeting, while on the phone with a client...in disturbing and realistic nightmares.

"Why does he want to see me after all these years?" He began to invent all kinds of questions the sergeant could ask. "Maybe he wants to trick me."

Maria was the only one he felt he could confide in but she was loathe to discussing it if she didn't have to. Regardless, he needed to talk to someone and looked forward to the lunch he had set up with her almost immediately after the arrangement was made with Arrondondo.

On this gray, teeming day, Alex rented a car and drove to Huntington; she had said she wasn't up to coming into the city and he thought nothing of it.

After a few pleasantries—they talked enough so both knew most of what was going on in each other's lives—Alex brought up the subject both were not comfortable discussing. He told her about the meeting planned for the following morning.

"Lately I've been thinking about when Sergeant Arrondondo interviewed the two of us. I'm worried that before long someone, somehow, will solve the disappearance of Robert Steeter; that someone will unearth the details—incredulous as it is that they are still unknown—and solve the mystery. I'm worried about the impact it will have on both our lives if and when that someone succeeds; and Sergeant Arrondondo could easily be that someone.

"I know you don't like talking about it," he continued, "but I want us to refresh our recollection before time completely covers over the details and we forget, which then may become a problem. I want to get the details straight in my mind for our meeting."

"Alex," Maria interrupted, "you know I don't like discussing anything to do with the convent, but I realize that what I want and what will be are two entirely different things. I don't want to think about anything back then; especially in any detail, with you or with anyone, but I know I must—inevitably; but, this morning, if I find it too revolting, appalling or reprehensible I'll get up from this table, thank you for the nice lunch, and leave. I can't help it; I can't help the way I feel, especially today; today I am not in the mood. Fair enough?"

"I know Maria. Don't you realize that I don't want to think about it, talk about it, either? It scares me. I wish I did not think about it, but I do, and I worry. And I worry about you, too!"

They looked at each other for a moment, neither saying anything, looking at each other but staring into nowhere, but their minds were not at ease.

Alex went on, "I did not give much thought at the time to the answers I gave the sergeant. We were both very young back then, so when he asked about Robert's disappearance I was scared—answered I don't know, or I don't remember to most of his questions. However, now that years have passed I wonder about those answers, how did he interpret them, did they run up red flags that indicated we knew more that we were letting on?

"I think he believes that Robert ran away," Alex continued, "but I don't think he is absolutely convinced. I think he wants to prove that it was the old janitor who was somehow involved, but now, as I look back at the conversation with him from the distance of time, I probably left room for doubt with my feeble 'I don't know' and my 'I don't remember.'

"They put him in jail for something else and I often wonder, during all his time in jail, when Sergeant Arrondondo could go see him any time he wanted and most probably did—I wonder how many unanswered questions the sergeant actually has remaining."

"Well," Maria answered, "I've had some of those same thoughts. At the time he questioned me, fortunately or unfortunately we'll never really know, I don't recall saying anything; I just cried. It seems at one point he was getting frustrated, told me, quite harshly I recall, to 'stop that crying, I'm not going to hurt you and neither are my questions, so stop it!' Rather harsh, don't you think?"

"Perhaps, but the less you said the better. Let the good sergeant believe what he wants."

Maria did not know that Alex was still seeing Maureen. Actually, she never had any notion of what went on between them and certainly never gave a moment's thought to the likelihood that they ever talked to each other since the day Maureen left the convent to go with the foster parents. So, there was no ulterior motive when Maria responded to Alex.

"Have you ever had occasion to talk to Maureen about what she thought of the sergeant's questioning," she innocently asked, "she is the only other convent kid I know that he talked to?"

"We have talked," he answered, "in fact we still talk. She was one of the kids I felt comfortable with and we seemed to be able to talk freely, realizing that neither of us would gossip about each other to anyone else. So yes, we've talked. Maureen believes like I do that the sergeant is on a quest to find Robert because he believes the janitor knows where he is, and, for some reason the janitor is hiding it, and he wants to get to the bottom of it."

"If that is the case, what possible reason would possess the sergeant to think the janitor would purposely hide knowing where Robert is? What would be his purpose in keeping his whereabouts secret? Isn't that the conclusion the sergeant would come to? I certainly would. Although as you said, the sergeant is not stupid, so there must be something we are missing, don't you think?"

"Well, I do but I hardly remember that janitor. Perhaps, since it is pretty well confirmed that he gave Robert the pocketknife and everyone knows that it was one of his most valuable possessions—it would seem that there must be more to the story. Maybe the sergeant thinks the janitor is afraid that if he tells where Robert is, the next thing that happens is that he gets charged with something quite serious—so the sergeant figures he knows but isn't telling, don't you think?"

"That's a good point. It gets complicated," Maria answered after a few moments of recollection. For another half-hour, Alex and Maria discussed the details of what they had previously agreed had happened.

Then she added, "I'm glad we are having this talk. It is important that both of our stories match. I don't feel any better about the whole thing and it will give me more to worry about, but there is nothing you or I can do about it. Actually, the less we think about it the better off we will be. I don't think we have anything to worry about, the janitor is the one who has to worry."

"Yes, you are right; I know you are right." He looked at his watch, "I have to get back to work. Thanks for coming to meet me, and I will call you next week. Say hi to Eric for me and tell him too bad he missed lunch today."

He gave Maria a kiss on the cheek; she went on ahead, turning at the doorway to give him a last look. He paid the bill, left the restaurant, and went to a hastily setup client meeting, though not feeling any better.

19

Alex joined CCG right after he completed his stint in the Army and worked himself up to senior executive. Essentially, it was the only job he ever had, not considering the little stuff to earn spending money during college.

CCG was a private partnership of six people and a tough firm to work for. Their battle cry was *feed the lion*. As in most firms of this type—consultants, lawyers, accountants—CCG had a pyramid structure, whereby the person at the top of the pyramid, Alex in this case, was supported by the number of people he had working on his projects. The more projects he had, the more people working on them, meant more fees that went to paying the salaries and generous bonuses to the partners, with more than enough left over for the Alex's.

The objective for each client was to generate more fees—through more work, more referrals and more references—in that order. Hence, *feed the lion*. The firm's few partners were never satisfied. It took a long lead-time and cost a lot of money to secure a new client from scratch, whereas to get *more work* from a current client cost relatively nothing.

A *referral* was next in terms of cost: to have a top client refer CCG to one of his or her business associates would greatly reduce the sales and development cost to get a new client.

Lastly, merely getting a current client to be a *reference* was better than nothing—using them to provide testimony as to the "high value" CCG provided. By the same token, in the end if you could not get a client to become a reference it generally meant that *here's one who isn't satisfied,* and a few of these and the Alex's of the firm were gently advised that this was not the career they were best suited for.

Feeding the lion was essentially what Alex was paid to do. "Anyone with a little technical skill could manage a CCG project," or so the mantra went; one's value to the firm was the amount of more work and referrals that were generated; it was all that mattered and all that was measured. Of course, *more* was never enough.

Major Henderson, one of the partners at CCG had Alex in his office.

"We've been reviewing your section Alex, and our lead generating department tells us that the percentage of more work you brought in last quarter from the New York area fell far short based on the potential out there."

"We" referred to the partners. The Chicago office's lead generating department consisted of the staff whose job was to comb various listings of organizations that met certain requirements and select those that could then be considered potential clients for CCG. Their information was essentially used by sales, but through some magic mumbo-jumbo, they also came up with a potential for more work, expressed as a percentage that each partner could use to prod his executives to maximize their "hunt."

"Is there something we should be discussing?"

Major Henderson was subtly asking Alex *what's the matter, how come you are not meeting your percentage?*

"What are you doing when you visit New York? Do you have a little something on the side?" It was in jest of course, but Henderson had been at this game for a long time and knew the ropes. He knew from his own experience—as well as what he gained from managing a whole lot of Alex's—the signs that one of his senior executives was having a little love tryst on the side, that was interfering with *feeding the lion.*

Alex dismissed the jibe. "I've got some things in the works; should be closing a few pretty soon," he lied as he handed Henderson a list of his clients with the status of each in terms of more work and referrals. He hastily put it together between the time he was advised of the impending meeting and being in Major's office.

"I don't know Alex," Henderson continued. "I get the feeling something is wrong. Something is bothering you. If it is related to the firm I want to help, and I can help, it's what I'm here for. However, if it is something else that is bothering you, personal stuff, you'll have to get it taken care of. Know what I mean?"

"I don't believe there is anything going on Major," Alex answered. "Nothing serious, that is. I get the message. Thanks, you know how it is, sometimes you have to be reminded of what's important and I got the message."

"There is one other thing Alex," Henderson stood up, walked around his desk and put his hand on Alex's shoulder. "We've been fortunate to hire a 'go-getter' that we have high hopes for. He seems a natural in coming up with unique solutions to our clients' problems. You have been one of our top people and I want you to take this new guy under your wing, develop him. Furthermore, I think he could be a great asset to a few of the clients you are wrestling with in New York. I want him to accompany you on the next trip, put him to the test. I think you will both benefit."

"Sure," Alex answered, "what's his name?"

"He's outside, his name is Dave Crowley, originally from Kansas somewhere, went to MIT and knows his engineering." Major Henderson opened his office door and invited Dave in.

"Dave, this is Alex Fazio. Alex, this is Dave Crowley. You two will be working together for a while so get to know each other and good luck. Dave, as we've already discussed, you'll report to Alex so both of you arrange when you can spend a little time together to work out the details. Any questions?"

"Pleased to meet you," Alex shook hands with his new protégé.

"Likewise." Dave answered.

"We can meet right away. Come to my office in half an hour, I have a few things to clear up then we can talk, okay?"

20

Sergeant Arrondondo was sitting across from an average looking man— dressed nicely enough; a little short of six feet tall, slightly stocky with a trimmed mustache. He had straw colored hair, brown eyes and appeared very much in control of himself. His name was Earl Stasser; his occupation: janitor.

He recently worked for a maintenance company that was in turn hired by building owners to maintain their offices. I say recently because it was very likely he would be the guest of the Department of Corrections for the foreseeable future.

"Earl," Sergeant Arrondondo was saying, "we could make this easy or we could be here a long while. I've got a lot of time and the way it is looking, so will you. The evidence is overwhelming so it will be to your advantage to cooperate. It is up to you. What do you say?"

"I don't have anything to say. If you say you've got evidence and it is overwhelming then what do you want from me? You don't have any evidence of anything. You've got someone's word against mine, just like the last time; that's not evidence. I didn't do anything against the law and you know it." Earl the janitor was slouched back in the metal chair.

"I still want to know what happened to Robert Steeter. It has been almost twenty-five years since he disappeared and I think you know where he is, or at least where he went when he supposedly ran away. If you cooperate I will do what I can to get you the minimum sentence."

137

"I don't know what you are talking about. Like I told you back then, I read about the kid in the newspaper so that is as much as I know. I got set up by that old busybody lady, the judge's wife. The kid was scared of her so he agreed with everything she made up. I did my time, too."

"I don't think so Earl. Here comes the bad news. We got the judge to sign an order to search your apartment yesterday afternoon and it was quite enlightening."

Earl stiffened up quickly. "You searched my apartment? Why?"

"Easy, in case you forgot, you were arrested because you were exposing yourself in the train station men's room. I convinced the judge that you know more than you are telling us about Robert Steeter."

"So he said you could search my apartment?" Earl asked incredulously.

"Yes. Know what we found? I'll tell you what we found." Sergeant Arrondondo, who was sitting on the edge of his desk, got up and walked around to his chair. He sat down and opened the left hand drawer. He pulled out a small camera and showed it to Earl.

"This is what we found. Nice camera, isn't it? I especially like this feature where you set this little timer and if you quickly run around in front of the camera before the timer goes off, CLICK, it takes a self-portrait. It is very nice; comes in handy sometimes, doesn't it?"

Earl didn't answer; he looked at his fingernails as if to decide if he needed a manicure.

Next Sergeant Arrondondo pulled out a manila envelope, opened it and withdrew three photographs. He passed them across the desk to Earl.

"Did you take these photos with this camera? We already know you did, they match." Of course the police lab could not match a photo with a specific camera but Arrondondo took the chance that the janitor was oblivious to this fact. "Who are these kids? Actually, I already know who two of them are, you conveniently wrote their names on the back; who is the third?"

Earl glanced at the photos without picking any up. They clearly showed Earl and young boys in compromising positions, but the photos were grainy and blurred; it looked like they were taken a while ago and developed with one of those home-developing kits. He didn't say anything for a while.

"I don't remember their names, " he answered.

"This is what I am interested in," Sergeant Arrondondo continued as he drew another envelope out of the drawer. Inside were newspaper clippings of Robert Steeter's disappearance. The clipping included the photo that the grade school provided to the newspaper at the time.

"Why do you have this newspaper clipping among your things in your apartment if you don't know anything about him?"

"It is no crime. I forgot I had the stuff. I must have clipped it out because I used to work at the school. Doesn't mean anything."

"You gave Robert a pocketknife with 'Ruby Falls' printed on it, didn't you? Before you answer, I have quite a few people from back then, who are now adults, and they will swear that you did, so tell me, why did you give it to him?"

"Sure, I gave the kid the knife. I found it; he helped me do some chores one day so I gave it to him."

"What were the chores?"

"How do you expect me to remember? It was a long time ago."

"One of these pictures, it is hard to make out who it is—is this a picture of the boy Robert? It looks like the newspaper photo."

"No, of course not. I don't remember his name, but it was not the runaway if that is what you are thinking."

"Where was this taken? Two of the pictures were taken inside an apartment or house. This one looks like it was taken outside; the wall is brick, doesn't it look like brick to you?" Sergeant Arrondondo picked up the picture and handed it to Earl. "Where was it taken?"

Earl answered promptly after taking a quick glance at the photo. "I don't remember; behind the house I was living at probably."

"Where were you living at the time?"

"I don't remember. I move around a lot. It goes with the jobs I've had. Jobs often include a small apartment; then I get tired of the job or find another that pays more or has a nicer flat and I move on. Nothing wrong with that is there?"

Sergeant Arrondondo reached into the envelope one more time and pulled out a long slim switchblade. "Where did this come from? It's illegal, in case you don't know, to have a switchblade more than three and a half inches long and this one is closer to four; where did it come from, where did you get it? You certainly don't look like a hunter."

"I found it," Earl quickly responded. "Besides, I ain't carrying it so I'm not doing anything wrong. I know the law."

"Sorry Earl, you've served time; so it's illegal but that is not what this is all about...unless of course you don't cooperate; so I am going to ask one more time. Who is this boy?" referring to the picture that was not very clear, "and exactly where was it taken? You can answer now, make it easy on yourself, or I will eventually find out and I'll see to it that you are sent away for a very long time. What will it be?"

"I don't remember," was Earl's response.

✦ ✦ ✦

Alex and Maureen were again in Manhattan, at Il Vagabondo, sitting near the entrance. They had just been served the glass of wine they ordered and were examining the menu, preparing a strategy in case the waiter wanted to decide for them what they should order for dinner and it didn't appeal to them. They were both looking down intently, studying the menu, when their table was bumped...just slightly. As is natural, Alex looked up and saw that it was the maître d' who inadvertently bumped them; he was followed by a sleek young lady who was followed by Dave Crowley.

Alex and Dave looked at each other, startled. Alex spoke first. "Hello Dave, this is a surprise...seeing you here."

"Well, you told me it was a great restaurant and not to miss it, so here I am," Dave answered as he reached to shake hands with Alex who was getting up off his chair.

"Dave, this is Maureen. Maureen, this is Dave Crowley. I work with him; one of the rising stars of CCG, I might add." Turning to Dave, Alex added, "I don't mean to embarrass you Dave, but you are and we are lucky to have you on our team."

"Thanks," Dave answered, obviously appreciating the compliment, and shook Maureen's outstretched hand. "My pleasure," he said.

Meanwhile, Dave's guest, who had continued following the maître d', stopped, turned around and returned to the table.

"I'd like to introduce my wife Shelly," Dave said to both Alex and Maureen and continued, "instead of me going home to Chicago this weekend, Shelly decided to come to Manhattan. She'll return Sunday night. We have been looking forward to this for a while...Shelly's first time in Manhattan."

"You can do a lot in a few days," offered Maureen to Shelly, "I am sure you will enjoy the city."

Not knowing any better, Shelly asked Maureen if she, too, was here for the weekend. She never gave a thought to Maureen not being Alex's wife and obviously looked forward to the answer, readying her next question, which was going to be how often do you make the trip.

"No," Maureen answered, she too not thinking. I live here, have all my life, so I suppose I get enough of the city."

It was an awkward moment for Alex when he realized that Dave quickly got the panoramic view of what was going on, and in order to ward off embarrassment for both of them, Alex said. "Would you like to join us?"

Dave quickly responded, "Thanks for the invitation, we planned this to be a little get-away you know, from the kids, a chance to be alone. Could we take a rain-check, perhaps back in Chicago?"

Maureen answered for both of them by looking directly at Shelly. "I understand," and, realizing that the cat was out of the bag and feeling pissy, turned to Alex, snuggled too close and said, "I don't blame them wanting to enjoy each other's company," and, tauntingly, "just because you aren't a romantic..." and trailed off.

"Yes, enjoy yourselves," Alex picked up where Maureen trailed off. Dave and Alex shook hands again; "I'll see you at our appointment tomorrow. I think you'll enjoy the food here and don't miss watching the bocce game." Alex and Maureen sat down as Dave and Shelly followed the maître d'.

"That was awkward," an annoyed Alex whispered to Maureen.

"Who is he?" Maureen looked at Alex, "I gather he is one of your guys, will he blabber that you are having an affair?" she said in her typical pissy way.

"I hope not. Let's order, I'm starved."

21

Arrondondo arrived Wednesday morning promptly at eight a.m.

"Thank you for taking the time to see me," he said stepping through the doorway and shaking hands with Alex.

"No problem," Alex answered while thinking just the opposite. He did not at all relish talking about his past, no less the disappearance of Robert Steeter. The entire subject put him on guard.

The hotel room was one of those business suites where the main room is separated from the bedroom, and contained a sofa, chair, desk, and television. It also had a small dining table with four chairs. Alex pulled out one of the chairs and asked the sergeant if he'd like to sit down.

"Can I make you a cup of coffee? I don't particularly like coffee that comes in an envelope but it is all there is. I especially don't like powdered whitener either, how about you? If you prefer I can order real coffee, with cream, from room service. It may take a while, though."

"No thank you," the sergeant answered as he took the chair and sat down. "I don't care for hotel room coffee either, but a glass of water would do." He put his briefcase on the table, took out a notepad and pen, crossed his legs and leaned into the table with his folded hands resting on the edge. To Alex it was an intimidating posture. It signified that the sergeant was no nonsense and here for business.

"You said you have a person of interest, may I ask who it is?" Alex asked while filling two glasses with water and trying mightily to stifle his apprehension. He had been thinking since the original call about who the person of interest could be...the old janitor of course, but then again wasn't he suspected of being involved all along?

"Of course," Sergeant Arrondondo answered, "it is a man; I'd rather not give out his name at this time, but just before Robert Steeter disappeared...or ran away, he was connected to the school. I'd rather not go into too much detail about him. However, we had occasion to search his home and we found a picture we believe is of Robert Steeter. Also this man had a folder with newspaper clippings from the time the boy disappeared.

"My purpose in contacting you," the sergeant continued, "is to hopefully identify the boy in the picture. It is grainy and the shadows make a positive identification difficult. Since you knew Robert better than any of us it is possible you could identify him...perhaps by his clothing, his stance, anything to make the identification more positive. Almost as important, we would like to know the location where the picture was taken. We have other incriminating photos we found in his apartment, however they were taken inside; whereas the picture we believe is Robert was taken outside, and knowing the whereabouts would prove helpful."

The sergeant opened his briefcase and withdrew a folder, opened it and handed a picture to Alex.

"It *is* Robert," Alex said, "I am sure it is Robert; I recognize his clothing, the striped shirt, even after all these years. I surprise myself that that time in my life must have made an impact. I don't usually remember much of my past but I remember him and I am almost certain this is a picture of Robert."

"Does the picture surprise you, the two of them...what they are doing and all? You don't seem surprised?" Alex handed the picture back to Sergeant Arrondondo while answering the sergeant's question.

"Does it surprise me? I suppose nothing surprises me any more. You have to understand orphans in an orphanage Sergeant. I wasn't an orphan, my father was still living, but Robert was. Both his parents died before he was one, maybe two years old, I don't remember exactly, so the only thing he knew was the orphanage...run by nuns. God bless them, they believed they were doing their best but, in fact, I got the feeling the orphans were a side-line with them, a charitable works project...help God's children...feed them and clothe them...not necessarily mold their character, or nurture them, or love them.

"Robert and the other orphans hardly had any visitors, as I recall. The only thing they knew was the convent, the nuns, each other. I know for certain that he and his sister acted just like two of the many inmates; they didn't consider each other as brother and sister in the same way you and I would, if indeed you have a brother or sister, but you understand what I am saying. They were just two of many pups in the litter.

"I remember once having a conversation with Robert— remember, we were ten, eleven, twelve years old at the time, I

147

don't remember exactly how the conversation went, but Robert didn't have feelings about anyone and sex with a girl or a boy, man or a woman didn't make any difference to him. He was complex for his age.

"He had no *feelings* for anyone either. It seemed like he just did not care if he hurt someone either physically or mentally. He was very strange, so does the picture surprise me? No, I guess it really doesn't surprise me. It's who Robert was."

"Do you recognize where the photo may have been taken; was it near the convent?" the sergeant asked.

"No, I don't recognize anything else, although it is quite grainy, as you said, and shadows. Do *you* have any ideas?" Alex asked.

He knew exactly where the photo was taken and hoped it didn't show in his answer.

Neither said anything more; the sergeant took a sip of water just before he put the photos back into the envelope. He took his time doing this, obviously thinking about what Alex had told him; coyly waiting for more, finally...

"Do we have any ideas? I first wanted to get confirmation that this picture was of Robert. We had no difficulty identifying the two others, the man we suspect had written their names on the back of the originals. It also appears there was a time lapse between the picture you believe is Robert and the others...we are guessing six months.

"We also believe the man, lets call him John Doe, moved during the interval between the pictures. Again, we know where he lived when the two later pictures were taken but we cannot determine where he lived when the first one was taken. So again, do the surroundings ring a bell, do you have an inkling where the photo may have been taken?"

"No Sergeant, sorry I can't be more helpful. What will you do next?"

"Keep searching. As I said, now that we know with a little more certainty that the picture is Robert, we will look around the convent. It has been several years now and things change but we will take another look."

Sergeant Arrondondo put the envelope back into his briefcase. He seemed, to Alex, that he was deciding whether to bring something else up.

"I have a question about the night Robert disappeared. I believe you maintain that you and Robert didn't have any conversation during the evening, is that correct?"

"Yes, as I recall," Alex answered.

"I also understand that your sister and you walked back to the convent together. I want to make sure that you didn't see anyone during that time or didn't talk to anyone during that time, is that correct?"

"Yes, that is correct."

"What I don't understand is that it took a half-hour. Now then, after all this time to perhaps re-consider your answer, don't you think that is a long time to walk across the street?"

"No, not if you are walking slowly, enjoying the evening with your sister. No, I don't believe it is too long at all."

"One more thing, one of the teachers maintains she saw three children outside the church at approximately eight o'clock. You maintain that it was not Robert Steeter that she saw with you and your sister, is that correct?"

"Sergeant, I have no idea whom she may have seen. She may have seen Maria and me but if she saw a third person I do not know who that could have been. I can be no help there. It is not that I have forgotten, I just did not see any other children around us at the time."

Sergeant Arrondondo got up off his chair, pushed it in closer to the table, and shook hands with Alex.

"Thank you for your time. You have been helpful. If anything comes up I will let you know and, by the same token, if you think of anything, here is my card, give me a call anytime...and no matter how inconsequential you may think it is, let me know."

"I will Sergeant. Good luck," Alex said although he didn't mean it.

✦ ✦ ✦

After the sergeant left, Alex sat down. He knew exactly where the picture was taken and believed it would not take long before the sergeant also found out.

He also knew that the teacher probably did see three children...Robert, Maria and himself, just before they went back behind the church. To admit that, however would lead to divulging that Robert threatened to rape Maria and she was adamant; that was something she never wanted to think about again, didn't want anyone to know about, and certainly didn't want to discuss with anyone.

No sooner did he sit down, he immediately got up, looked at the clock that hung on the wall over the short counter that contained the sink and coffee machine, and underneath, a small refrigerator—eight thirty-five. He bent down, opened the door and took out an overpriced orange juice bottle from the top shelf, took one sip and sat down again.

When he next looked up at the clock it was five minutes after ten—his meeting was at ten-thirty and the orange juice bottle had not been touched again. He'd be late but it didn't register; he continued sitting and began a conversation with himself.

Out loud.

"They are going to blame this guy, I know it. That sergeant will figure out where the picture was taken and blame that ass-hole janitor," he was looking down at the floor.

"I'm surprised it's taken this long. They've had him in-and-out of jail, how many times now? Well, perhaps he'll get what's due him. He had no business taking advantage of the fact that Robert was a little jerk-off who didn't care shit about anyone but himself; spent his days...oh sure, what about the nights? Spent the nights too...terrorizing me and the other kids, so it is only fair that the janitor terrorized him.

"But maybe he didn't terrorize him. Maybe Robert egged him on. He was like that, you know, lived for the moment. What the hell, he was fucking his sister, how bad can it get, fucking your sister?

"I hated him, I hated him for how he terrorized Maria. Every time she looked at him she would shiver and I was too much of a fucking coward to do something about it. I could have told Father Mike, he'd understand...but no, I was *afraid* of Robert. I was afraid what he'd do—to *me*."

Alex grimaced as he said this and bent over, put his head in his hands, elbows resting on his knees, visualizing Robert describing how he'd fuck him and how he'd like it as much as Robert did when the janitor fucked him! He sat quietly for a few seconds, thinking.

"Maureen, what about her? She was no saint. Didn't she egg Robert on? Always showing off her little cunt, letting...no grabbing boys' hands to fondle it. She didn't care if Sister saw her; she didn't care that Robert fucked her...his own sister. Now I'm fucking her...and I'm married, got two kids, fucking up my job over her...making unnecessary trips to this fucking place just to fuck her.

"I hate her, I hate Robert, I hate that fucking priest and that fucking sergeant; fuck them all.

"I'm royally screwed; my mind is fucked up. What am I going to do?"

✦ ✦ ✦

Alex missed his appointment at ten thirty and two others he had scheduled for later in the afternoon. "Let Crowley go," he explained to the hotel room.

He threw himself on the bed about noon; without lunch and didn't have supper. He woke up about nine in the evening, undressed, dropped his clothes on the floor, and went back to sleep again.

He woke up early Thursday morning and called the airline to book the first flight back to Chicago; there was one at eight but it was already full and Alex wanted to be gone from New York as quickly as could be. He was able to book a reservation for the flight at noon.

This was a time when airlines made a distinction between business and vacation travelers, and Alex's company was a good customer of United, which flew predominately east and west. Fortunately, in times of need, being a good customer had its perks, and now was the time to take advantage of one.

An agent at the United counter in Chicago knew Alex was a frequent business traveler and supplied him with a book of ticket-tags. Each airline used identical passenger tickets which consisted of a piece of card-stock with the itinerary printed on it: flight number, time of departure, seat assignment and fee code; or, the information could be handwritten if the ticket was purchased at the last minute at the departure gate.

Ticket-tags, also used by all airlines, were small sticky-labels about an inch and a half long and three-quarters of an inch high with a place to re-write a flight number, departure time, and seat assignment. Having a book of these little ticket-tags came in handy for frequent travelers like Alex.

If a flight was full or cancelled or going to be late, you looked for an alternate in your Official Airline Guide—a monthly publication to which most frequent travelers subscribed, and which showed every flight from every airport—and you filled out a ticket tag and the problem was solved.

Some little old lady, or more likely a smart-assed kid who thought it was cool to be the last one on the plane, would find his seat taken and the stewardess (that's what they called them in the early seventies) gave her apologies and sent him back to the counter to get his own little tag...this one, unfortunately for him, filled in by the ticket agent for the next flight.

This way, Alex got on the originally booked eight o'clock flight, and devoid of any traveler's guilt walked into his house a little before noon.

22

When Alex arrived home, Sara was surprised. "What are you doing home, I thought you would be home tomorrow night, what happened, did you get fired?"

Lately Alex took notice that there was a change in Sara. She was her same old self but there was something brewing; he could feel it like a slight breeze from a window opened just a crack. The breeze was not enough to make you totally aware of it, but it was there, gently trying to get your attention. It was only a matter of time and it would succeed; it was beginning to.

"Your sister called...said she tried to reach you at your hotel...in NY; left a message but obviously you aren't in New York, are you? So you missed it. She didn't know you were coming home early...either. I had told her Friday night." Sara said this just a little caustically; the breeze wasn't so gentle any more.

"Did she say what she wanted?"

"She said to call her as soon as you get a chance."

"Is there something wrong?"

"How should I know?" A stronger breeze...Sara and Maria normally talked small talk for an hour and kept no secrets...well, on second thought, didn't keep secrets except for Maria's big one.

Sara continued. "We didn't talk long. Maria just said to call her, that was it."

"Don't you two normally talk forever?" a little caustically, "was she in a hurry or something? Are you sure there is nothing wrong?"

"Call her," Sara said in a frustrated tone, like she wanted this conversation to be over with...now.

"Okay, thanks, I'll call her later."

"Alex, you don't get it. She didn't say call her later, she said 'call her' that means now, not later."

✦ ✦ ✦

"What the fuck is wrong with her?" Meaning Sara—Alex mumbled as he began unpacking his suitcase in the bedroom. "What's eating her? I hope that sergeant hasn't been bothering her," meaning Maria—"what else could it be? Very unlike her to be short on the phone with Sara; that's probably what pissed Sara off—she does not like it when she knows something is going on and she doesn't know every little detail about it."

Alex closed the door a little too hard then dialed Maria's number at work.

"She isn't in today, can I take a message?"

"This is her brother Alex, did she take the day off?"

"Alex, I thought I recognized your voice, this is Vivian; Maria called in sick again this morning; sounded terrible. You know the flu is going around and everyone, I mean everyone is catching it. I'll be next, no doubt about it, if anyone in this office gets sick I always catch whatever it is a few days later...."

"Thanks, Vivian, I'll call her at home. Be careful, don't get too close to people, then you won't catch anything."

"Stupid bitch," Alex said out loud as he put the phone back on the nightstand. Then he caught himself. He sat down on the edge of the bed, and folded his hands on his lap; his head was lowered, looking down at the floor.

"Christ...Jesus Christ...I don't talk like that. I never call someone a bitch. Why all of a sudden? What is wrong with me...yesterday at the hotel; the language...this isn't me. What's going on, what's happening to me?"

He sat...contemplating for a few more minutes...then got up, went into the bathroom, leaned over the sink with his hands on the edge and looked into the mirror. He saw a young man ageing.

Alex was a good-looking man. He wasn't vain but he could tell that most people saw him as attractive. He was just shy of six feet, controlled his weight and was born with his dad's roman features: dark brown hair that was easily manageable, and was conscious of how he dressed—shoes shined, clothing fresh; some people's clothing fit nicely and some didn't. It had to do with body shape, an unexplained way of selecting whatever you were going to wear, and the combination of the movements of your body combined with the movement of the clothing.

He looked directly at you, listening intently, rather than through you as you talked to him; with large, dark-brown eyes and broad eyebrows set in a chiseled face half cherub and half imp.

What he saw in the mirror, however, was vastly different today. His skin looked like the tallow of a yellowed, one-hundred percent bees-wax altar candle; his eyes were too moist; his lips were turned down at the corners; he looked like he felt: miserable, apprehensive, and no longer in control.

✦ ✦ ✦

He reached for the phone a second time and dialed Maria's number at home.

He noticed that she answered the phone on the first ring and realized, apprehensively, she's waiting for me to call. He felt his face flush...something is wrong, something is not right... fucking shit!

"Hi, it's me, Alex. You tried reaching me...Sara told me you called?"

"Yes, where are you? You're still in New York, aren't you? Can you come to my house later on? I need to talk to you. Do you have some time before you leave for Chicago?"

"No Maria, I'm not in New York, I'm back home; I'm in Chicago. What's up?"

"Oh, I thought you were in New York. Well, I'd rather not talk over the phone; I'd rather talk to you in person. When are you coming back here...to New York?"

"I'm not sure. Actually, I screwed up." He meant of course that he screwed up at work but didn't say so and the detail went over Maria's head. He continued.

"I have to tell you about my visit yesterday with Arrondondo," Alex jumped right in.... "His reason for coming to the hotel was to show me a picture. It was Robert Steeter and that janitor...Robert pulling his shorts up; his trousers down around his knees...it was an incriminating picture! There was no question it was Steeter; he had that shirt with the stripes, you know, the one he always wore. I think it was the only one he owned!

"It looked like the janitor took it with one of those self-snapping cameras then developed the film himself...looks like a home developing kit; that's what the sergeant thinks. I tried to not look startled or surprised, but it was difficult and that sergeant is like a hawk; eagle eyes, notices every grimace. It was Robert, no doubt about it and I had to tell him so—he already knew, I could tell he already knew." Alex kept going and going.

"...What he did *not* know...at least I *think* maybe he didn't know...was *where* the picture was taken. That's what he asked me about, that's why he wanted to show me the picture. Can you imagine, he was going to come all the way to Chicago just to show me a picture? I'm worried Maria."

"Well," Maria answered, "first of all where was the picture taken, behind the church?" Maria saw the dilemma immediately. "It was, wasn't it?"

"Yes," Alex continued, "you could make out the wall between the church and the street. You couldn't see the church, only the wall, but those bricks are pretty distinctive aren't they, so maybe he already knew but wanted to see if I knew. That's why I'm worried. If he has the picture of the janitor and Robert doing that kind of stuff and he knows the picture is near the church, he probably is wondering if I'm involved somehow. I don't think he believed me when I told him I didn't know where it was taken, I could tell by the way he looked at me."

"So what? What's there to believe? What are you going to do?" asked Maria.

"I don't know. Do you think I should come to New York and go back to the convent; see if I can find anything before the sergeant figures things out and goes there to look?"

"Alex, of course not. Don't get excited, don't do anything stupid. What if someone were to see you? That's how luck goes, they would...for sure, let it be. They'll blame anything they find on the janitor. He probably deserves it anyway...the picture. Don't you think so? Even if Robert was mean; a weird bully...that janitor had no business...Robert was just a kid; it's against the law...so he is going to jail no matter what."

"Yes, yes, you're right. But it bothers me and I'm still worried...but you are right. I've got enough problems right now, I don't need any more." Alex took a breath then asked, "What did you want to see me about; did you want to find out about the sergeant's visit? What's up?"

"I'd rather be telling you this in person, but I got some disturbing news. I hadn't been feeling that great so I went to the doctor. He said I have cancer. He was not very optimistic."

There was silence.

Finally, Alex spoke first. "Cancer? What kind of cancer? Is he sure...the doctor you saw? Who is he? Are you going to see a different one, get another opinion?" Alex felt weak all of a sudden. He had three sisters but Maria was like his Siamese twin. Dolores was the older sister, didn't seem to be on the same wavelength as he and Maria. Francine, the youngest...they only saw her once in a while.

It had more to do with him always trying to protect Maria—first from Robert; then from boyfriends as she was growing up. Alex felt responsible for her, and now there was something happening to her, and he knew he had to take care of it; but he feared...he knew...it was something that would be out of his control.

"I don't think I need to see any more doctors Alex. There were three of them involved. It's certain. It is in my pancreas and none of them was optimistic. The question is the treatment. The doctor wants me to have radiation—more to manage pain than as a cure. He said he couldn't guarantee anything but feels it is worth it; might prolong things or at least reduce any un-comfortableness." Maria was stoically calm.

"Do you want me to come back to New York? I could get a flight this afternoon. Have you told Eric?"

"Of course."

"What did he say?"

"Alex, I don't think it has registered with him, God bless him. You know Eric, he's the eternal optimist...'Everything will be fine, I know it,' that's Eric and why wouldn't I believe him?

161

"What's the worst that can happen if I believe what Eric says? What's the alternative? ...Alex, I'm scared."

Alex realized that Maria was holding back, didn't want to cry; didn't want to share her emotions with anyone, even her brother whom she loved so dearly.

"Maria, I'll make arrangements to come to New York tomorrow...is it okay if I spend the weekend at your house? ...But if you rather, I can get a room. You haven't told Sara, have you?"

"No Alex, I haven't. I couldn't. It's embarrassing...to be sick. It's like you're inferior, only inferior people get sick. I don't want Sara to know. I don't want anyone to know...but she has to, doesn't she? Will you tell her for me? But don't make a big thing out of it. Let's assume the radiation will work, I'll be all right and all will be as it is supposed to be. We've had worse, haven't we? We endured Mom dying, living with our stupid relatives, the convent, Robert...and even after all that, it's been okay, hasn't it?"

"Maria...yes." Alex thought for a second then continued, "I have this feeling. You're strong; you'll kick this just like you survived everything else. I'll see you tomorrow." Alex was clueless about the destruction going on inside Maria.

"Alex," Maria answered, "Eric and I would love to have you visit over the weekend, but believe me, it is not necessary. Stay home; be with Sara and the kids; your next trip here will be soon enough, believe me. I love you."

"Okay sure, I'll probably have to return to New York next week anyway. Are you sure you don't want me to come tomorrow?"

"No, brother dear, next Monday or Tuesday is fine. So, till then, I love you."

They both hung up their phones to contemplate their grief in private, just like always.

✦ ✦ ✦

Alex was in no mood to talk to Sara. Something was happening to him. "What is it?" he sat down again and tried to think.

There were too many problems and they all hinged on each other. Maria was now at the top of his list. Then the rest:

"It is only a matter of time before Sara finds out about Maureen.

"It is only a matter of time before Maureen finds out what happened to her brother.

"It is only a matter of time before Sergeant Arrondondo finds out about the picture.

"It is only a matter of time before I fuck up my job even more than I already have and get fired.

"It is only a matter of time..." He continued sitting on the edge of the bed. Finally, after a long time, he resumed talking to himself.

"If Maria dies, who's left? Me. I'll have to deal with both of them alone...Father Mike and the sergeant. How do I explain everything to my kids?

"My job, that's done with, I've fucked that up royally already. That fucking Dave and his fucking wife, they are just waiting to get my job, I knew it the first time I met the fuckers. I'll bet he's with fucking Major Henderson right now, telling him everything...about Maureen...me.

"The way Sara's been acting lately she probably suspects something about Maureen. Why wouldn't she?"

After all this wretchedness, recognizing what he was doing to himself, he murmured, "I need to get a grip...but I can't; what am I going to do?"

Alex was confused; he realized it. He looked around the bedroom like it was the first time he'd ever been there. One of his pet peeves was a picture that was not hanging straight, yet both the ones in the bedroom were crooked. He looked carefully at the first one. "What an ugly picture that is. Why would anyone waste his time painting that piece of shit? It looks like paint-by-numbers. Maybe if it was real, an original by some famous ass-hole it might be okay, maybe it would even be more attractive—if you could tell what it was—the way it is it's a piece of shit. No wonder it's crooked.

"The other one...they don't even match. A ballerina that you can hardly make out that she is a ballerina; looks like one big smudge and a few pencil lines standing on one skinny leg; another piece of shit. Where was I when we bought them, I don't even remember?"

He felt his world collapsing and felt powerless to do anything about it. He realized for certain when he again mumbled, "What am I going to do?" He didn't feel well.

23

Friday morning he drove to his Chicago office. When he walked in, it surprised his secretary; she didn't expect him until after the weekend; Monday the earliest. Often, after an extended trip, Alex wouldn't even go to his office on Monday, he'd work from home and come to the office on Tuesday. She gave him a second look.

About an hour after arriving Dolores called. She told him she had just got off the phone with Maria who asked her to call Alex and tell him what she, Maria, had failed to tell him when they talked the previous day, that she hadn't told him all the details.

"Alex, she's known she's had cancer for going on six months now and the doctors did not give her much encouragement as to the prognosis even back then."

"She never said anything about that," Alex answered, "Why didn't she tell me...why did *you* wait this long to tell me? She's my sister as much as yours; why did she tell you and not me? Have you known all this time?

"Take it easy Alex. No, I haven't known all this time, only a few weeks; she knew it would devastate both of us, told me you have enough to keep you busy with your job and all and, Alex, in true Fazio fashion, you know bad stuff is not talked about. The Fazio family motto is 'I don't want to talk about it'—let's face it Alex, you are the motto's champion."

There was a moment's silence on both ends.

"I feel so bad for her," Dolores continued, "she's all alone except for Eric and he's almost useless when there's a crisis like this, don't you think so? He's a wonderful guy and all, but Maria needs one of us."

Dolores lived in Texas with her husband and three kids. She said she could leave immediately for New York but with the weekend coming it would be inconvenient and difficult, so she decided she'd wait a little while for when Maria really needed her, and by planning ahead she could stay for as long as she was needed. Eric and his uselessness could still manage for now.

Alex could not believe what he was hearing...didn't want to believe it, and tried to convince himself that all he had recently heard was wrong.

"I just talked to her yesterday," Alex began repeating out loud to Dolores what he was thinking inside, more for something to say... "It is all arranged, I'm flying to New York early next week, first thing Monday morning probably, and I plan to spend the night at their house. I'll make a reservation as soon as I get off the phone. I'm all set."

"Will you call me as soon as you get there?" Dolores asked, "tell me how she's doing. I think doctors always give you the worst scenario; that's what they always do. They want to prepare you for the worst; don't you think so?"

"You can't be sure. That's why I want to go see her." But then he went too far in his optimism.

"I hope I can convince her to see another doctor; get another opinion, and when she does I will let you know right away."

"Alex," Dolores countered, "there is no need for a second opinion. She has known for months, too many in fact. I don't know any other way to tell you this...this is not something that is going to end well. She didn't want to upset you until it was absolutely necessary.

"She knows it too, when I spoke to her this morning she asked me to be the bearer of the bad news that it's terminal. Alex, the doctors give her weeks, a few months at most."

"But I just saw her," Alex still didn't want to believe what he was hearing, "she looked fine."

"It's an insidious disease, she has good days and bad days, but it is there and there is nothing either you or I can do about it. Frankly, let's not discuss it any longer; let's wait until you get there, find out for yourself, and then call me, okay? Do you mind if we change the subject?"

Dolores noticed the pause on the other end of the line. She could tell that Alex was holding back. She knew he would take her advice and try his best to not think about Maria's illness; it was his way of handling problems anyway: don't think about them. Dolores hoped he was right that she'd recover—but not this time; realistically she new better. As for Alex, she was concerned about him too. One never knew at times like this exactly what was going on inside another's head, regardless of how close you believed you were to them.

She tried changing the subject.

"I heard some interesting news the other day, have you heard? I get the New Hyde Park local newspaper, have for years and years, and they are going to demolish our old church; it is too small for the growing crowds, and they are going to build a new one—*build the church for Easter Sunday*," she said lightly, "supposedly demolition begins in a few months. They are going to use our chapel in the convent for services, isn't that something? If we go to mass after they begin construction it will be like going back in time...at our old chapel. If I was in New York I'd go to the last mass at the old church then the next Sunday go to the first mass in the convent chapel. Did you know about it, have you heard anything?"

"No, this is the first I'm hearing it. Doesn't surprise me though, the church was tiny for such a growing community. No, it doesn't surprise me. How is Maria feeling right *now*? Is she in pain, and how is she taking it? How is Eric taking it? They don't have any kids so that's a blessing...well not really but you know what I mean. They didn't want to have kids. Maria told me so a long time ago."

"Alex, Maria will be strong. If she is having a hard time she won't tell anyone. You know how she is."

"I do, Dolores, you are right, I do."

"I had the craziest idea the other day," Dolores tried once more to diffuse the situation, "after I read about the church. What if we have a reunion, you know, the kids we were with. We could invite the nuns...see if they are any different...now that we are grown up and they are a bit older. See if the cranky ones are still

170

cranky and if the nice ones are still nice." Alex could feel the feisty little smile that he detected in her voice.

"Dolores, that is the worst idea I think I've ever heard. Do you really want to see that bunch of mutants, those inmates as well as their wardens? Or should I say animals and keepers, if I never see any of them again it will be way too soon."

"Every once in a while I hear from Arlene Stern," Dolores added, "she's the only one. She told me a few months back that she ran into Maureen Steeter, you remember the kid who ran away or disappeared; his sister Maureen...what ever happened to him, did you ever find out?"

"I don't know, I haven't heard any more and don't know anymore than at the time he took off."

"You're full of it, Alex, Arlene Stern told me you see Maureen regularly...you do, don't you?"

Dolores wasn't snitching; it just slipped out.

"But I never said anything to anyone until now," Dolores confessed. The last time I saw Maureen was just after Dad died; what was that four years ago?"

"Okay, I see Maureen once in a while; we bump into each other sometimes when I'm in Manhattan, so what? We go out to dinner, that's it."

"I don't think so, brother dear, Arlene talked like it was general knowledge that you two are more than casual acquaintances...you are, aren't you?

His older sister could hear him swallow hard.

She won't understand—a lot of thoughts ran through Alex's mind in an instant—nobody does, only Maureen and I understand. She thinks it is wrong, Dolores does; it isn't. It's only wrong if you look at Maureen and me as lovers. We aren't lovers; we are old friends. We're two people who have been together forever, like two views of the same scene...and, is one view right and the other wrong? Of course not.

We don't talk like lovers; we don't look into each other's eyes and swoon, any of that lover stuff, we communicate, both having the same ideas springing from the same source. If we were lovers we'd talk about each other to each other. We don't. We can sit for hours and not even want to say anything, not even care if we are with each other except that like those multiple views of the same scene we can't be separated. How could anyone understand?

"Dolores, you don't understand, she's not my lover; we're friends, that's all."

"Alex, I don't want to pry. Besides, I'm not your confessor either, but as your older sister I feel compelled to give you advice. It's not about what *you* think; it's what others think. You have a lot to lose...Sara, the kids, maybe even your job, I don't know about that part, but just promise me you'll think about what you are doing. Especially at this time...Maria and all...what would Mom think?"

"Don't start with me on that, Dolores. Mother has nothing to do with it."

"Okay, okay, I've said my piece, I get the picture. But don't say I didn't warn you." Dolores didn't want the conversation to end on a sour note and tried to think of some way to diffuse any potential bad feelings before the call ended.

"I am curious though"—if this was diffusion, it was of dubious quality—"do you ever talk about her brother? She always seemed like a nice girl but neither of them, her or Robert, seemed particularly close, not like the three of us. They always reminded me of strangers with the same last name, if you know what I mean. Don't you think so?"

"They were different. We don't talk too much about her brother. Naturally she wonders what happened to him. She vacillates between: he ran away; he took off with his buddy the janitor or he got hit by a bus and is buried in Potter's field...."

"So which do you believe?"

Dolores wanted to know more now that she was entertaining the idea of a reunion.

"I'd like to have him come to my reunion," she continued, "you think I am kidding? I'm serious. We could make a fund-raiser out of it and donate a window or a pew or an altar candlestick. I think it would be fun."

"Dolores, you're nuts. First you'll never find any of them, it's not like they settled down and became model citizens with their names on a suburban do-gooder roster; more likely on the bulletin board of the post office."

"But I want to know about Robert. He's the most exciting thing that happened during all those years, don't you want to know what happened?"

"No, not particularly," Alex answered.

Dolores decided she wasn't finished with the news yet, so she brought up the current gossip.

"Just one more thing, then I'll let you go. Last weekend I was visiting my foster parents—Rose and Joe are doing great by the way, considering their age. Well, my stepsister Katie told us a sad story. Her husband Paul, you know Paul of course, well it seems his father was sentenced to prison for twenty years. Katie's parents don't see her in-laws that often, but it seems Paul's father murdered a liquor-store owner during a robbery. Isn't that something? Maybe you read about it in the newspaper, his name is Bateman, George Bateman. His poor wife Erica, I've met both of them, Paul's mom and dad, at Thanksgiving a few years ago; she's a nice woman. I never liked the father though, gave me the creeps so I can't say I was completely surprised when I heard he is going to prison; but it makes you wonder why someone like her would marry a creep like him?"

"As Aunt Anna used to say, every pot has a lid," was Alex's only response.

"Yes, but think of the damage something like that does to the entire family. Think of what his kids now have to go through. Paul's the oldest and married, but he has a younger brother and sister, and neither of them are married yet. What will it do to them? How do they explain to their friends, 'my father was sent up for murder!'

174

"Oh, of course," Dolores continued, "that is sure to make it easier to find a wife or husband, no doubt about it! Katie already said to me that she is concerned that it runs in the family. Now she's worried about her baby. How is *he* going to turn out? Alex, do you think there is such a thing as *bad blood*?"

"I hope not," Alex pondered.

"Dolores, I've got to go. I'll be in New York Monday morning and I have a lot to do before I leave. I'll call you after I've seen Maria, okay? Love you." Alex hung up the phone.

Including his desk, his office had four swivel chairs set around a small conference table that was positioned near the corner of the room. The door was closed. He pulled a chair out, sat down, and slid it further away from the table. He resumed his seemingly normal pose of late: his elbows resting on his knees, holding his head in his hands.

He pondered Dolores' conversation. "I have two kids, what if something like what she just told me happened to me, how would my kids react. What would *their* friends say? Who'd marry them? I hate even thinking of it."

He sat there for a while until he noticed that he began to feel strange, ready to faint. He felt like he needed a sip of water from the thermos on the credenza that was kept full by the unseen office staff. When he got up to pour a glass for himself he felt nauseous.

24

The next day was Saturday and Alex hadn't felt well all day, but Sara insisted that they not cancel the dinner they had committed to almost immediately after Dave Crowley joined CCG and was assigned to work with Alex. Rightfully so, she argued, Dave would think poorly of them for canceling the afternoon of their arranged date. Besides, she gathered that Alex didn't feel sick, he just felt miserable for some unexplained reason—to Sara, at least.

"What is wrong with you," she began around three in the afternoon, "you look fine, you just seem mopey? A pleasant dinner in a nice restaurant will do you good. Besides, I want to meet Dave and his wife. Lately we have not spent time with any of the people you work with—not like we used to.

"I know it happens eventually," she continued, "after a while people who work together get comfortable in their rut; camaraderie falls by the wayside. Is that what is happening at CCG? When was the last time we were out with Major Henderson and his wife? It has to be at least a year."

Alex merely grunted acknowledgement that he heard her, not that he was agreeing or disagreeing with what she was saying.

So she continued.

"What is Crowley like? Have you met his wife? Will I like her? Will you please answer me?"

"What do you want me to say?" Alex responded. "He's nice enough, he's a go-getter. He'd do anything, say anything to have my accounts and would feel no compunction whatsoever after taking them away from me. His plan is to endear himself to Henderson somehow, and he is the type who would subtly drop hints to disadvantage anyone he feels he is in competition with. Do you still want to have dinner with him?"

"Don't be a smart-ass Alex. Besides, has he done anything to you? No, he hasn't. You are in a bad mood; snap out of it. If you go to dinner with an attitude like that you will only spite yourself."

Alex didn't answer.

"Besides, I'm looking forward to meeting his wife."

Nothing more was said for the remainder of the afternoon. Sara busied herself getting the children taken care of. The babysitter who was coming had been there before so there was no problem in that regard. Still, she had to make dinner for them, have snacks ready, have their pajamas laid out and have a breakfast that they could help themselves to in the morning in lieu of waking up their parents. As if that wasn't going to happen.

Sara was already getting more annoyed at Alex, and it didn't subside as she thought this through: at six in the morning, which one of them would they wake up? Certainly not him, they may want to crawl into the bed and begin wrestling with him, but as soon as he let out an "enough" they'd be off to wake her.

Meanwhile Alex watched T.V.

✦ ✦ ✦

When it was time to dress Sara tried to snap him out of his bad mood. She couldn't decide if it was because he didn't really feel well or because he didn't want to socialize with Dave Crowley and his wife.

"Are you feeling any better Alex?"

"Yes," he answered what she wanted to hear. He was almost dressed, was sitting on the edge of their bed with his foot up on the corner of the frame so he could tie his shoelace.

Sara was sitting in front of the mirror, finishing "putting on my face" as she referred to it; she could look through the mirror and see Alex.

I don't know what has happened to him but lately he seems to be in a funk, she thought, I wish he'd tell me what is wrong. Does he think I don't notice that the problem is not that he doesn't feel well physically, but that the problem is something going on? This has been a month at least.

Finally she said out loud, "Alex, no matter how you feel I still think you are one of the best looking men I know."

He looked over towards where she was sitting and mumbled, "Thanks."

"Well," she responded...

Alex got the hint and added, "And you are by far the best looking and greatest wife in the world," and he meant it.

As it happens, they both for that moment realized that they were telling the truth to each other and it made them feel good. It especially seemed to work on Alex. He got up, walked over and gave Sara a little kiss on the back of her neck.

Feeling confident, Sara continued the second-degree she started earlier. "So, tell me again, what should I expect when I meet Dave and Shelly. You know I don't like surprises and I believe I am not quite as boring when I know a little about someone and have some things prepared to talk about."

"Dave's a likeable person," Alex answered, "you will not have to worry about finding something to say. Conversation comes easily to him. He will have you charmed in no time."

"Good," Sara answered. "Now I feel better. What about his wife? I asked earlier if you have met her, have you?"

"Not really. We bumped into each other in New York not long ago and I don't remember saying anything more than 'pleased to meet you,' that's all."

"What is she like? Will I like her?"

"Hard to say. If you feel you need to prepare things to talk about, you'd better get busy—unless I'm misjudging her, and hopefully I'm wrong, but she strikes me as a scatter-brain, and there is truth to the saying 'opposites attract' especially pertaining to personality. But again, I could well be wrong. Hope so. Are you ready, we'd better be going."

As it worked out, Alex and Sara arrived a few minutes early and decided to take the table that was offered and to sit and wait for Dave and Shelly. A few minutes later they arrived. Alex stood and shook hands with Dave then introduced his wife Sara. Dave took over and introduced Shelly.

She was attractive enough, not what you'd call a raving beauty, yet her nice clothes certainly contributed to her pleasant appearance. Unfortunately *boring* or a more kindly *average* would immediately come to mind in describing her.

Both Alex and Sara held that it was a recipe for a long evening if the men began conversing among themselves and the women were left to do likewise, so they had developed a pact long ago to make sure that if there were four people everyone would talk about the same thing. That essentially left out talking shop: sports, office, as well as recipes and kids.

Politics and religion were out unless there was certainty that everyone was on the same page; so Alex and Sara had come up with a way to get things moving: ask the other couple how they originally met. It worked every time. People like to talk about themselves, especially in an arms-length way, and answering that question usually works well. Besides, it often ends up in jovial disagreement about some inconsequential aspect of their romantic history, which contributes to the overall enjoyment of the evening.

It worked well tonight.

✦ ✦ ✦

The couples ordered dinner and part way through, Shelly brought up her recent trip to New York.

By this time Sara had realized that it was problematic to ask Shelly a question, because she took forever to answer and went into excruciating detail; and didn't disappoint when describing her maiden voyage to New York.

"Well," hesitation, "I couldn't decide which suitcase to take. I wanted to take enough clothing to cover any contingency but the large suitcase is too big and the small suitcase is too small, so I asked David, and well," hesitation, "he said bring the small one, it is only for two days.

"So," hesitation, "with that problem solved I was off to a good start. Wasn't I David?" as she snuggled up to him and kissed his neck.

"Yes you were, dear," Dave answered. He preferred being called Dave—she preferred calling him David. I guess they worked it out somehow.

"So," hesitation, "that's where I met Alex," Shelly continued, "well," hesitation, "Alex had told David about this great restaurant, Il Vagabondo and, would you believe, we decided to go there the very night I arrived. Isn't that something? That's where we met them..."

There was that millionth of a second where the synapses in Sara, Alex and David's brains played musical chairs; when the music stopped the one that was left standing was in Sara's, and whoops, it was the one that carried the message that something was askew.

Shelly, of course, was oblivious to what she had just said and Sara, not actually suspecting that it would not be work related, looked at Alex, and to keep the conversation on point, innocently asked, "Do I know who you were with?"

"No," he answered with the distinct need to change the conversation. So he continued, looking at Shelly and Dave, "I never did ask you if you two enjoyed the food that night; did you play bocce or just watch?"

✢ ✢ ✢

Later, in the car driving home, Sara asked, "So, who was the woman you were with the night you met Shelly?"

"Who said it was a woman," Alex answered.

How can reasonably intelligent men not realize that in a situation like this, first, answering a question with a question is a dead giveaway and second, not having immediately given the woman's name was as good as saying *whatever I answer is going to be a lie*?

"Well then, who was it?" Sara insisted.

Quickly Alex had to make a decision: lie about it being a woman, in which case he could be found out easily enough by Sara confirming it with Shelly the next morning in a phone call she was sure to make, and that ostensibly was going to be about the wonderful time they had the previous evening; or he could lie and give the name of a woman whom he identified as a client— again he could be caught in a variation on the previous maneuver; or he could lie and say it was someone he knew from boarding school, recently ran into on the street, and arranged to have dinner with in order to talk about old times! Poor Alex. It was too late. No matter which one he decided on, Sara was not going to believe him.

"What is her name?" This conversation was not going to end either quickly or satisfactorily.

Here's Alex's second stupid question, "Who's?"

"The woman in the restaurant...in New York."

"Her name is Maureen, one of the girls I was in the convent with. Check it out with Maria the next time you talk to her." Mistake number three, assuming the other person won't believe you. "She knows her from back when we were little kids thrown together by our parents, or in her case, lack of parents."

"Do you see her often?"

Alex waited a second before answering, "She works in Manhattan (lie) and we bump into each other occasionally (lie)."

Sara merely answered, "Oh."

25

Arrondondo couldn't remember what year he was promoted to sergeant. Randy Stillerman, had asked him recently and Arrondondo could only snicker, "Too long ago."

He admitted to himself that he could not complain: he liked what he did, knew he was good at it; you couldn't call it dangerous duty and he had regular hours—usually, and a good pension.

Randy had been his sidekick for a couple of years now. He was a sharp kid, would make a great detective and obviously liked and respected Arrondondo.

"I am stumped with my meeting with Alex Fazio on the Robert Steeter case Randy, too many things don't add up."

It was the morning after Arrondondo's meeting with Alex at the hotel in New York. "The guy lived in that convent for what, four or five years? Was an altar boy for what, two of them? Yet he couldn't identify that the wall in the picture was next to the church? I recognized it right away. What do you make of it?"

"You didn't, I suppose, bring up the fact that you already knew where the wall was...while you were talking to him...did you?"

"No Randy, something told me I had to test him. He maintains that he has a weak memory for unpleasant things from the time they happened, like his mother's death...he specifically brought that up one time when we were discussing the Steeter case. Frankly, I found that a somewhat interesting statement so I even made note of it in my notebook. But why would a wall bring up the same sort of reaction as something like his mother's death? Something doesn't add up."

"One explanation," Randy offered, "could be that you've been back there to see Father Mike—off and on all these years—so you've seen the wall more recently than he has; he lives in Chicago and probably hasn't been back since he originally left a long time ago. That could explain not recognizing it, couldn't it?"

"Maybe, but I don't think so. I believe he knew where the picture was taken but didn't want to let on to me that he knew."

"And you never found anything unusual when you checked around the church property?" Randy asked.

"Haven't been there to investigate for a long time now; not since the time of the disappearance. Back then I didn't see anything that was out of the ordinary; but of course there wasn't anything in particular I was looking for either.

"It's the wall okay; I found some cigarette butts; but that's about it if I remember correctly. I didn't think they were that unusual, hell you see them everywhere. I did make a note, however; I didn't find anything else." Arrondondo was thinking out loud.

"Perhaps it's time you go back, or do you want me to go take another look, Sarge?" Randy volunteered. "I know it's been a while, but even so, maybe it wouldn't hurt if I went and took another look around."

"Actually, I was thinking we'd go see the priest first, you and I...Father Mike. It has been a couple of months since we've spoken; he's as interested in this case as I am; besides, he feels responsible, especially if something happened to the boy. He hasn't turned up...it's been a long time now. They usually turn up...a relative finds out about them, they get in trouble; even a little fender-bender traffic accident, something usually brings them forward. But not this time, so the priest and I...we're stumped.

"Sooner or later," Arrondondo continued, "he'll show up. I'd like you to come along Randy. We'll ask Father and I'm certain we'll get the okay to snoop around; then the two of us looking may turn up something. What have you got going this afternoon...after lunch?"

"I'm open," Randy answered, "I could use an hour to finish up a few things but I can be ready whenever you are."

"Good, I'll call him right away and let you know if we are on."

✦ ✦ ✦

"Father Mike? Sergeant Arrondondo here; did I catch you at a bad time?"

"Sergeant? No...you caught me at a good time. Anything new on the Steeter case?" It was not unusual for Father Mike to jump right in to the probable reason for a phone call.

"Well Father, we had a few interesting things happen recently in the case and I was wondering if we could get together for a little while later this afternoon, say after lunch?"

"Sure, as I said, I don't have anything on my plate that I can't postpone. After lunch you say? Do you want to come here or would you prefer I meet you at the precinct?"

"I'll come to the rectory Father, and if you don't mind I'd like to bring Detective Randy Stillerman. He works with me and he too has taken a special interest in this case.

"Father Mike," Arrondondo couldn't help venting his frustration, "why do you think we are having so much difficulty with this case? Why, after all these years can't we put it to bed?"

"I don't know Sergeant, unfinished business I'd say; something's keeping us from just stamping the file: *Runaway—Case Closed,* isn't it? What else could it be? That's the question don't you think? Unfortunately, I think neither of us believes the boy merely ran away."

"For me it is unfinished business," emphasizing *is* —"but it's more than that," Sergeant Arrondondo responded, "I've always had a strange sense about this disappearance, it just never seemed right; but I can't put my finger on it."

"Same here," Father Mike agreed, "I'll think about it often. Perhaps there is something there, something that *neither* of us can put our finger on. If we could, it would answer whatever questions we have. What makes it worse Sergeant, I'm not sure I even know the questions," Father chuckled. He had to do something to add levity to what he knew was a serious and disturbingly unsolved case.

✦ ✦ ✦

After introductions, Father Mike invited Sergeant Arrondondo and Detective Randy Stillerman to have a seat. They were in the parlor room of the parish rectory and the housekeeper had put a fresh pot of coffee on the sideboard. The aroma enticed the three of them. They each poured themselves a cup, sat down, and were ready for business.

"First of all Father, how much time do we have before your next appointment?"

"I'm free until a little before five o'clock, then I have to get ready for dinner. We're having a special guest from the Archbishop's office—parish business—so it is important that I attend. Afterwards I'm off to the hospital. One of our dear parishioners is very sick and has asked for a priest. I find early evening a good time to visit; gets them settled down and I like to think they sleep better."

"In that case," Sergeant Arrondondo continued, "I'd like to review what we know. It will help bring Detective Stillerman here along and perhaps he might pick up on something that we have overlooked."

"Fine," answered Father Mike, glancing at Stillerman.

"To begin with, here is what we know." Sergeant Arrondondo flipped open his notebook and began.

"According to Alex Fazio, the two of them, he and Robert, served the Wednesday night service. Father, you maintain that you didn't observe anything unusual during the service, and had to leave the church immediately after it ended."

Arrondondo looked up from his notes and continued, "Alex told you and confirmed with me, that he and Robert didn't have any conversation either before, during or after the service. Father, you told me you believed this was unusual, since Robert was normally a non-stop talker—a smoocher, someone referred to him, is that right?"

"Yes," Father nodded and answered. So Arrondondo continued.

"A Mrs. Jean Reilly, wife of Judge Patrick Reilly, saw three kids standing outside the front of the church at about eight p.m.; the service ended at approximately seven forty-five; add fifteen minutes to tidy up, put everything away; correct?"

Again Father Mike nodded and confirmed.

"According to Sister Kostich, the brother and his sister, Alex and Maria Fazio, did not return to the convent until almost eight thirty...that's a half hour later; isn't that right Father?"

"Yes." Father Mike confirmed. "However, there is a discrepancy with what we've learned from Mrs. Reilly and what both Alex and Maria have told us. Mrs. Reilly maintains that she saw *three* children who suddenly seemed to vanish and then, when she looked again, there was only one. The Fazios maintain that they met after the Benediction and walked—just the two of them—directly back to the convent."

"Yes Father, that is what we know as of right now and we don't have an answer. It could be important, it could be the Fazio kids are not telling the truth; I don't see any reason for Mrs. Reilly to lie, can you? Of course, she could also have made an honest mistake in what she thinks she saw. Besides, it was night remember, but let's keep this in mind and come back to it. However, there is more..."

Sergeant Arrondondo leaned forward and looked directly at Father Mike, "There is a new development. We got a court order to search the former janitor, Earl Sasser's apartment—from Judge Reilly, no less—and found these."

He motioned to Stillerman who pulled the photos out of one envelope and passed them over to Father Mike and while Father was looking at them, Randy pulled the newspaper clippings out of another and held on to them until he got the nod from Arrondondo to pass them over as well.

"You know that Earl has been in and out of jail since the disappearance and there was always something gnawing at me that he had more to do with Robert Steeter's disappearance than he let on. These photos, to me at least, confirm my suspicions. Yes, there is more to this story than we know.

"Father, we know for certain who two of the boys are, our janitor wrote their names on the back of the photos. The third picture is Robert, or at least Alex Fazio confirmed what I already believed, it is Robert; he identified the shirt as definitely belonging to Robert. However Father, here is the strange part," the sergeant continued.

"I showed these pictures to Alex and asked him if he knew where this one with Robert was taken and he said he didn't know. Unless I'm mistaken Father, you know where it was taken; you do, don't you?"

"Of course," Father answered, "against the wall by the church. You'll notice that the church wall is quite different than the one around the convent—take a look the next time you get a chance—the convent wall is constructed of smooth, gray, sandy-looking blocks; around the church they resemble rough concrete, more pebbles rather than just sand...embedded in the blocks; quite unusual actually."

This was Father Mike's way of confirming his answer to himself; he didn't want to agree to something unless he was absolutely sure.

"I realized immediately it was the church wall," Sergeant Arrondondo looked again at the picture, almost as if he too was verifying what Father had just described. "The question is, if you and I can identify the location right away, was Alex lying or holding back or, as he told me, 'it was a long time ago and I tend to not remember unpleasant things from my past.' Do you buy that, Father? I don't. There is something going on here and that is why I can't let this case drop. I want to get to the bottom of it. It is how I am; I don't like 'unfinished business,' so to speak."

"I can't answer for Alex," Father Mike responded to the sergeant's original question and looked at Detective Randy...like he was looking for support even though he knew there would be no reason to expect any; perhaps, therefore, support that meant, "You understand what I'm agreeing to, don't you." Detective

Stillerman gave a reciprocal look but also figured it was a cue to make a clarifying statement.

Randy began, "We don't know the whereabouts of Earl Stasser the janitor during the time of the disappearance; so we don't know if he was involved in any way. Therefore, these pictures, though incriminating in their own right, and unless I am missing something, unfortunately they do not lead us any closer to solving the disappearance, do they?"

"Wait a minute," Father Mike looked at Sergeant Arrondondo then back at Randy Stillerman, "did you say you don't know where the janitor was during the time of the disappearance?"

"Yes," Sergeant Arrondondo answered for Stillerman. "Why?" He had a puzzled look.

"Well, a few days before Robert Steeter disappeared, the janitor came to see me. He asked for his old job back, told me he was unemployed and needed a job.

"Unfortunately I hesitated before saying no! He certainly knew why I hesitated and repeated what he maintained all the while, that he never did anything wrong, that someone was out to get him for some reason and whoever it was had lied.

"I didn't agree or disagree; I was in no mood to rehash an old subject, so I merely said I was sorry, we don't need any help at the present time."

"What did he say?" Sergeant Arrondondo perked up with this new information.

"As I recall," Father Mike continued, "nothing specific that I can remember, he just said 'thank you' and left. I thought you knew Sergeant?"

"No I don't recall having heard that Father, but I'm glad you remembered and that you told me. I'll certainly take note of it."

"But there's more," Father Mike continued, "I saw him again—on Wednesday afternoon. I was coming out of the convent; I had just met with Sister Hortense, the Mother Superior and he was on the other side of the street, about two-thirty; he probably didn't see me, but I just figured he had been at the school, asking our principal if she had any work for him."

"What do you make of it Father?" Sergeant Arrondondo asked.

"Well, nothing special; just a coincidence."

"Perhaps," Sergeant Arrondondo answered, "but it adds a little more light on the subject. I always figured the janitor may have something to do with the disappearance but until now it was just a long-shot."

"Sergeant," Father Mike looked at both men before continuing. You could tell what was going on inside his mind.

"I find these pictures so disturbing. Why is it that grown men go after little boys; I feel responsible. Robert was ultimately in my care and this happens? I feel responsible for his disappearance, too. If he ran away, why didn't he come to me first; discuss whatever was bothering him. If he was abducted by someone like this janitor, why didn't I prevent it? I only found out what was going on with the janitor after it was too late. We fired him; I was concerned about what the parishioners would think so we just fired him. I should have turned him over to the police. It is my fault."

Arrondondo agreed but did not say so out loud. Instead he answered, "We treat these things too lightly...until it is too late. If more people worried less about what others think and more about the right thing to do, perhaps we'd see less of this." He was frustrated about all the crimes he witnessed, not only this one. It didn't dawn on him that he was lecturing the priest.

"But Father, getting back to Stasser being near the church on Wednesday afternoon," Sergeant Arrondondo was persistent. "Could it be that he was the third person Mrs. Reilly saw? If Robert and the Fazio boy didn't talk all during the Benediction Service—we'll have to get to the reason why later on—and if the janitor *was* around and *was* indeed the third person Mrs. Reilly saw, then that would confirm what the children said about just the two of them walking home together. The next question becomes '...was he waiting for Robert and therefore complicit in helping him run away...?' Or should I say *disappear*?"

"I think you may be on the right track Sergeant," Father Mike responded. "It's the most plausible explanation so far. What are you going to do next and is there anything I can do?"

"Let me think that through Father. Meanwhile, Detective Stillerman and I would like to take another look around...if you don't mind? It's been a long time but this picture, the wall and all, with Randy as a fresh set of eyes, we'd like to take another look."

195

"Of course Sergeant, by all means." Father Mike looked at his watch. "I'll be available until just before five so if you need me again don't hesitate."

They shook hands and Sergeant Arrondondo and Detective Stillerman walked from the rectory to the church.

It was a bright sunny day, no wind but a little on the crisp side. Both the detectives had on light jackets.

"He has a lot of responsibility," Detective Stillerman offered, "first of all a lot of kids and secondly they are not his own. When they are your own and you are with them all the time, you get to know them really well. How can Father Mike possibly spend all his time with his kids, and even if he did, would he know them as well as a parent would?" Stillerman was trying, in vain, to come to terms with orphans and other kids who were, for whatever reason, placed in an institution like Holy Ghost Convent.

"It must be difficult for both sides, the kids as well as the priest and nuns," he continued talking to Sergeant Arrondondo, who may or may not have been listening. More likely, Randy was just thinking out loud while they walked the block to the church.

26

The two men stopped in front of the church. Sergeant Arrondondo turned and pointed to the front door of the school. "Where we are standing is where Mrs. Reilly said she saw the children while she was inside that school door waiting for her husband to pick her up.

"It was dark so it is possible she didn't recognize precisely who was standing here...could even have been three other kids, not convent kids, but what she says she saw *does* fit with the latest information we got from Father Mike; so let's count on it being Alex, Maria and Stasser the janitor. After all, what reason does she have to make something up, unlike the two kids who may have been involved and don't want to admit it?"

He pointed to the wall just to the right of the church to show Stillerman which way they were heading, then continued his musing. "She said that when she looked again, after getting into her husband's car, there was only one of them. Where did the two go and which two was it. No help from our Mrs. Reilly there."

Stillerman added another possibility. "Perhaps she saw the three, like you said, but then the boy and the girl went towards the convent and the third person, the janitor, stayed behind. The question then is, did the boy and girl know the janitor was nearby?"

"Good point," mumbled Arrondondo.

They walked toward the space between the wall and the church.

"One of the times I had Earl in the interrogation room, he inferred that he and the Steeter kid sometimes would go behind the church and smoke cigarettes. I asked him because I saw butts on the ground among all the junk that is tossed back there, but of course anyone smoking behind the bushes could just toss them over the wall, that would explain it, no?"

"You said inferred," Detective Randy Stillerman asked, "do you mean he didn't fess up, or what?"

"No, once Earl realized what I was asking he said he misunderstood the question; said only *he* went back there, never would dream of giving cigarettes to any kids."

"I see."

"There are two corners back there, the one on the street side and the other one beyond, on the left, but that's a very tight squeeze. It's a good thing you are as skinny as a drink of water," Sergeant Arrondondo said to Randy, "it is very tight, but we'll see if you can squeeze through."

"Sure is a lot of junk," Randy said, as they got further into the space on the right; "got to be careful you don't trip, or worse, twist your ankle."

"Yes," Sergeant Arrondondo agreed, "which adds to the difficulty thinking that two of the kids came back here in the dark. But, if the boys liked to smoke cigarettes after serving at the church devotions, it would account for what Mrs. Reilly said. It would also explain her seeing only one kid when she looked again...after getting into the car...the girl most probably, either waiting for the other two, Alex and Robert, to finish their smoke or something. However, that scenario leaves the janitor unaccounted for."

"What's in this hole?" While the sergeant was talking, Detective Stillerman had gone beyond, into the left corner, ahead of the sergeant. Being so skinny he was able to slip between the rounded sacristy and the rear wall. The left quadrant behind the church was a copy of the right side where he had left the sergeant standing. The space was so narrow it never dawned on the sergeant that anyone could readily slip through; with the place where he was standing so hidden from view, why go any deeper? Besides, you had to step over a barrier of more bricks about a foot and a half high, as well as to squeeze through.

"What hole? I don't see any hole."

"There is a step over here, just like on your side, a doorway that has been bricked over. Beyond the step is a large hole, like going into the basement. Too bad it is getting dusk, I can't see anything inside."

"There is a flashlight in the car, isn't there?"

"I think so."

"Run back and get it, I'll look around on this side. I don't know if I can squeeze through there." Then to himself, "fat-ass."

Detective Stillerman was slightly out of breath when he returned with the flashlight. It was getting dark and something in his head told him the hole next to the step was important.

"Got it," referring to the large, powerful flashlight, "let's take a look."

He squeezed through the space again, switched on the light and peered into the hole.

"Holy crap," he exclaimed. "What do we have here?"

"What is it?" Sergeant exhaled and through sheer will power got himself through the narrow space and looked down as Detective Stillerman crawled a little further into the hole. "Bones Sergeant, human remains. We found him Sergeant, the striped shirt matches the picture."

"Get out of there!" the sergeant yelled, "I don't want anything disturbed."

"Get back to the car and radio for Jordy. Tell him what we've got. Get someone to set up a ladder from over the wall. Jordy is fatter than I am, he'll never get through here. Get some lights, too. I'll go back to the rectory. This is going to be a sad day for Father Mike."

✦ ✦ ✦

Jordan Saydorf. Only Sergeant Arrondondo called him Jordy. He hated the nickname and long ago made the mistake of telling his good friend Arrondondo that he hated it, and so embedded the moniker forever.

Jordy was the county medical examiner for life, or so it seemed. He continued to get reelected over and over without having to do any campaigning. No one ever ran against him; he did his job quietly and effectively and, most importantly, got good marks for "works well with others" especially from Sergeant Arrondondo and all the other detectives throughout Nassau County—the people who relied on him.

Detective Stillerman quickly gave him just enough background and information for him to assemble the correct staff and equipment. Jordan had a few questions, but in the main, Stillerman painted a quite accurate picture of what Jordan would find as well as the difficulty he'd have with the small entry to the space under the church sacristy.

Stillerman was sure to emphasize that Sergeant Arrondondo was waiting at the church; Jordan got the message and immediately got the response team into high gear.

Stillerman next called the fire department, was fortunate that he was put through to someone he casually knew through playing softball, described the problem with the wall, and they too got on it immediately. As he was walking back from the car where he made the calls, he saw Sergeant Arrondondo coming from behind the church; he'd been taking advantage of the waning light to look for anything unusual before heading over to the rectory to see Father Mike. The sergeant saw Stillerman walking toward him, stopped, waited until he caught up and asked him, "You go to church here, don't you?"

"Yeah, it's my parish, but I don't go as often as I should. My parents are always on my case; I go with my girlfriend every couple, three weeks; yes, I guess you could say I go to church here, why?"

"I'll bet you and the other parishioners had no idea a body was decomposing beneath the altar. As you know, I don't go to this church, but it's probably not any different than mine: High Mass at eleven on Sundays with a lot of incense; Benediction on Wednesdays, with more incense; what, two or three funerals a week? Again, more incense. No wonder, with a ton of incense each week...that would mask any odor coming from the crawl space. Besides, this church was built when they figured it would be here for five-hundred years; layer upon layer of wood, stone and mortar."

Sergeant Arrondondo took a hard look at the front of the church and Detective Randy followed his gaze. "I hate doing this," Sergeant Arrondondo finally said to no one in particular, "this is going to be hard on Father Mike, poor guy."

He turned to Randy and said, "Did you get hold of Jordan?"

"Yes, I expect him here within fifteen, twenty minutes. I talked to a buddy of mine at the fire house, they are on their way; should be hearing their sirens momentarily."

"Good, you wait here for the fire department boys; send them to the next street to get access or maybe they can do something from this side, I don't think so though; and as soon as Jordy gets here, come and get me at the rectory. I don't want him or his men to go in until I get back here, you understand?"

"Will do Sergeant." Detective Randy Stillerman straightened up as he responded.

27

Father Mike Monahan knew there was going to be bad news as soon as the housekeeper informed him that Sergeant Arrondondo was waiting in the parlor, confirmed when Father saw the look on the sergeant's face.

"Mike," Arrondondo said. For the first time he felt the need to be informal. "I'm afraid I have some bad news. We found Robert Steeter."

Instinctively, Father Mike put his hand up to his mouth, covering it; he closed his eyes for a second and gave his head a momentary side-to-side shiver.

"There is a space under the church altar," Sergeant Arrondondo continued, "the entrance is next to an old step, no longer used and not even with access; there is no question; the shirt is Robert's...exactly like in the picture. I've called the county medical examiner, should be there in a few minutes. They will call me; I want to be there before they touch anything."

Sergeant Arrondondo reverted to his "take charge" manner.

"You are welcome to come along Father. If you'd rather not, then have your dinner, visit the hospital and I'll keep you informed. Sorry to bring bad news Father." Sergeant Arrondondo touched Father Mike on his forearm in a gesture of understanding, "I'd better get over there. It is important that this be handled properly and I only trust myself to see that it is."

"I understand, and yes, it is important that I attend this meeting and that I visit the hospital. I know you will keep me informed Sergeant."

"Do you know the cause of death Sergeant?" Father Mike asked.

"No, not yet. It may be difficult; the body is decomposed, but I will let you know as soon as I find out anything. I'll see myself out."

✦ ✦ ✦

Arrondondo hurried back to the church. He saw Jordan's van drive up and he and four of his team got out.

"Hello Jordy," Sergeant Arrondondo said as he approached the van. He then acknowledged the assistants with a nod. "We'll have to wait here until the fire department finishes getting us access; the remains are behind that church and we will never be able to squeeze through the space between the church and the wall, especially with any equipment. We'll have to see if they can get us in on this side of that rear wall or from the backyard behind the church. Sergeant Arrondondo pointed to the area he was talking about. Let me fill you in while we are waiting."

Sergeant Arrondondo gave a quick summary of what he perceived happened. "You will find the remains of a youngster, maybe fourteen years old, been missing for twenty-plus years. I've been following this case Jordy, for all that time. I knew it was going to come to this.

"If he was murdered, which I will bet you a hundred bucks he was, I think I know who did it. I'll need you to be extra careful; every detail could be important. I've got to know how he died. I'm counting on you."

"Understand," Jordan answered. He was a man of few words but was known for writing one hell of a report!

✦ ✦ ✦

Actually, the fire department boys were already in the neighbor's backyard on the street to the west of the church, erecting a platform on top of the wall with a ladder going up and then down into the quadrant. It was a narrow space so they also erected a small crane-like piece of equipment to haul items up and over the wall.

The first person in was one of Jordan's staff. He wore rubber gloves, was dressed in a white coverall, a mask on his face and a hairnet. He had a flashlight even though the fire department had a light on a short stand just outside the hole. It was obvious that it could be readily moved inside.

After spending a few minutes under the sacristy, he came out; squatted by the entrance to the space; looked first to his boss who was kneeling at the entrance to the hole, then to Sergeant Arrondondo and Stillerman who were standing on the platform looking over the wall, and gave a quick summary: "A decomposed body, fully dressed including shoes, looks to be a young male, looks like it was dragged into the hole."

He stood up, removed his gloves and continued, "The space is, and I'm estimating, five feet high and forty to fifty feet deep by about thirty-five feet wide. The body is about ten feet beyond the entrance."

"Okay," the medical examiner said, "first I want pictures; carefully examine every inch of the place, then bring the body out. You know, typical routine. Okay, get on it. Is the photographer here?"

Jordan went up and over the platform and there the photographer was, at the ready.

"I was thinking Jordy," Sergeant Arrondondo said, after Jordan gave instructions to the photographer, "this is like a mausoleum, it's likely even an animal couldn't get in over that brick barrier. I'd like your opinion if anything has been disturbed between the time he died and today."

"I'll get a sense from the pictures," Jordan answered, "I saw that the arms are raised over the skull and the boy—Robert Steeter you said his name was—is on his stomach, he could have crawled in himself and then died or he was dragged in. We'll know more after we determine the cause of death, although like my technician said, seemingly he was dead before he was moved to where he is now."

"I'll need your preliminary report as soon as possible. We will not be able to keep this out of the news and I'd like to question my suspect before he finds out we've found the body."

"Give me a few hours and I'll have a good idea of what we are up against."

Sergeant Arrondondo was on his way back to the squad car he and Stillerman arrived in, when one of Jordan's technicians came up to him.

"Sergeant, we found something you'll be interested in, a cigar box up in the rafters. Appears the intent was for it to be hidden. Jordan said you'd want to know right away.

Sergeant Arrondondo responded, "I'll be curious what's in the box; probably not cigars; my guess is that the kid kept cigarettes in it. Is that what's inside?

"Don't know, Jordan wants it taken to the lab so it can be opened and examined very carefully, told me to tell you he'll let you know as soon as possible."

"Okay, and incidentally, can we get someone to examine those butts that are back there among the junk, before they have been stepped on?"

When the technician reported the sergeant's request, Jordan immediately understood the possible connection that Arrondondo was getting at with the cigar box, and told another of his men to collect the butts and secure them in a plastic bag.

28

It normally took an hour, more or less, for Alex to get from home to his office. He preferred to drive, believing that he wasted less time that way. If he drove, he could listen to the news or, alternatively, he could have the radio off, thereby leaving him time to think about work, home, anything and everything. In a quiet car he could strategize, plan or daydream, whereby on the train, so he believed, he totally wasted his time because he could not stop himself from scrutinizing people.

Where is that one going? What type of work does she do? That guy looks pathetic; does he realize it? The one over there, with the ass you could set your coffee cup on, what does she have to smile about? He'd look at folks blankly; listen to their conversation; some people he'd find attractive, others he'd find repulsive; some he'd like to know better, occasionally there was one he'd like to throw off the train—usually a loud, useless, obnoxious, punk kid. It was more and more difficult to find nice people; nicely dressed commuters. Lately the people in his office annoyed him too.

Suddenly Dolores came to mind. Specifically her "news" that Paul's father was sentenced to prison. "The old guy undoubtedly deserved what he got; it is the kid that has to bear the brunt of it. Just got married. I've met him, nice guy, right for Katie. Now what have we got, nine, ten people's lives ruined by the fact one of them, a father, is going to prison for murder.

"What if it were my kids? What then? Their lives would be ruined, they'd probably think twice about having kids of their own, afraid that the *murder-gene* would be passed down. Of course...there is no such thing. Really? Can anyone be certain? Maybe it's like when everyone was convinced the earth is flat; who's to say?

"I've always maintained that one should never, never say something cannot exist or cannot be done, because sure as hell, someone will find it or do it. There is no such thing as can't. I'll bet if you asked Caesar if a man could fly he'd say, 'No, of course not, can't be done,' and he pass out if he could get up from his grave today and have an airplane fly over his head.

"Katie and Paul. I wonder if they will have any children now? I wonder if they have talked about it in the same way I'm thinking about it right now?"

Most of the time he'd talk to himself like he was doing now, only in the car, not on the train...

Sometimes he'd think things, not say them out loud; like...I hope that sergeant gets himself wasted was today's conversation; then he caught himself, snapped his head in a circular motion in an effort to clear it; he realized how negative he was becoming, how intolerant, the foul language; I need to get hold of myself, he admitted.

His office was in the Loop. Today, he parked his car in the underground garage under Grant Park, a few blocks east of his office. He figured it would be a bad day because as he was walking up the stairs from the garage, all of a sudden he felt dizzy. It was happening more and more frequently; he missed his step and landed on his wrist. It hurt like hell.

So he was not in a good mood when he walked through the glass doors into the CCG reception room. The receptionist, who of course recognized him but he could not recall her name even though she'd been there forever, said in her high-pitched voice that Alex found so sugary and sweet it almost made him throw up; "Mr. Fazio, Mr. Henderson asked me to tell you as soon as you came in that he would like to see you. He said you should go right into his office, he'll be waiting."

Well, he will have to wait, Alex thought, I have to pee.

But instead he responded, "Thank you."

He put his briefcase on his desk and went into the men's room. He stood at the urinal for an actual seven minutes, though he didn't realize how much time had elapsed, and eventually came to the realization that he hadn't thought of anything at all—all that while. Nothing.

I just stood here, didn't pee a drop, yet my mind was absolutely blank. That's incredible...like I'm in a coma. What does that ass-hole want now? Doesn't he realize I have enough to worry about; can't he give me a break; lay off just a little?

Oh well, let's get it over with.

The door to Major Henderson's office was open as usual. Look at that fat-ass, sitting at his desk, pretending he's important, doesn't do squat.

"Major, good morning, you wanted to see me right away? What's up?" Alex tried putting on a happy face.

"Alex yes, come on in. Close the door. Have a seat. Let's have a little chat."

Alex took a seat across from the huge powerful desk and the huge powerful Major Henderson. His life was in Henderson's hands. His wrist still hurt so he massaged it, but he realized it was nothing compared to the hurt that was on its way.

"Alex, Alex, Alex, what am I going to do with you? You know you are one of my favorites, like my own son?"

What a bunch of bullshit, went through Alex's mind as Henderson pushed back in his great big leather chair.

"You've done one hell of a job for us; you've gotten the biggest, most profitable clients; they are always happy...but what the hell is going on? The last time we talked I was kidding about some bimbo in New York but now I find I wasn't kidding; but before you go off half-cocked and figure Dave Crowley has been gossiping about you, he didn't spill the goods, I drew it out of him so eventually he told me her name, Maureen isn't it?

"What is she doing to you, what are you doing to yourself? I'm not your confessor but I got to tell you, you are getting yourself into deep shit...I know Sara, she is not going to like hearing about any Maureens."

For anyone watching Alex during this tirade it would be difficult to figure out exactly what was going on inside his head...if anything. There was a slight upturn of his lower lip but he didn't move a bit; the look on his face portrayed interest in what he was hearing...sort of, but if Henderson was looking for feedback, he wasn't getting any. In any case, he continued.

"But, that is all your business. It becomes mine when it interferes with your job. Besides, you hung Crowley out on a limb last week; he showed up at your client meeting just like the two of you planned, but knew nothing of what the meeting was about and found himself stumbling like an idiot when you never showed up, never said a word, that's incredible! He told me he finally had to beg forgiveness for not knowing what was going on, saying he didn't want to miss-speak himself, made a lame-brain excuse for your not being there and told the client he'd get back to them. Do I have that correct?"

Alex changed positions, inhaled a little and answered blankly, "No excuse, every once in a while shit happens."

He realized as soon as the words were out that he should have responded differently.

"Major, that's not what I meant. Every once in a while we all find ourselves in some difficulty, like right now. You are right, of course, I've been through a few troubling weeks; my sister is sick, probably won't survive much longer; it's taking its toll; perhaps I need a few weeks leave, maybe a month, to take care of my personal stuff."

"I'm sorry about your sister, I didn't know, you should have told me. Does Crowley know?"

"No, I haven't told anyone. In fact I just found out that the doctors do not give her much hope."

Why am I making excuses to this ass-hole, Alex thought to himself, he could care less about my sister—Maureen a bimbo? Fuck you. You have no idea what's going on. I've got this cop on my ass, my other sister's relative is going to jail for murder, Sara's being a pain in the ass, and you're worried about your fucking clients?

"I thought," Alex continued out loud, "I could handle work too but, frankly, I guess I can't. I think I need some time off," he said to Major Henderson, "I can tie things up with Crowley today and tomorrow, and if it is okay, I'll take a few weeks off and let you know how it's going."

"Well, of course, do you have any vacation coming?"

Oh you mother! Alex thought, vacation? I've brought in millions to this firm and you are worried about a few fucking weeks of vacation? However, he answered, "Yes I've got some, I'll work it out."

"But that doesn't solve the problem of this Maureen person, does it Alex?" Henderson continued.

"I understand about your sister, but Maureen is a bigger problem. I've told you before it doesn't work to have a 'sideline' in some far off city. You start making your business fit your personal life instead of the other way around. If Dave Crowley can take over your clients while you are away, why can't he take them over permanently? That's what I have to decide. If you are going to be more worried about Maureen or whatever her name is than focusing on why you are in New York in the first place, don't you think it will be a problem?"

What was going through Alex's mind was, who the hell does this guy think he is, my father, my confessor...I don't believe what I'm hearing. If he doesn't shut up pretty soon I'm going to say something I'll be sorry for.

Henderson continued, "Sure, take some vacation time, but I'm not so sure things will be the same when you come back. This isn't something that just came up, I was aware of something going on in New York for a while now and the rest of management does not treat it lightly, they are on me to have Crowley take over. Know what I mean?"

Alex couldn't stand it any longer.

"No, I don't know what you mean. Like you just said, I've brought in quite a few clients, good clients, if you think Dave Crowley, that little mother-fucking motor mouth can do better, then take your job and shove it up your ass. I quit." Alex got up, walked out of the office and slammed Henderson's door.

✦ ✦ ✦

That was brilliant! Alex went back to his office, closed the door and sat in his usual position when he was in a funk: head in his hands, elbows on his spread-apart knees. He didn't sit long.

He got up, went around to his desk and dialed Maureen's phone number. She answered promptly.

"Hi. I just quit my job." There was a moment of silence on the phone.

"Why," Maureen asked.

"I don't want to talk about it now. I'm still at my office. I am going to go home, pack a bag and get a flight to New York later this afternoon. I'll call you when I get in. Is it too short notice for you to plan on meeting me in Manhattan?"

"Yes, we've got plans for tonight but I'll see you tomorrow. Can't you give me a hint? What happened?"

"It's complicated. We'll talk tomorrow."

When Alex got home, Sara was out. He quickly packed and left a note that he had to make an unexpected trip. This happened frequently enough that Sara would not give it much thought; he didn't feel it necessary to go into detail. He knew that they didn't have any plans for the evening so that eliminated one potential problem. He stopped at a restaurant a few blocks from his house and used the pay phone to call the airline and hotel for reservations. There was no problem getting either.

He drove slowly to the airport, parked in the long-term lot, waited two hours in the terminal watching people, and then boarded the flight.

29

Sergeant Arrondondo spent the last forty-five minutes reviewing every detail of the Robert Steeter disappearance case with the chief of police and the district attorney. They were in the chief's office. The meeting was being held to determine if there was enough evidence to bind Earl Stasser over for the murder of Robert Steeter.

Sergeant Arrondondo explained how Detective Stillerman stumbled onto the hole under the church sacristy and discovered the bones of a juvenile, identified as the missing boy Robert Steeter.

He explained the preliminary report by the medical examiner, Jordan Saydorf, that the probable cause of death was multiple blows to the head; the probable weapon was a piece of wood approximately four and one-half feet long, resembling a broom handle," which was found outside the entrance to the space under the church. The suspect was known to be in the vicinity of the crime at the time it was committed; this last item fairly well rounded out the impeachable evidence.

At issue, and more significant, was a letter found in a cigar box tucked into the rafters above the body. Sergeant Arrondondo explained how they found a box containing cigarettes and a handwritten note, later determined to have been written by the deceased and dated two days before he disappeared.

At the moment, the district attorney was speaking—"The law is unclear regarding evidence from a dead person. If the letter you found in the cigar box had been written as the boy was dying

217

it would not be impeachable; the fact that it is dated two days before his disappearance makes it a little more dicey.

"I'm not saying you don't have a case. Considering the other evidence, you do have; and my guess is any judge would agree you have sufficient cause to convene a grand jury, especially since you already have him in jail on a related charge. Perhaps when you confront him with the scenario he'll confess, what do you think?" The district attorney looked first at the chief of police and then at Sergeant Arrondondo, seemingly for affirmation.

The chief of police raised his hand for a question, or at least that is how it looked to Sergeant Arrondondo. He had to chuckle to himself; it looked funny, his boss raising his hand to ask to speak. "Could you go over it again Sergeant, what exactly was in the letter?"

"Sure Chief," Sergeant Arrondondo picked up the copy of the letter that had been typed from the original handwritten one they found in the cigar box. The original was a scrap of paper, written in pencil and, although there was no absolute proof that it was written by the boy, the handwriting was judged to be juvenile in appearance, it was dated two days before he disappeared, and it was signed Robert Steeter.

Sergeant Arrondondo read the following:

To Maureen
If anything happens to me bring this to the police and tell them that if any thing happens to me it was Earl S. who did it. I want him to pay me 50.00 dollars or I will tell the police what he did to me in the picture he has because

it is a crime and he will go to jail. Signed Robert Steeter.

Sergeant Arrondondo added that what he just read was typed exactly as it was written, then he put the paper back down on the table and waited for a response.

It was the chief who asked, "So as I understand it, Earl Stasser does not know about the existence of this letter, correct?"

"That is what we believe Chief," Arrondondo answered. "But we can't be sure. As I see it, the boy wanted money to keep quiet. Whether he told Stasser that he wrote an *insurance* letter, we don't know. I want to be sure of what to expect in terms of how it can be used for evidence before I bring it up to him. If the letter is good evidence I will handle it one way, but as I understand from this meeting, it may not be good evidence so I will have to think through carefully exactly *how* I am going to handle it."

Sergeant Arrondondo looked toward the district attorney before continuing, "This is what I think happened: the Steeter boy extorted fifty dollars from the janitor who planned to meet him after the evening church service. The young girl waited in front of the church until her brother came out, then she and her brother walked back to the convent while the Steeter boy stayed behind to wait for our man Stasser."

The sergeant continued, "The boy was expecting to be paid, but our murderer had other plans. The boy demanded fifty dollars, so he realized this situation might turn into a long-term blackmail and would have none of it. His solution was to get the kid to go behind the church, ostensibly for a cigarette, and at the opportune moment hit him over the head, drag his body into the space, and figure he'd save fifty dollars, which he probably didn't have anyway—shut him up and get away with murder; all at the same time."

The sergeant paused a moment, as if to check a fact in his memory, then continued, "This confirms what Mrs. Reilly, Judge Reilly's wife saw. She maintains she saw three kids standing in front of the church, next time she looks they are gone, but admits that she was momentarily blinded by car headlights; then moments later she sees only one kid. She says she isn't absolutely sure it *was* the girl, but she isn't absolutely sure it *wasn't*, so it fits that it could have been Stasser waiting for the two Fazio kids to begin walking back to the convent, at which time he'd then go to meet Steeter behind the church.

"It also fits with Alex's statement that he and the Steeter kid never had any conversation all the while they were in the church as altar boys for the evening service; that he left the church before Robert; met his sister outside; and the both of them walked back to the convent—albeit taking a half hour for a five-minute walk.

"What I have to find out is if the janitor knew where the boy hid his cigarettes or not. We know he didn't find the letter or he would have taken it, right? Or, perhaps he hit Robert over the head before the boy went in to get his cigarettes. In that case he could have known about the hidden cigar box but it did not occur to him to search it after he hit the boy—not suspecting that the kid left a letter.

"Meanwhile, the other two went back to the convent and didn't know anything happened until much later when the Steeter boy did not return. By then they were too scared to say anything.

Besides, those convent kids, I found out, never told on each other; they had a strict code of sorts; it seems they don't talk to *outsiders*."

Sergeant Arrondondo paused, then almost as an after thought said, "Jordan Saydorf's preliminary suggests blows to the head as the cause of death. My question to you is: should I wait until I have the full medical examination report and take the chance this letter leaks out to Stasser or go with the information I have right now? Since he's in jail I could impose a gag on the information he receives."

The district attorney and chief of police looked at each other seeking agreement before the district attorney answered for both of them, "Around here trying to control information never works; go with the preliminary. Saydorf doesn't usually stick his neck out unless he is pretty sure; what do you think Chief?"

The chief nodded in agreement.

"Then I'll go see Earl Stasser this afternoon and formally charge him with the murder of Robert Steeter," Sergeant Arrondondo said. The meeting was over.

✦ ✦ ✦

Maureen came to Alex's hotel a little before ten. "So what's going on?" was her introduction. "You've been acting strangely lately, what's this all about?"

"Do you want some coffee, some breakfast?" Alex answered. "I haven't had anything, what would you like?"

"If you are ordering, just coffee thanks."

Alex ordered two coffees, toast and jelly; they both sat at the little table that was in the room. Alex usually stayed at the same hotel, mostly because of that little table in the suite.

Maureen repeated herself, "You've been acting strangely lately, what's going on?"

"Well, first things first, do you remember that evening at Il Vagabondo's when that little ass-hole Dave Crowley and his wife bumped into us? Well, I knew from the beginning he was after my job so he made it a point to let Henderson know all about us; probably exaggerated. Henderson pretends he's a 'goody-two-shoes' and began lecturing me, called you a bimbo.

"I wasn't in the mood Maureen," he looked at her, "I told him to shove his fucking job up his ass. Aren't you proud of me?"

Maureen continued her somewhat blank stare but didn't answer...so Alex continued.

He pulled his chair in closer to the table and leaned across. He looked at Maureen directly; one hand was almost in the center of the table, as if he were reaching for her.

There was a moment of silence; obviously Alex was deciding how best to bring up the next subject. Suddenly though, you could tell he made a shift in his thoughts and decided he'd discuss Maria first.

"Maria is not doing well. The doctors give her weeks; maybe a month or two—if she's lucky—is how they put it. Right now she is comfortable and her doctor told Dolores and me that he will do his best to keep her doped up toward the end."

Maureen continued to look somewhat blankly. There was a knock on the door and room service delivered the toast and coffee. After giving him a tip, getting everything poured and set, Alex resumed his seat.

"I've had a lot of time thinking about how I was going to tell you this...I decided I'd just tell you straight-out." Alex took a sip of coffee and began the story that he'd never told anyone for almost twenty-five years.

"I have to tell you what happened the night Robert disappeared."

The only change in Maureen was that she made a slight squeeze of her lips. Her left hand remained cradling her chin; the right remained around her cup of coffee. Alex continued to look at her.

"The night before everything happened, Robert told us that he was going to rape us both, behind the church, after the Benediction Service. He told us he'd kill us if we told anyone...why I didn't, I'll always be sorry for; there is no excuse." Alex hesitated, deep in thought, "What happened, happened." He looked directly at Maureen.

"There is a basement under the church sacristy and Robert and that old janitor would smoke and then have sex under there. After the Benediction, we went behind the church. He told Maria and me to wait while he went into the crawl space for his cigarettes.

"Maureen, I was scared—for myself but also for Maria; I didn't want him to hurt her. Then, as he was coming out of the basement, there was a stick lying on the ground right in front of me. I reached down, picked it up and hit him...hard...two times, maybe more. I hadn't planned it, it just happened; I reached down, picked up the stick and beat him on the head as hard as I could.

"We left him there. He wasn't moving. We got out of there as quickly as we could and walked back to the convent, and on the way the only thing we said to each other, Maria and me, was that we'd never bring up what happened to anyone, ever. And we didn't.

"Later, when he didn't come home and everyone said he ran away, Maria and I believed it. We figured he was afraid Sister Kostich would find out what he was going to do to us and he'd be in trouble, so he ran away. That's what we thought: that he came to, got up, and ran away.

"The next night I went back behind the church, I was so scared, but he wasn't there. So I believed it...that he'd run away. Then...I don't know what made me look in that hidden hole under the church, but there he was. He was just lying there, on his stomach. I knew he was dead. I knew he crawled in there and died. I killed him Maureen. I killed your brother. I didn't mean to." Alex was fighting back tears.

"You can understand why I never told you before today, can't you?"

If he expected a response from Maureen, he didn't notice that he didn't get one.

224

"I'm only telling you now because I believe the policeman who was called up on the case back then has reopened it. He came to see me last week and showed me a picture he had of Robert and the janitor. It was taken behind the church. He asked me if I recognized Robert, I told him I did. Then he asked me if I knew where the picture was taken. I told him I didn't but I know he didn't believe me.

"The janitor is in serious trouble because the picture shows Robert pulling up his shorts; his trousers are down around his knees so I am sure he'll go to jail. But now they'll accuse him of worse...of killing Robert, too. He'll be blamed for what I did.

"Say something Maureen, just don't sit there."

"What do you want me to say? I'm not surprised that you knew more about what happened than you let on. I didn't care then, I don't care now. Tell the police what happened..."

Maureen merely shrugged as her way of ending the thought.

After a few moments of silence, she asked, "What about your job? What are you going to tell Sara? Are you going to be stupid enough to tell her about me? It would be stupid, you know, unless she suspects anything—does she?"

Alex took a while to answer. "I don't know, I don't think so."

"Then go home," Maureen leaned back, folded her arms across her chest and continued, "first of all, apologize to Major Henderson, he'll understand...your sister and all." She unfolded her arms; pushed away from the table and said, "Don't call me anymore. I don't want to see you. If and when I'm ready I'll get in touch."

She stood up, walked to the door and before opening it she turned around for one final look.

30

After their marriage it was easy for the new Mrs. Sara Fazio to decide that she enjoyed sleeping in the same bed as Mr. Fazio. Of course once he joined CCG he was off—frequent business trips—she'd have to sleep alone.

Two or three nights gone, he'd return—away exactly the number of nights required for her to get used to sleeping without him—then he'd be back beside her. After several iterations of this, she found that it was much too difficult to change what she had to get used to, so she he had him permanently repair to the guest room bed.

She was surprised when she got home earlier in the day and saw Alex's note. However, since it did not describe an out-of-the-norm occurrence, she went about her routine: make dinner for the kids; put them to bed; straighten up the house; read a little; and get to bed early.

The morning after Alex's note, Sara didn't give much thought to his being away, in fact, although she was aware he was not at home, for a short while she hadn't thought about the fact that he left town on such short notice.

Suddenly she stopped what she was doing and put her hand to the side of her neck. "That's odd," she said to no one in particular, "with him being moody," she paused, then continued, "and not feeling well lately...trouble at the office, this is not like me, but I find it worrisome that he left so suddenly. I don't like it!"

Sara decided then and there that she would call CCG to find out where he went, get the name of the hotel, and call him just to check that he was all right. It would make her feel better and she could then get on with her event-filled day.

The busybody at CCG who answered the phone told her that she was unaware that he was out-of-town and was sorry but did not know where he was—since he wasn't in his office either.

This unnerved Sara tremendously. Her immediate explanation was that he had a client problem and hadn't yet told his office that he had to travel; then she recalled their recent discussion about Maria being sick; then their argument in the car after their dinner with the Crowleys; and eventually she found herself beginning to think all sorts of strange scenarios to explain where he was and why he took off so suddenly—and why...had he failed to notify his office?

Meanwhile, the busybody found it imperative that she inform Major Henderson that "Alex was AWOL"—not in those terms of course, but certainly by her pigeon-chested delivery. Everyone at CCG was aware of the spat between Alex and Major, and especially Ms. Busybody, who was only too happy to be the bearer of breaking news to one of her bosses.

Sara meanwhile, as she considered all the scenarios that put her on edge, it was the one about the *discussion in the car* that won out, and since she knew the hotel in NY where Alex usually stayed—too frequently lately come to think about it, and this was integral to the selecting of this scenario, although she didn't think it through in exactly that way—she called, expecting to leave a message since it was an hour later in NY; already nine-thirty in the morning. She figured that if it *was* a business trip he'd not be in his room to answer the phone.

It was typical in the early seventies, after the phone in a guest's room rang several times and no one picked up the receiver, the call was automatically transferred back to the hotel desk and the caller was asked to leave a message. When they did, a little red light on the room's phone blinked. Because Sara didn't have to leave a message, since he was still in his room, and answered on the second ring, her imagination was aroused.

"Hello? ...Alex?"

"Hello Sara."

"I was worried...you left suddenly, is everything all right?"

"Of course, why wouldn't it be?"

"Well, I called your office and they didn't know where you were, so I got worried. Did you get a call from one of your clients or something?"

Alex thought through a whole list of things in a few moments, yet couldn't figure out where to start.

"I've got a few things I have to take care of," he settled on this one; "I quit my job." A few seconds of silence followed. Then, "Remember when I told you Crowley was after it? Well he can have it now...I've quit."

There were a few more moments of silence.

"I don't understand," Sara broke in, "why did you quit and when, this morning?"

"No, yesterday. Henderson and I had an argument, I got pissed off and quit, that's all. You wouldn't understand."

"Well, you're right, I don't understand." Sara was getting pissed herself. "Don't you think you should have discussed it with me first?"

Alex shook his head no, as if she was there in front of him, but she wasn't, she was nine hundred miles away.

She continued, "Tell me what happened, what did you argue about and is it final? No, of course not, it isn't final, you should call him right away, apologize, tell him you are sorry you got excited or whatever; use the excuse about Maria being sick; tell him that's why you had to leave for New York so suddenly; then tell him you will come see him as soon as you return to Chicago." Sara had it straightaway worked out.

There was no immediate answer. First, he thought, it isn't that simple. True I can explain that I'm in New York because of my sister, but Henderson will figure out that I'm also going to see Maureen while I'm here. I could tell him that I need to see her to break it off—yes, I've taken your advice, I am going to tell her I don't want to see her again.

It won't be difficult, he continued thinking this through, Maureen already broke it off, didn't she? *Don't call me anymore. I don't want to see you. If and when I'm ready I'll get in touch—* that's how she put it.

230

"Sara, you caught me at a bad time. I'm not in a very good mood; I'm not in the mood to discuss this, especially over the phone. My mind is made up, I've quit, so if you don't mind, I'd prefer we finish this conversation when I get back to Chicago, not over the phone and really, not now."

"Well, that's all right for you to say; what am I supposed to do, go about my business...my husband quits his job, isn't that wonderful. Perhaps I should cancel my plans for today and go look for work. Which should I look for, part time or full time? Will you be taking care of the children and the house? Great, you can go shopping, cook dinner, clean, wash the clothing...don't you worry, I can find work."

There was no response on the Alex end.

"Are you still there? ...Alex?"

"Yes, I'm here, but one more time, I don't want to discuss this now and not on the phone, and I don't want to hang up on you, but listen to me...please, I'm going to say goodbye, okay?"

"No, it is not okay. Do you expect me to put it out of my mind? ...Alex? ...Alex? You stupid shit, you hung up!"

✦ ✦ ✦

Alex lay back on the bed. He looked up at the ceiling and noticed the smoke alarm. He decided that unlike the ones he had at home, these were hard-wired to the hotel's electric, whereas his at home were powered by batteries. He could not remember the last time he changed them.

231

He began working out the details of how he could hard-wire his. He could do the boy's bedrooms easily enough because he had access to the attic. For the same reason, the master bedroom would be easy, but the smoke alarm at the top of the stairs would be more challenging because access was limited. However, he concluded, in case of a fire, three hard-wired alarms were better than none.

Besides, there really was no reason to think the battery operated smoke alarms wouldn't be sufficient; and chances were the fire would start downstairs, and the smoke would be picked up by the battery-operated units down there.

Now that he had that figured out, for the next ten minutes or so—or so it seemed to him—there was nothing going through his brain. Then he noticed that nauseous feeling again that he'd been getting off and on lately, and this time his arms hurt. If not for that he probably would have fallen asleep. It was what made him realize, that since Sara's phone call he hadn't been thinking of anything; it concerned him that his mind had been such a blank, and it caused him to snap back and consider Sara—his new predicament.

However, he became aware of the splitting headache he suddenly developed, and was at a loss as to what to do next. He had not showered or dressed, and decided that perhaps he needed to have something to eat. That, he figured, was what was causing his dizziness—and the headache. There upon he decided—but first he needed to make an appointment to see Father Mike Monahan.

All his religious training paid off. Alex knew that a priest was prohibited from divulging anything he heard in the confessional—*the seal of confession*—regardless of the seriousness of the sin. Alex would then be safe; using the confession to not only tell Father what had happened, but get his advice on how to handle it.

After I have some breakfast, he thought, my mind will have cleared up and I'll begin feeling better. Sara made sense, he agreed, he had better call the office and make up with the asshole. He pictured Ms. Busybody, looking like Lilly Tomlinson as Ernestine, adjusting her bra strap at the old-fashioned switchboard, plugging him into Henderson.

He had no doubt that Father Mike would tell him what to do. It was self-defense, but the important thing was that in Alex's mind the janitor should not be blamed—under no circumstance could that happen. He would not be able to live with himself, absolutely not; the janitor was not involved and, he thought, *anyone who places blame on him will spend eternity in hell.*

Alex felt certain that by stepping forward he would completely exonerate himself as well, and of course, he would not be charged with the murder of Robert Steeter; he was certain of that, too.

His boys—didn't Dolores just get finished telling him how devastated Paul was when he had to confront the fact that his father was going to prison for murder? Although, Alex was sure, *he* would not have to go, nevertheless the stigma of just being mixed up in a murder would be sufficiently devastating to them. "This is a problem I'll have to figure out later," he said out loud.

He also figured he could get Father Mike to telephone Sara and explain that the relationship between Maureen and him was not a sin; Alex was sure of it. So there was nothing for Sara to forgive, was there?

That left Maria. Poor Maria! Alex would suggest to Father Mike that he stay in NY for a few weeks, maybe a month, to be at Maria's bedside. By the time she died and was buried, Sara would have forgotten Maureen; she would have forgiven Alex; and his relationship with Henderson's would have returned to the way it always was; everyone would make up and everything would return to normal!

Perfect. Alex felt much better. All the loose ends would tie together. Now all he had to do was make an appointment with Father Mike.

But it wasn't perfect. He forgot about ordering breakfast and by the time he was showered he felt miserable again. He could not come to terms with how cavalier he was about these serious faults in his life, his person, his behavior, his morals and his image of himself.

Nothing would be the same. It would *never* be the same anymore. Sara was not going to forgive him. Why should she? What had he done for her lately besides screw around?

Maria...he was ready to use her and then discard her. He had protected her all her life, for what? So now she could run interference for him; she could die so Sara would conveniently forget about his transgressions, and he'd have a ready-made excuse to explain his behavior to Henderson?

What about his kids? What would their life be like, knowing their father killed someone? Would it really make any difference that there was a good reason? Unlikely. Not to them, not to their friends. Would future girlfriends want to become engaged to sons of a murderer?

And...Henderson, the least of his problems; but nevertheless, would he rehire someone who was a known murderer? Did it make a difference that it was a long time ago...when Alex was just a little kid? Murder at any age is still murder.

His headache got worse and soon after, the dizziness too; severe enough that Alex had to lie down on the bed again. He fell asleep for a few more hours.

31

The phonebook in the drawer of the bedside table had the number listed for the rectory at Holy Ghost parish.

A pleasant enough woman answered and explained that Father Monahan was with an electrician at the church right now but she expected him back any moment. "Can I have him call you, I don't expect it will be more than a few minutes, ten at the most, and he would like to call you back. Would you like to leave your name and phone number?"

Then, in order to close the sale she added in her little Irish brogue, "You know, he'll blame *me* if we don't get your name and number, and we wouldn't want that, would we?" She said this in a manner that it would not have been easy to refuse. You could picture what she looked like.

Alex gave both name and phone number to her and hung up the phone. "I am definitely doing the right thing," he sighed audibly, "this whole thing has made me feel sick. No, it has made me miserable and pathetic. It's no wonder I've been getting dizzy all the time, and headaches. Even my chest hurts and my muscles ache. This must be done and done immediately."

He stopped for a moment then continued. "Am I going nuts, talking to the walls?"

Alex shook his head and walked into the bathroom to brush his teeth, but instead he glanced at himself in the mirror for a second then turned away; quickly; disgusted.

No one would understand what I am going through, he reflected. And it isn't even my fault. Was it intentional that Steeter got himself killed? No, besides...hitting him on the head...who would have thought *that* would kill the little motherfucker. It was just a broom handle, for Christ's sake. Was he that much of a pussy; couldn't even handle a broomstick?

And he thought he was a big man...that's how I will explain it to Father; nobody's fault; he must have had a soft spot on his head and the broom handle connected just right. How was I to know he wasn't as tough as he thought he was?

A soft spot on his head killed him; it would have happened eventually: playing stickball or if he bumped into something; the corner of a cabinet. See, it wasn't intentional; we just wanted to prevent him from raping us. I'll have to say hurting.

Right, I can't say raping to Father, no sir. He'll understand hurting of course. He'll know exactly what I mean. Yes, both of us were scared Father, it wasn't premeditated or anything like that; spur of the moment; that's how they refer to it.

Would we do it again you ask? Of course we would Father, so does that make it a mortal sin? For a mortal sin there must be sufficient reflection. There was none in this case. Grievous matter? I'll give you that one Father. No question, we killed him. Deader than a doorknob.

Full consent of the will? Father, I'll have to leave that one to you. That one needs to have someone who is once removed, not involved, an innocent bystander. Yes Father, that's your call. You decide, was there full consent of the will?

Alex was splashing warm water on his face when he noticed that the phone was ringing. "I'm loosing my mind," out loud, "didn't even realize the phone was ringing. I'm coming." While hurrying to the phone he grabbed a towel; it was Father Mike.

"Father Mike...thanks for returning my call. Do you remember me...I lived in the convent about twenty-five years ago. Yes, that was a long time ago. No Father, I don't miss it."

Well, Alex thought, he certainly has a sense of humor...something I need right now. He's sharp, I'll have to remember that technique; a good way to disarm someone you figure is nervous or almost sorry after it is too late...that he made the call...no going back now...if I hang up the phone he still has my name, doesn't he?

"Father, I don't know how else to put this but I need to make a confession. Could you hear my confession today?" After a moment he added, "If you can fit me in please?"

Alex listened carefully to how Father Mike responded then said in response to Father's question, "Yes, I was hoping this afternoon, if it is possible?" Pause. "One o'clock would be perfect yes, I understand; no, we don't have to meet in church; if you hear my confession at the rectory it is the same as in the confessional in church; yes I understand. Thank you Father, I will see you at one o'clock...at the rectory. And Father, thank you."

Alex sat down at the table, put his elbows on the edge of the table and cupped his cheeks in his hands. His eyes blurred with salty water.

I feel better already he thought, I can't let that brainless janitor go to jail forever for something he didn't do. I can't blame that detective either; the evidence is crushing and that's not the sergeant's fault, is it? The sergeant is not arresting him on purpose...because he has nothing else to do. Besides, why should anyone suspect Maria and me of being involved? Yes...for sure...I feel better.

Alex got up from the table, called room service and ordered a breakfast of scrambled eggs, bacon, an English muffin without butter; and orange juice and coffee. He finished dressing while the hotel kitchen prepared it. "Hey," he felt relieved, "my last meal, but at least I feel like a human again."

He made it a point to not look in the mirror any longer than he had to.

32

The Monahan family was not what you would call religious—that was what Farther Mike's dad explained to anyone who inquired: how it is that your son became a priest?

Mr. And Mrs. went to church every Sunday and of course on Christmas, but that was about the extent of their outward practice of religion. Inside however, was another story. The family was intense about living a wholesome life, not necessarily full of prayer or good works in the religious sense, but following the precept "don't do anything you would not want *everyone* to know about."

They often discussed among themselves how lucky they were that their six children turned out so well. That didn't necessarily mean rich or famous, but rather just good, wholesome, well-adjusted and happy kids.

Mike wanted to be a priest for as long as he could remember. He liked going to church not, he was perfectly aware from the very beginning, because of the ceremony or the doctrine or the trappings of religion, but rather because he believed in a God and felt strongly that He wanted him to help Him in the overwhelming job of getting everyone, or at least as many people as possible, to get along, be happy, see the positive side of this short gift of life and not commit mortal sins. Since his family was Catholic, becoming a priest seemed like the route to take.

Father Mike believed that committing a mortal sin was actually not real easy to do. You had to be very determined: a difficult and genuinely mean person...to dogs or cats or to your fellow man.

Mike liked people regardless of how they decided to go through life. If a person chose a "sinful" path, Father Mike was not going to be their judge, but he believed that God wanted him to try and influence that person, not necessarily to completely change him—Mike was a realist—but he hoped he could at least open the person's eyes to the reality that he was sinning and that doing so was not prudent.

Prudence was, for Father Mike, the ultimate determinant of how one should act. If you were going to do something that would land you in jail, it wasn't prudent. If you were going to do something that was likely going to result in a mortal sin, it wasn't prudent. Otherwise, all actions were fair game. He was a proponent of "if it feels good and makes you happy, it is good—as long as it doesn't interfere with someone else...and it is prudent."

Father Mike appreciated the historical component of the Catholic Church. He recoiled at the notion of Jesus walking on water, or Mary being a virgin or any of the other beliefs that were still taught as "gospel."

Although he would not admit it to anyone, he took comfort in these beliefs from the historical perspective and believed that they were created for a purpose; served their purpose and became the fabric of what it meant to be Catholic. When he had to discuss them it was a discussion about faith, not the controversial. History is history; it isn't prudent to change history—not for yourself; not for the government; not for the church.

Did George Washington cut down a cherry tree? Who knows, who cares—it serves to describe in a relatively few sentences the time, place and society in which George lived, what was important, and how he interacted; and the story did immeasurable good in terms of defining the fabric of what the new country would be made of.

So too during the formation of Christianity, with an essentially ignorant following, these beliefs defined what Jesus was about.

Father Mike received his education at the seminary in Huntington, not far from where Maria and Eric lived. He graduated with honors and was fought over by several parishes that saw his potential.

He liked Holy Ghost; he liked the other priest and their pastor and liked working with the school children; and in particular felt a special obligation to take care of the orphans. He thought a lot about Robert Steeter and his disappearance, believed wholeheartedly that there was foul play involved, but was at a loss to put his finger on precisely why he believed it.

While waiting for Alex to arrive for confession, Father Mike thought about him too, tried to picture what he was going to look like.

Of course he remembered him as a boy, a rather impetuous youngster who enjoyed getting into trouble by doing whatever he wanted to do, when he wanted, regardless of what the nuns wanted him to do.

If he was supposed to use the dustpan to team up with the person sweeping the floor, he would be off kibitzing with the person cleaning the bathroom sinks.

If it was time to light the altar candles for Sunday Mass, he'd be trying to fix the broken clasp on the incense pot.

Alex and his sisters were close, unlike many of the other children in the convent and Father Mike attributed that to their dad. He came quite frequently and if he couldn't, someone would; usually their Aunt Catherine—often their Uncle Bart, Aunt Margaret and their cousins.

Father Mike figured out what this confession was going to be about and was anxious about it. He knew that Sergeant Arrondondo and Alex had recently met to discuss the new developments with the janitor, and he figured that all along Alex was holding back on something, and now felt it was important to come forward. But why "confession"…it was what made Father anxious.

Mrs. Corbett, the rectory housekeeper, showed Alex to the parlor before she called Father Mike, and when he entered Alex stood up and they shook hands. Father looked for and found the signs he was afraid of—Alex looked nervous, pale and his eyes were not as bright as one would expect. They hadn't seen each other for a long time but still; Father Mike was able to discern that this was a troubled soul.

"Good afternoon Alex, it is nice to see you again. Make yourself comfortable. I would like a cup of coffee, how about you? I am sure it is already made and Mrs. Corbett will be more than happy to bring us some." He turned to her and nodded his head; she was standing there in anticipation, "Two cups please.

"Do you take cream and sugar Alex?" The "just cream, please" was acknowledged by Mrs. Corbett and she left the room. Father Mike took a seat across from Alex.

"So Alex, how have you been and please, tell me about your family, your sisters, your dad, your aunts? I remember all of them and hope each is doing well. And what have you been doing? I'd like to hear about you—married? Children? We've got as much time as you want, I don't have any appointments until much later, so we can take as long as is needed." Father Mike was stalling until the coffee was brought in and until Mrs. Corbett set the tray down, walked out of the room and closed the door behind her. Now they were alone.

"Yes Father, my family is fine, except my sister and that is one of the reasons I wanted to see you." Alex paused for a moment. Father Mike was comfortably seated in an armchair, perfectly still, with his fingers together like when you pray; his hands, with his thumbs in the shape of a church steeple were resting above his stomach. He wasn't smiling but he had a contented look on his face that told you he was confident that whatever he was about to hear would not be the first nor the last time and that whatever it was, he would be able to help.

"She has cancer Father, the doctors don't give her any hope at all. It's pancreatic cancer, the worst kind of all. They are telling us that it will only be a matter of a month, not much more."

Father Mike, without changing his expression said, "Yes, I understand, when we have to face the coming of the end of a life it is very difficult; yes Alex, I understand. But tell me, what can I do? Do you want me to go see her, would that comfort her in some way? It does, you know, even for people who haven't thought about their religion for a long time."

Father Mike was not in the habit of discoursing nor was he full of soothing words about going to a better place, none of that ritual. He was a realist, and he felt the best he could do for someone at the end was to comfort them and their family by having them look back on all their wonderful memories, and to thank God for the life He provided.

"Tell me Alex, would she want to see me?"

"I don't know Father," Alex answered, "I will ask her. Can I do that and then call you? She and her husband, his name is Eric, they don't have any children; they live in Huntington, maybe twenty miles. I think they go to church, maybe not every Sunday, maybe once a month...like I do."

"Yes," Father Mike answered when Alex clearly had finished that thought, "you find out and let me know. Does she remember me...do you think...and what kind of memories would I bring back? Remember though, that one of the glories of life is reflecting on all the memories, the good with the bad. It is what makes us human and only humans are eternal—through our memories; the memories we have of loved ones who have died years, and for some, centuries ago—but I wouldn't want memories of me or her time in the convent to upset her.

"And what about you Alex, how can I help you? You must tell me how *you* feel. Grief is powerful but it is necessary. It too is what makes us human, and a wonderful thing it is. Where would we be without it?

"You don't need to give me an answer about grief—unless of course it would make you feel better—it is something to think about though, perhaps to pray about. God is powerful and prayer is a way to tap into that power especially in times like this: grief, disappointments, feelings of helplessness or uselessness.

"Would it help...for you to tell me how you are feeling right now, sitting here with me?"

There was quiet. Alex had a great deal to tell Father Mike. Maria was at the top of the list, but Father was right. That problem would last only a short while longer, then he would have only the memories of her, of all they'd been through, how he loved her so much and would be filled to overflowing with grief when she was gone. But what can you do? Nothing. Spend as much time with her as she wants, talk about their life together, savor the memories—they could all be good, it depended on how you talked about them.

All except Robert Steeter.

That popped Alex back into reality, the reality he saw when his eyes focused on Father Mike, still sitting in the same position, waiting for him to tell him how he felt, and how he could be of help. Alex realized that Father knew what was going on in his mind for those last few moments; knew that Alex was answering the question he had posed—about grief—and that Alex was making up his mind how he would use it to comfort Maria and himself.

Father Mike saw something in Alex too; that he was having difficulty bringing up the next item on his list—and knew unhesitatingly that the next item was the real reason for the visit. After all, Alex had discussed *confession* when he made the appointment didn't he?

"You said Maria was *one* of the reasons you came to see me Alex?"

"Yes, of course. Father...I've been married for twelve years...to Sara. We have two boys. We are lucky, they are good kids; not like I was."

Father Mike saw what was coming, how difficult it was going to be, and felt the need to put Alex at ease—give him a few seconds to ease into it. So he said, "Alex, you were taught, right across the street as a matter of fact, that confession is another of the wonderful gifts from God. It is a magical and mystical way of rinsing off our soul...so from that viewpoint it is comforting.

"I think," Father continued, "I know where this is going, so you won't shock me regardless of what you have to confess. Besides—adding levity—though you may not see it this way, priests have a much easier time committing sins; believe me, I have experience."

It worked. Alex hesitated a few moments then continued, "Do you remember Maureen Steeter Father? Her brother, his name was Robert, ran away from the convent years ago. Maureen and I, way back then, began sinning. It has continued all this while, up to today. My wife Sara does not know, although I believe lately she suspects."

He continued, "Maureen's husband Tom...they have two girls the same ages as my two boys...Maureen thinks Tom knows. In fact she is quite sure of it, but it seems he lives with it. Sara won't. I quit my job the other day because my company found out about Maureen, and I got angry, took it out on Sara. I'm afraid she knows Father, about Maureen. Can you talk to her, tell her I am sorry, it is over, that Maureen and I will never see each other again?"

This last was a question, and Father Mike recognized it for what it was.

"Alex, help me to understand something, and in so doing, perhaps you will get a better understanding of yourself. You said you and Maureen have been together for all the years since you left the convent. I know it is rather late to be asking this question, but why didn't you and she stay together? Didn't the two of you ever discuss it? Weren't you in love with each other? What caused the two of you to seek other partners?"

"Yes Father, we've discussed it and no, we don't love each other. You wouldn't understand. It is how we grew up. Especially her Father, no parents, essentially no one else in the world; she was alone and still is. Maybe I felt sorry for her, maybe I still do. We are friends. I tell her things that I would not tell anyone else in the entire world, and the same with her...although a lot of times I don't think she cares about anyone else in the world, including me. Can you understand what I am saying?"

"Of course I can. You have a predicament. Unless I am mistaken, Sara will not understand, will she?"

"No, of course not." Alex leaned forward a little and lowered his head a few moments. He looked up at Father Mike and added, "Would it help if you talked to her. Explain how Maureen and I are like brother and sister. I know it sounds silly, but how else can I explain it?"

✦ ✦ ✦

Father Mike's next move was done with sufficient reflection, full consent of the will, and was a grievous matter. He was going to commit one of those sins he referred to—in this instance the mortal sin of selfishness—he was going to take advantage of the willingness of Alex to openly discuss the past; it was a selfish opportunity to change the subject and bring up the disappearance of Robert Steeter.

"Tell me more about Maureen's brother."

Alex stopped to question himself. Had he already gone too far with Father Mike, told him too much...his affair with Maureen, its impact on Sara, his predicament? But this is why he came here, wasn't it? The janitor—wasn't it about the janitor, not himself?

Father saw in Alex the change in his facial appearance. It was amazing, how one could morph so quickly from a penitent husband to an *unapologetic*. Suddenly he looked a little angry, like he had a problem that wasn't of his own making and probably not the least repentant about.

"I killed him, Father, it was an accident. The janitor that Sergeant Arrondondo is holding had nothing to do with it. Well, not with *killing* Robert Steeter that is."

Alex and Father Mike stared at each other, each taking in and processing the magnitude of what was just spoken. In an instant, Alex realized that he was not shocking Father; it was like he already knew.

For his part, a hundred thoughts raced through Father Mike's brain in a second: how could a youngster possibly kill someone; how could he keep it to himself for all these years; what prompted such a diabolical act; what is it in a human being that would allow such a thing...? What will happen to him; the Steeter boy is beyond saving...how am I going to save this one?

"Do you want to tell me how it happened Alex? It would be important since the janitor is going to be charged with murder; and you know that he is, don't you? Of course if he had nothing to do with it; I know you couldn't let that happen, could you?"

"No of course not Father. I need you to help me. I am hesitant to go to the police. I have my family to think about. Robert Steeter deserved to die, even though it was an accident. He wanted to harm Maria. Father, I couldn't let that happen, so I hit him...on the head, with a stick I found behind the church. I didn't want to kill him, I just wanted to prevent him from harming Maria; it was an accident.

"There is more Father. Maria doesn't want to talk about it. She knows we are not to blame; it was Robert's own fault, he brought it on himself, and besides, she feels the janitor deserves to get punished too, not only for what he had been doing to

Robert, but because Robert told us the janitor was invited that evening. Robert said the janitor would pay him to participate, or just to watch. So, she feels, he was not innocent. She is worried about me Father; she knows if the truth came out that I killed him it would change my life because of my children. Even though she knows that she doesn't have long, neither of us can explain it, so please, promise me Father, you won't get her involved."

"Certainly not. But tell me something. You told both the sergeant and me that you and Robert didn't talk during or after the church service that night, then you told him that you and Maria walked back to the convent, but that it took about a half hour, is that when it happened, or is there more?"

"Yes Father. Although it is true that Robert and I did not say anything of consequence to each other during church, except for the few things we *had* to say to each other—about the service itself; he earlier made Maria wait for us in front so we could all go behind the church. He liked to smoke and kept his cigarettes under the back step. Once we got behind the church, he said he was going to harm Maria, then me. After I hit him, he just lay there. Maria and I went back to the convent.

"The next day, or maybe that evening, that part is blurry, we heard that Robert ran away. Father, we believed it because we figured Robert was afraid; afraid we'd tell Sister what he was going to do to us.

"The next night I sneaked behind the church, being very careful there was no one around; he wasn't there so I figured that it was true, he'd run away. But then, I don't know why, but I looked under the step...where he kept his cigarettes."

Alex stopped telling his story. Father noticed that he was becoming more and more pale; all the blood was rushing from his face, which had become very white. He just looked at Father Mike and didn't move at all. Finally Father Mike helped Alex finish the thought, "He was dead, wasn't he? He didn't run away, and you knew he was dead because you hit him on the head, is that what happened?"

"Yes," Alex said softly, "I didn't mean to kill him."

"Alex," Father Mike sat upright and looked directly at him. "Why are you telling me this? It is important for you to figure out why, after all these years, why do you want to confess this. Is it because confessing at the time would have jeopardized your affair with his sister? Is it because now your wife has found out about you sleeping with Maureen, which has been going on some twenty years?

"Is it because your sister is dying and you need someone to corroborate your story? Is it because you are concerned that the janitor will be convicted of a crime he didn't do? Is it because you need to confess for your own selfish reasons...in order to make you feel better? Why Alex, why are you telling me this now?"

"Because it is the right thing to do Father. That's all."

"Well, you and I both have to know, if it is the right thing to do today, why wasn't it the right thing to do yesterday, last week, last month, last year? Why wasn't it the right thing to do when you found Robert's body and realized he was dead? Was it the right thing to do allowing everyone to continue to believe he ran away?"

Alex looked at Father Mike while trying to come up with an answer. But he couldn't. "I don't know Father; help me...I don't know."

"I cannot judge why people do what they do. But it seems to me, that if you are being honest with yourself, then you will be forgiven. But what do you want from me Alex? You know you should tell Sergeant Arrondondo what you have just told me, don't you? I can accompany you if it would make it easier. It is your decision. I will keep what you have confessed to me absolutely to myself, you know that, so what happens next is entirely yours to decide."

Alex waited a second before he answered, "I cannot let that janitor go to prison for what was an accident. Yes, it would make it easier...if you could explain to Sergeant Arrondondo what happened. He visited me the other day, showed me some pictures that were clearly of Robert and the janitor. The police will think the janitor killed him to keep him quiet...but that is not what happened. I did it, it was an accident; I could never kill anyone on purpose."

Alex didn't add anything more; he leaned back and rested his head on the back of the high-back chair. He looked like he slipped into another world.

"Let's change the subject for a moment, Alex, tell me about your children, what are their names, how old are they?"

"Father," Alex answered, "can I have a glass of water, I don't feel well?"

"Sure." Father Mike got up and went to the door. He called his housekeeper who came immediately; he asked her to get a glass of water...and please hurry.

He turned back to Alex who, he noticed, was now quite pale. "Are you all right?"

"I feel very strange Father, something is wrong; I don't feel well at all, everything is spinning around in my head and I feel nauseous. My arms hurt; it's happened before so I think I'll be okay in a few minutes; a glass of water would help."

Father Mike recognized the symptoms. "Alex, just rest a moment, lie still, I will be right back."

He went into the hallway where the telephone was on a little table under the stairs and he dialed the operator. "Could you please call an ambulance to come to the Holy Ghost Rectory...yes, on Sixth Street...and please hurry, one of my visitors is having a heart attack."

Father Mike quickly went back into the parlor. "Alex, I've called for a ambulance, just relax, take it easy, they will be here shortly. You will be all right; here, lie still...." Father pulled a pillow over from the large sofa and was going to put it behind Alex's head and the side of the high-back chair.

Alex didn't respond. He was staring into space. Father Mike became alarmed. "Alex, Alex." Father gently touched his shoulder. "Alex, are you all right? Alex?"

There was no answer.

Father Mike shook Alex's shoulder. "Alex!" Still, there was no response. He walked back to the telephone, dialed "O" again and asked to be connected to the police station. The call went through immediately.

"This is Father Mike Monahan at the Holy Ghost Rectory on Sixth Street, I believe one of my parishioners just died, he won't respond. Can you send someone right away? An ambulance? Yes, I've called them moments ago; they are on the way. Yes, at the rectory. We were talking in the parlor and I believe he had a heart attack. No, he hasn't been moved. Thank you."

Next, Father Mike looked up Sergeant Arrondondo's phone number and dialed it. Fortunately he answered the phone himself. "Sergeant, this is Mike Monahan, you know, Father Mike, at Holy Ghost Parish...is it possible for you to come here right away? Alex Fazio was visiting me and he suddenly passed away. Yes, probably a heart attack, it was very sudden. He is still here and I am waiting for an ambulance and the police. I just telephoned them; they are on their way. Could you come too?"

Father Mike got an affirmative and responded, "Thank you."

33

The ambulance arrived first. The technician checked Alex's pulse and listened at his chest with a stethoscope, and then looked at Father Mike...the slight nod confirmed what was evident. "I believe I heard you say you called the police?"

"Yes, they should be here any moment."

"We will have to wait for the medical examiner to confirm the death and sign the certificate before we move him. Do you know any next of kin?"

"Well, that is a little bit of a problem. I know who his wife is, they live in Chicago or, I should say, near Chicago, but I do not know how to contact her. Do you, by chance, know Sergeant Arrondondo, the detective? I've telephoned him and he should be here momentarily. I believe he will know how to contact his wife."

"Yes, I know Arrondondo, a good man. It should make things easier if he is here. We will wait outside Father. You'll want to leave everything as it is, won't you?"

✦ ✦ ✦

When Mrs. Corbett showed Sergeant Arrondondo into the parlor, Father Mike was seated across from Alex. He appeared deep in thought, perhaps praying.

For Father Mike, prayer in this instance was asking God to help him figure out how he was going to get everyone involved to forgive each other. And why not, what was the alternative, to continue struggling through life with bitterness about something that was absolutely impossible to undo? For what purpose?

Father Mike began ticking off the players in the drama. Robert and now Alex were dead. Robert died so long ago that his cause of death no longer mattered—except for the janitor—and Father figured he and Arrondondo would be able to rectify that.

Except for a few persons—Maria, Maureen and Sara—as far as Father Mike could determine, no one else had any reason to know what darkened Alex's soul.

"Almighty God," Father prayed, "that is where I need Your help. How am I going to reconcile Sara? I somewhat understand the relationship he had with Maureen, having worked with the convent kids all these years, but our understanding, Yours and mine dear Lord, though commendable, isn't going to help unless we can arrive at some way for Sara to think of herself as something other than a jilted wife."

Father turned when he felt someone come into the room...escorted by Mrs. Corbett. He stood.

"Well Sergeant," Father Mike's greeting was said with a heavy heart while he was getting up from the chair, "it would seem that now the case is closed or at least I believe it is closed," as he was shaking hands with Sergeant Arrondondo.

He continued, "Alex just confessed that he was the one who killed Robert Steeter. He maintains it was an accident, self-defense. Robert was intending to rape the two youngsters; the boy went into a space under the church for cigarettes and when he came out Alex hit him over the head with a stick that was lying on the ground. He came back later because he'd heard that Robert ran away and wanted to make sure he wasn't where he last saw him. He found the body, figured he'd crawled under the sacristy before he died, realized he had killed him, and with his sister decided they would never tell anyone what happened.

"Before he died I heard his confession. I want you to know that he specifically asked me to accompany him to see you and I agreed so I am not revealing without his permission what he told me in confession."

Sergeant Arrondondo nodded that he understood. "This will be good news for Earl Stasser," the sergeant said, "I may have to set him free. I have no reason to hold him unless I can find the others in those pictures and get them to press charges. Too bad; he needs to be off the streets."

Father Mike looked down, obviously processing what the sergeant just finished saying. He slowly looked at him and said, "We will have to notify Alex's wife and sister. I have no idea where to contact them, hopefully you do. Please tell them that I was with him when he died and I am available to talk to them if they wish."

The two men were interrupted when Jordan arrived. After introductions he spent a few minutes examining Alex then told the ambulance men to remove the body. Since everything was now under control, Sergeant Arrondondo said, "Father, I will take care of notifying his wife and sister. This may get complicated and I don't want you involved if you do not need to be. I will, however, tell them what you said. I have to take care of Stasser too, so I will say goodbye for now. Thank you for all your help in this case, it is too bad this occurred under your roof. I will see myself out."

259

Sergeant Arrondondo found this part of his job distressing; something he certainly did not look forward to doing, yet he believed that if it had to be done he was the best one to do it. He was good at it, "If that is something to be good at," he admitted to no one in particular.

Unfortunately, in this situation, the gruesome task of notifying the next of kin would have to be turned over to the police department in the town where Sara lived. Sergeant Arrondondo hoped they would do it as well as he would. No matter how you looked at it, it was not easy.

However, he could help by accumulating all the information they would need thereby adding to the professionalism that most people appreciated in times like this. The police would send two persons to Sara's home, and if she happened to be alone, one or both would stay until a relative arrived.

Also, the sergeant needed to coordinate the notification to Alex's sister, which he would do himself—Sergeant Arrondondo needed to talk to her to confirm what happened before he could put the release of the janitor into motion.

Chances are, he figured, Sara will be told of Alex's death first, then she or a relative will telephone Maria, so he would be catching her during the height of her grief. The timing would be a dicey situation and hopefully the police in Sara's town would be able to confirm if and when, in fact, the wife had been notified.

He called them the next morning and in pure bureaucratic efficiency they couldn't be sure—they'd check and call back! He decided to call Maria's house and ask if he could visit her, and in that way determine if she had heard from Sara...without specifically asking. He could then arrange an appointment correspondingly.

When he got her on the phone she was sobbing. Arrondondo made a decision that the best way to handle this was the straightforward way. After introducing himself he said, "I apologize for having to telephone you at this time, but I need to see you as soon as possible. If you would like, I can contact Father Mike Monahan; Alex died while he was visiting Father, so he asked me to tell you that if you want, he can accompany me. You can think about it and let me know."

However, it was imperative that he talk to her immediately, so he persisted, "I will need to see you as soon as possible, this afternoon would be preferable, can we arrange a convenient time?"

There was no answer on the other end.

"Maria, I'll need an answer. I know it is difficult but I must see you."

Through the sobs she answered, "Three o'clock."

"Thank you, I will be there at three o'clock. Would you like Father Mike to accompany me?" She answered affirmatively, they both said goodbye, and signed off.

Sergeant Arrondondo then called Father Mike, brought him up to date and asked if he was available at two-thirty to go to Huntington. "Of course," the priest answered, "I can easily rearrange my schedule. I will see you then. Will you stop here and pick me up?"

34

On the way to visit Maria, Father Mike asked Sergeant Arrondondo if he knew about her cancer and that, according to Alex, she did not have long to live. Father stressed that although he heard it in confession, he concluded that it was not something one would "confess" so in that regard, Alex would not hesitate to have Father inform the sergeant.

"No, I did not know, so thank you for the head's up. I need to see her however, so it doesn't alter that. It does seem that too often you find that things pile up on top of each other; she has one all-consuming problem and now there is this other. I will have to think carefully about how I am going to handle this, and I hope which ever way I select it is the right one."

When they got to Maria's house—Sergeant Arrondondo was relieved that she was alone—considering what they needed to discuss, and in response to a question about the whereabouts of her husband, she said he was at home when Sara called last night and they both decided it would be best if he went to work today. Maria said she wanted to be alone for a while. "He's called me several times today," she volunteered with sadness.

Her first question was how did it happen. "Sara told me that he was visiting you Father. Was it sudden and can you tell me why he was visiting you?"

Sergeant Arrondondo took the question. "That is why we are here Maria. Alex asked Father if he could hear his confession so that is why he was at the rectory. Father assures me that afterwards, Alex asked Father to help him by accompanying him to the police so Alex could explain the part you and he had in the disappearance of Robert Steeter."

The sergeant then looked at Father Mike as he continued, "We believe he had a heart attack, it was over in an instant, is that what happened, Father?"

"Yes," is all Father Mike said, accompanied with a nod.

"What did he tell you?" Maria asked while looking first at Arrondondo then at Father Monahan.

Father Mike answered. "He said that the three of you: Alex, you, and Robert, went behind the church. Robert went under the church crawl space to get some cigarettes and when he came out, Alex hit him on the head with a stick he found lying on the ground. You both then returned to the convent and later, after hearing about Robert having run away, Alex returned to the space under the church, saw that Robert was dead, and concluded that he had caused it.

"I asked him why he was confessing this now...he'd kept it inside him all this time; so why now," Father Mike added, "his answer to me was that he did not want the janitor who is being held in Robert Steeter's death to be charged for something *he* did. So we have to be clear, is that what happened?"

Maria didn't answer. She started sobbing uncontrollably. She had been sitting on the couch; Father Mike was sitting next to her. Sergeant Arrondondo was seated on a small chair across from them. The men decided they would remain silent; give her time to compose herself.

Finally Maria said, "I am sorry, where are my manners? Can I get you something to drink, a glass of water or tea perhaps; we don't drink coffee?"

Sergeant Arrondondo answered, "Yes, a glass of water would be nice." He looked at Father Mike, who got the message conveyed through the sergeant's eyes, and also answered affirmatively.

While Maria was out of the room, Sergeant Arrondondo whispered to the priest, "I could have done without the water, but I believe it is helpful for her to have something to do for a few moments; it gives her some time alone to compose herself."

Father Mike nodded that he understood.

After the men took the glass which Maria handed to each of them, and after she sat back down again, Sergeant Arrondondo returned to the reason he was there.

"Maria, we are holding a man for the murder of Robert Steeter, his name is Earl Stasser, a former janitor at Holy Ghost Parish. If he did not do it then it is not right that we hold him in jail. Alex's confession is no longer sufficient now that he is no longer alive. Therefore, I must know what happened when Robert Steeter died. Can you please help me?"

Maria looked up at the sergeant then over at the priest. You could tell she was trying to decide how to put into words what she had been holding inside for all these years.

She shocked both men.

"No, that is not what happened. Alex didn't hit Robert, I did. He told you he did it because he is trying to protect me. It is not how it happened at all. He was lighting another cigarette...he was telling Alex to smoke it...'smoke it like a man,' is what he said. I will never forget...'because I am going to fuck your little sister, then you...and if you are a man you'll fuck this little cunt too.' Those were the exact words. I haven't forgotten them all this time. I apologize for the language Father, but that is exactly what Robert said."

Her head drooped down and she closed her eyes for a second. Then she continued. "I saw a stick, a broom stick, lying on the ground. I picked it up and hit him hard. I hated Robert, I'm not sorry I did it. He didn't deserve to live."

Both Sergeant Arrondondo and Father Mike looked at each other—confused. You could tell that both were thinking the same thing: which one do we believe?

Both men figured that the brother and sister were trying to protect each other. Although Maria ostensibly knew her time was limited, Alex didn't know that his was. So that, to the two men, seemed to be an important factor—it seemed more likely that Maria was trying to take the blame to protect Alex than the other way around.

"Maria," Sergeant Arrondondo continued, "A woman, Mrs. Reilly, told me that she saw three children standing in front of the church about eight o'clock on the Wednesday when you say you hit Robert on his head. What I want to know is, was it you three and if so, was it before you went behind the church?

266

"Secondly," he continued, "Mrs. Reilly said a few minutes later she again looked but only saw one person. Who was it she saw? She said she thought it might have been you? If she is correct, if you are the person she saw, then you could not have hit Robert with a stick, could you?"

Meanwhile, Father Mike noticed that Maria appeared less emotional. Seeing that, he believed she *was* telling the truth...he figured that having removed this major problem from her soul she felt relieved. Nevertheless, it took her a while to answer the sergeant's questions.

"Yes, we met after Benediction...out in front of the church. Robert wanted to wait until there was no one around to see us going behind the church. It wasn't one of us the lady saw, I told you, all three of us walked behind the church together. It happened like I said."

"I apologize for troubling you at this time Maria," Sergeant Arrondondo said, "a man is in jail for something he didn't do...so I think you understand, don't you? Unless you recant your statement, I may have to take you into custody, you know that don't you? But, we'll leave that for another day."

"Yes, don't worry, I am not planning to go anywhere." She said this with both resignation and what appeared to be a look of relief.

"One more thing Maria, there is something I cannot understand," Father Monahan, with a quizzical look asked, "why did you and your brother agree to wait outside the church for Robert? Why didn't you tell someone if you knew why he wanted you to wait for him? Why didn't you tell Sister Kostich or one of the other nuns, or your teacher, or even me? Didn't you think someone would have understood what was happening? How could Robert so easily have lured you, convinced you and Alex, to go with him behind the church, if you knew what was going to happen?

"You would had to have been there Father; it was easy for a little girl and a young scared boy. Earlier in the day, Robert told me what to do. He said to wait outside the church, tell my friends to go home without me because I wanted to wait for my brother and, he told me, that if I said anything to anyone he would get the janitor that used to work at the church to beat up my brother; beat him severely. He said the janitor would break his legs or arms and he would be seriously hurt. Then he told my brother that if *he* said anything to anyone, the janitor would do the same to me. Robert said the janitor was afraid of him and would do anything he told him to do.

"Now it seems we could have just told you or Sister, but at the time we were both afraid. We were afraid of Robert, everyone was; he was mean; the worst kind of mean, that comes from not being afraid of any thing or any body. Can you understand what I am telling you? It is hard to explain. Don't you think I haven't thought a thousand times about how stupid I was not to tell?"

"Maria," Father leaned forward in his chair, "it has been over twenty years since this happened, I can see why you would not have told anyone back then, but why have you never told anyone since...all those years? You must have known it was wrong?"

There was no immediate answer.

"I don't have a good reason Father. I promised my brother never to say a word and until now I haven't. He always put anything distasteful out of his mind forever; that is not an excuse for me I realize, but this was just one more distasteful thing for him.

"I understood him," she continued, "and I can also see where you cannot understand. But frankly Father, and with all respect, please try to understand *me*, I don't really care what you think. I don't care what anyone thinks. Neither of us saw any good reason to tell anyone."

There was quiet while the two men contemplated the bizarre lives of these several children, who were now adults.

"Did you see the janitor that night?" Sergeant Arrondondo asked after the pause and after having pondered but not fully understanding what Maria had told them.

"No, I didn't. Only my brother and Robert and me were there. Robert said the janitor was coming and we should wait for him. Robert said he was going to rape me and that the janitor was going to rape Alex, then Robert was going to charge him a lot of money...but he wasn't there. Robert was annoyed that he wasn't there; he didn't say anything, but you could tell he was annoyed; he said he was going to smoke a cigarette while he waited for him; so he went under the church for his cigarettes. When he came out he lit one for himself and then one for Alex. Alex didn't want it and Robert was trying to force him, like I said earlier. I saw the broom handle lying on the ground, I picked it up and with all I had in me I hit him from behind. He fell down. He didn't move so it scared Alex and me and we were afraid the janitor was coming, so we quickly left and went back to the convent. So Sergeant, no I never did see the janitor."

Sergeant Arrondondo stood up and said, "I have nothing more at this time. I will contact you as soon as possible if there is a need. Thank you for your time."

Father Mike then handed a card to Maria, "This has my phone number printed on it. If you feel you want to talk privately to me, please do not hesitate to call. I know you are going through a difficult time in more ways than one and I would be happy to spend as much time with you as you desire. God bless you, I will be thinking of you."

They left.

In the car, they discussed the newest twist in this bizarre case. "What do you think Sergeant," Father Mike began, "in some ways it makes little difference who actually hit Robert, except for the ones left behind. You realize don't you, that more than likely it is you who will have to decide who is ultimately responsible?"

"Perhaps not Father," Sergeant Arrondondo answered, "I don't profess to know all the details of the law, but it would not surprise me if the district attorney looks at it this way: Alex's confession was told to you, and you being the one to repeat it to me it could be construed as 'hear-say.' By the same token, Maria's confession is just that, a bona fide confession, so it seems likely that hers will stand."

"Yes, I suppose you are right. Perhaps it is for the best. Alex has a wife, two children, while Maria has no children. Yes, perhaps it is for the best that she confessed...whether she did it or not."

35

The district attorney, Bill Nelson, figured that his easily remembered name helped him initially get elected and it helped keep him there for several terms. He took pride in the fact that at least as far as he was concerned, he *looked* like a D.A. and liked to think that looking like one also played a part. He was beginning to gray, which made him look older and wiser. He was slightly rotund, always wore a black or very dark blue suit with a vest, a dark tie, and would have looked perfect with a pocket watch and chain across his ample belly—he didn't have one of course, he settled on a wristwatch with a Speidel band.

Sitting in the chief of police's office—the office and the D.A. looked like a pair—the office was from the thirties too: dark paneled walls; floor to ceiling windows that were completely bare; gray metal file cabinets in their appropriate location; and the proverbial massive oak desk behind which the chief, with his hands behind his head, was leaning back in his brown-leather, high-back, swivel-chair.

Fortunately there was not much crime occurring in the New Hyde Park area at the moment, so none of them, the chief, the D.A., nor Sergeant Arrondondo was in a hurry to conclude their discussion of the latest developments in the Steeter case. The D.A. was speaking.

"Yes, you are mostly correct in that hearsay would not be admissible in court. However, the fact that it was said to a priest in confession could have been an extenuating circumstance, especially if the sister hadn't confessed—after all, a man's life is in jeopardy; but it becomes moot now, doesn't it?"

273

"Not that what I am about to say makes any legal difference," the chief added a few seconds later, "but I understand your thinking in that each is trying to protect the other, isn't that what you believe is going on?" This was addressed to the sergeant.

"Yes, and like I've been saying," Sergeant Arrondondo answered, "we here, the three of us, have to consider what information we *have* to make public and what we can keep among ourselves. I for one do not see any good coming from announcing that Alex confessed to anything. He has a wife who is teetering on..." he lowered his voice for this next part, "...as I understand it from my interview yesterday with Maureen Steeter, deciding whether to believe whether her husband was having an affair—the affair Maureen admitted to me was very real and very current. Maureen told me she thought the wife might suspect something but wasn't sure if there was anything to it other than suspicion."

"So I take it *you* do not think the wife knows with certainty about anything to do with an alleged affair?" furthered the D.A. "Do you have any particulars as to why the wife would even suspect something?"

"Only recently has she begun to suspect," added the sergeant, "and amazingly, now after all the years of this illicit relationship. So here is the story as Maureen told it to me. Not long ago they were in a restaurant in Manhattan and one of Alex's fellow employees and his wife happened in. Alex subsequently told Maureen that his wife asked him about the encounter, and again, according to Maureen, he 'let on' to her that there was something between them. She, Maureen that is, made it clear to me that she didn't know to what extent 'let on' meant. Strangely, she then added, 'not that I really care'—rather an unusual comment don't you think?"

"Yes," the chief added, "didn't you once tell us that Maureen Steeter was a little strange to begin with...I seem to remember something about her and her brother not acting like brother and sister, more like acquaintances...something to that effect?"

"That's right Chief, I have in my notes from when we first began investigating that she had made it clear that they weren't what one would think of as brother and sister. She stressed that since they were in the orphanage almost from birth, along with others in the same situation, brother and sister relationships didn't exist. They didn't make those distinctions.

"At the time I thought perhaps it was her excuse so she wouldn't have to tell me what she knew about the disappearance. Then, later on, as I got to know Father Mike a little better, he intimated that it was true...and not atypical among the real orphans in the convent, though he made it clear that Alex and Maria Fazio very much acted like brother and sister, which brings us back to their confessions and what is really the truth."

The chief sat upright on his chair, rolled in toward his desk, flipped the switch on his intercom and said, "Tony, could you bring in a fresh pot of coffee...thanks?"

Silence followed for a short while, then Bill Nelson added, somewhat conclusively, "I submit that we keep Alex's confession quiet. Only the sister, the priest and we three know that he confessed—oh yes, his girlfriend told you—when was it, yesterday—that she knew, isn't that right Sergeant? You won't have any problem convincing the priest, will you?"

"No, of course not. In fact it wouldn't surprise me that he would feel relieved. Remember, Alex told him about the murder while in confession, and although Father Mike said that Alex asked him to go to the precinct station with him, which served as a release from the *seal of confession*...yes, I think we can safely say that Father will be relieved and nothing will leak out. To make sure no one else leaks it though, I will also discuss it with Maria and her husband—if in fact he knows anything—which I doubt."

There was a knock on the door and though they expected patrolman Tony with coffee, it was Jordan Saydorf, the medical examiner.

"Good morning gentlemen, am I disturbing anything?"

"Of course not," answered the chief of police, "we were discussing the Steeter case. Do you know we have a confession? The sister confessed yesterday to Sergeant Arrondondo. She was the one who hit the boy on the head. It seems he was going to abuse the little girl. We, Nelson and I, haven't talked about this yet, but I think we will both decide that it was self defense." The chief looked over at the D.A. seemingly for his agreement.

"Well, hold on," said Saydorf, "I'm here to report that the cause of Robert Steeter's death was not a blow to the skull, he died from stab wounds in the back. One of them pierced his right lung."

There was obvious and stunned silence.

Just then there was another knock on the door and Tony brought in a carafe of coffee and some crumb cake. "My wife made these; thought you'd enjoy them," he said as he put the coffee and plate of cut-up cakes on the chief's desk. He looked disconcerted when no one made any acknowledgement of what he had just said. He gave a slight shrug as if to say: don't forget to say thanks, fellas—walked out and closed the door.

"Are you sure?" Arrondondo finally said in a tone that was more of a statement than a question.

"Yes," Saydorf answered, "here is the report." He laid it on the desk. "It is all here, what little there is, but it is conclusive. I was attendant at the autopsy and there is no question that there are stab wounds; faint but visible. I'd say they were made by a sharp, pointed knife—a switchblade comes to mind; the weapon of choice when our Puerto Rican gangs bust each other up."

"Thanks Jordan," the chief said as he reached for the report.

"Anything else?" the efficient medical examiner responded. "You know where to find me." He left.

"Now what?" the D.A. said. "Looks like we are back to square one, doesn't it? I suppose you aren't going to be in a big hurry to release the janitor, are you Sergeant?"

They each had a piece of the crumb cake, without a thought to where it might have come from, discussed the three ew police cars that were delivered that morning while sipping their coffee, and said their goodbyes—"Let's take a breather...we'll talk later," Arrondondo said to the two others and left the room.

The Steeter case was more confused than ever.

36

"My brain hurts," the sergeant said to the traffic around him. He was driving home when suddenly he changed his mind. "I think I will go see Father Mike—if he's at the rectory—perhaps in the telling of this new development I'll come up with some little fact that will turn this case on its ear."

Father was home. "Would you like to join me? I'm heading over to that little Italian coffee shop on Jericho Turnpike. A change of scene might do us both good."

"Certainly," Father responded without hesitation. "There must be something wrong, you look upset...but I can wait until we get some coffee, then we can talk. Yes, a change of scenery will do us good." Both men were essentially quiet for the five minutes it took to drive to the coffee shop, park the sergeant's car, and walk in.

They sat down, a waiter came immediately, and they both ordered espresso. Sergeant ordered a small sandwich—that would make up for the lunch that consisted only of the little piece of crumb cake.

"Father, I'm irritable and hungry, probably the latter causing the former. This Steeter case is going to put me in the loony bin. I just came from a meeting with the chief and the D.A., we were meeting in order to decide on releasing Earl Stasser. Jordy Saydorf came in with a bombshell: the Steeter boy was murdered with a knife; stabbed in the back.

"The pathologist noticed something on his ribs, turns him over to investigate further of course, and is now telling us he was stabbed with a knife. Saydorff was at the autopsy and is certain the weapon was a switchblade; says it is just like what you see when the gangs go after each other. If you recall, we found a four-inch switchblade among Earl Stasser's things when we searched his apartment. I was trying to be a smart-ass back then and said to him, 'You don't look like a hunter,' also, I asked him but he could not remember where he got it. What do you make of that?"

"Whew! No wonder you're irritable and hungry...but I'd change it around; the former is causing the latter. When I'm feeling down I turn to eating...works wonders for me!"

Arrondondo chuckled.

"So," Father continued, "we now have three murderers, don't we? Alex, in his dying moments, tells me—ostensibly to protect his terminally ill sister—that he hit Robert over the head with a broomstick, but I have been wrestling with trying to figure out his real motivation for confessing. Then we've got Maria, tells us she was the one who actually hit the boy on the head, possibly because she knows she is dying and wants to protect her dead brother, and lastly we've got the pathologist telling us to disregard those two confessions because death was due to a knife wound, and we know the janitor, Earl Stasser, possessed such a knife because you found it among his things. Do I have this right Sergeant, and could it be any more complicated?"

"No, I don't think it could be any more complicated Father, and yes, essentially we have three murderers for one dead person."

"Back in Act One of this drama," Father added, "just a few days ago, we were certain the janitor killed the boy. The medical examiner was quite certain the cause of death was a blow to the back of his head. Then you find the cigar box with the boy's cigarettes and his letter that he is extorting money—I suspect that is a good enough motive for murder right? So, back then, all of us were as convinced as could be that the janitor killed the boy; and all indications were that the murder weapon was a broomstick found at the scene." Father stared into his espresso cup trying to come to terms with what he just summarized."

He looked up and continued, "Sergeant, I'm thinking that it is less the complexity of the case than trying to sort out the sequence of events and the motivation of each of the participants."

"Yes Father, a few days ago we believed we had the case solved. Clearly, it seemed, the boy was murdered in response to his attempting to extort fifty dollars from the janitor; and if he doesn't get paid, threatens to show the picture of the two of them to the police so that the janitor is then arrested for engaging in sex with a minor. Now admittedly, the evidence at the time was somewhat circumstantial. We knew the janitor was in the vicinity, had a good motive, and could not offer an alibi as to where he was on the night of the murder...but I am not so sure it would have been enough for a conviction...not for murder, that is.

"Then surprise!" Sergeant Arrondondo continued, "Alex tells you he is the one who hit Robert on the head; confirming Jody Saydoff's initial conclusion as to the cause of death. So, at that point we have a confession; again though, not on solid legal ground because it could be construed as hearsay since Alex told only you, and he is no longer here to confirm what he said. So, with Alex's confession we begin Act Two and we are ready to release the janitor. Unfortunately, Alex dies so we are prevented from interviewing him to get confirmation of his confession, or to get more detail on exactly what occurred...and therefore an opportunity to tie all the loose ends together.

"Next bombshell is that Maria confesses. As if that doesn't add to the puzzle we've got Jordy announcing that the official cause of death is a knife wound in the back. Now we are back where we originally were in Act One—with the janitor as the prime suspect, and fortunately I've got the murder weapon back at the precinct in Stasser's file.

"Father, the two Fazios have lied separately and have lied together. I've got to sort out the truth in order to construct a tight case." Sergeant Arrondondo followed with a suggestion: "Let's take this from the top. You have always been a good sounding board...especially since you seem to have all the details committed to your memory. Me? I have to consult my little book."

"Sure, do you want to start at the very beginning? Something inside tells me that is where we are mixing things up, or else we are missing some little detail that would clear up the loose ends, no?"

"By all means." Sergeant Arrondondo tilted his cup for the last drop; then raised his hand above his head to signal the waiter for another cup for himself and Father Mike—who confirmed the request with a slight nod. Sergeant Arrondondo continued.

"The first question Father, is why did the girl wait for her brother. That wasn't something she normally did, right? So what was different about that Wednesday night?"

According to her," Father answered, "Robert's threat was immediate and real; whereas rape—which she probably didn't understand in the same way you and I would—was not immediate. The only thing she knew was that if she didn't accompany Robert and Alex he'd get the janitor to beat up her brother. I think that would have been sufficient motivation for her to not only accompany the two boys, but to keep quiet as well. She was a very fragile young girl; scared of her own toes and certainly of Robert."

"Yes, I think I understand Father. To an adult it sounds unbelievable, but to her...? What about that strange comment from Alex about having no conversation whatsoever with Robert before, during, or after the church service? I think he was lying, what do you think?'

"I hadn't thought about that at all Sergeant, but now that you bring it up I believe you are right. If he had not lied, I would have asked him what they talked about, wouldn't I, and Alex would have been put on the spot. So, the easy way out was to tell this ridiculous lie—and I fell for it!"

"Don't fret Father, I fell for it too. Only now, while going through this with you, this is the first time the thought occurred to me that it could not have been true. One would think that some time during the night he would have whispered something to Alex; he'd want to confirm that his plans had not gone astray, wouldn't he? They also lied about not meeting Robert after church and immediately walking home together...taking a half hour to make a two or three minute walk.

"I'll go with what Mrs. Reilly saw. Yes, she saw the three of them, and when she turned away for a few moments, the kids

283

went behind the church. When she looks again, she sees the janitor, but to her at night and from a distance she thinks it is the girl because that's what she expected to see. What reason would she have to lie; there is none?"

"No, of course not. It also follows that the janitor saw the three kids too. After all, he's there to confront Robert about the fifty dollars. According to Maria, Robert was expecting him and got annoyed that he wasn't there. I'd say that the janitor didn't know about the letter, and wants to keep this little extortion strictly between Robert and himself. That would explain why he didn't meet up as Robert expected. Instead, our janitor decides to wait and see what happens; hoping to confront Robert alone."

Father Mike was on a roll. "So now we have what Maria told us. She is behind the church with the two boys, hears that the janitor is expected—which, in her mind, adds credence and a whole new dimension to the threat from Robert—there is the conversation she told us about...the part about smoking and raping...and she decides then and there to take action. Yes Sergeant, I believe what Maria told us is exactly what happened. Including that they were anxious to get away after she hit him. They didn't take a half-hour to get back; no, the walk across the street probably accounted for just a few minutes; the bulk of the half-hour took place behind the church."

"Going back a step Father, what prompted Alex to lie to you when he confessed that he did it? Do you think it was to protect Maria? He knew, because he told you so, that Maria had terminal cancer and that her doctors didn't give her long to live. Why would he lie about something so serious?"

"That Sergeant is something we can only speculate. Let's review the situation. He was distraught, first about his sister. They were very close, maintained this secret for many years—wholly believing that his sister murdered Robert Steeter. I could see that he wanted her to go to her grave without any blemish on her soul. He wasn't religious, but he believed in sin; he was practical and prudent. People's minds work in mystical ways. I could see how he could go through a bizarre logic that went like this: since Maria would never go to confession and he did not want her to die in sin, he convinced himself that he was responsible for the murder—who actually wielded the weapon was secondary. After all, he didn't protect her, he didn't stand up to Robert, he went along with the program; essentially it was his murder.

"Secondly, he confessed about the affair he was having with Maureen. He was devastated by this. I believe he saw his confession as a way out of his problem with his wife. I asked him, 'Alex, why after all the years of this affair are you confessing now?' He had no answer. That told me a lot. It was the recent problems: his affair itself; his wife; Dolores's recent experience with a relative's father being sent to prison for committing a murder during a robbery—and all the devastation *that* family had to deal with. Also, he recently had quit his job. I gather he assumed that confessing to a murder that he believed he was responsible for would solve all his problems. In fact Sergeant, he asked me to intercede in all of them, hoping I would be the catalyst for making everyone understand his remorse for each of the difficulties he was putting them through.

"Thirdly Sergeant, and perhaps the most crucial, I truly believe he could not abide by the janitor taking the blame for the crime that Alex believed he committed. When you showed him the picture of the young boy and the janitor standing next to a wall, he knew just like I did that it was the wall behind the church, and that is when he knew it was imminent that the murder scene would be discovered. He concluded, rightfully so, that the janitor would be blamed; this thinking was almost certainly the primary reason for the confession."

Sergeant Arrondondo listened carefully to Father Mike's explanation. Both men were silent for a while as they digested Father Mike's rationale. "I cannot find fault with what you say Father. You are a psychologist, not only through your formal education but because you constantly deal with these issues of the soul. Maria's confession is more straight forward," the sergeant continued, "of course she wanted to protect her brother's memory but I believe she told the truth. It all fits."

"One final question Sergeant, did the janitor witness the girl hitting the boy with the stick, knocking him unconscious?"

"Unless I get the janitor himself to answer that Father, I am afraid we won't know. I don't think it is a critical part of the case. Certainly it was the janitor who dragged the boy's body into the hole. However, I must make a note to ask Jordy and the pathologist to give me their expert opinion as to whether the boy was dead before he was dragged in or if he was stabbed inside the hole. Regardless of whatever the janitor says, their testimony will prevail.

"As I see it," Sergeant Arrondondo continued after sipping the last drop of espresso, "and I believe I'll get the details from Earl after I charge him with the murder. He kept himself hidden until the two Fazio kids headed back to the convent, figuring Robert would wait behind to collect the money. He had no

286

intention in participating in anything else—which confirms that cigarette smoking and collecting the fifty dollars were the primary events, and that the question of rape was, in fact, in everyone's mind just their typical 'dirty talk'—except maybe for Robert himself. The janitor wanted to see the Steeter boy alone. He saw him lying on the ground unconscious, used the switchblade we found in his flat to stab the boy and drag him under the church."

"Yes Sergeant, now he was rid of his problem—permanently; and since he didn't know the letter was in the cigar box..."

"Exactly. He believed he was safe; there was nothing to connect him to the murder, and furthermore, that is why Earl was so startled when I told him we found his switchblade. Probably could kick himself for not disposing of it. The last detail I need to know is who are all the people who knew about the murder—concealing a crime, you know. This will be something our D.A. will be interested in, but I submit that going way back in time, neither Alex nor Maria knew that the janitor killed the boy; they believed Maria killed him with the broomstick; what do you think?"

"I agree. Also, I'd be surprised if Maureen knew until just a couple of days ago...back in Act One when Alex told her, because if she did she likely would have told long ago...not having anything to lose or gain by withholding the information. On the other hand, Sara and Maria's husband Eric...none of them knew anything, I suspect."

"Well," Sergeant Arrondondo looked at his watch, "well done; that about wraps it up. I appreciate your help Father. Unless I'm mistaken, the case is closed...not officially until we get a conviction, but pretty damned close, if you will excuse my French!"

As they were walking to the car, Father said, "I think I'll walk the few blocks back to the rectory Sergeant. It will give me time to think and to pray. God knows how many people on whose behalf I need to intercede and He is waiting."

"I understand Father. I'll see you later."

37

The Funeral Mass was officiated by Father Mike. Sara had to make a difficult decision and in the end based it on several factors: Alex was with Father Mike when he died so evidently had close ties to him and would prefer he say the mass; he would be buried with his parents; it would be easier on his ill sister who was in no condition for extended travel; and Francine, the youngest, could readily attend, along with their many aunts, uncles and cousins still in and around New York City.

Traveling to New York from Texas would not be an untoward burden on his oldest sister Dolores, and Sara's immediate family—her dad, sister, and brother; and their spouses, told her they would support whatever arrangements she decided. Like their now deceased father who didn't attend his mother's funeral, her young boys would not attend his either. Some tried to talk her out of it but she held firm. How she was going to handle all of that in the near future was something she put away in the further-most part of her mind—she would store-up that pain for another day.

The more she thought of it, it made little sense to bring Alex back to Chicago and have his final resting place in a cemetery that she would have to select through a phone book or, more likely, the local priest whom she knew only marginally.

✦ ✦ ✦

The "Dies Irae," a beautifully sad, sobering, Latin hymn, with its haunting Gregorian Chant melody and often sung during a Funeral Mass, is a solemn backdrop in which to express one's grief while reflecting on the mystery of life and death:

> Dies irae, dies illa,
> Solvet saeculum in favilla,
> Teste David cum Sibylla.

...Reflecting is what Father Mike was doing while the hymn was being sung a capella at the mass.

His sermon was short wherein he repeated in a similar spirit, essentially what he had said to Alex when told about Maria's illness: God gives us a life we hopefully can fill with pleasant memories that are then shared and remembered by those we leave behind, and which become an element of the eternal life that God has provided for us.

He had temporal concerns to reflect on as well—he saw no reason for anyone to dwell on the revolting memories surrounding Robert Steeter. He saw no reason to dwell on Maureen either, yet he was anxious because she was at the wake the previous evening and he was very much aware that neither she nor Sara could keep from glancing at each other—though he suspected that neither spoke to the other, and he thought it likely that Sara was wondering who the stranger was.

The wake was held in the Donnelly and Parcel Funeral Home, the same place as Alex's mother's funeral; likewise the mass at Blessed Sacrament Church across the street. Father Mike, concerned about who all knew of Alex's confession, discussed the subject with Sergeant Arrondondo again, and was assured that on Alex's side, only Maria and Maureen knew. He likewise shared his concern that if Sara found out about Maureen and they got into an unpleasant conversation or worse an altercation, there was nothing to prevent Maureen from using her knowledge of Alex's confession as a weapon to hurt Sara.

"Any suggestions to keep that from happening Sergeant?" Father Mike asked.

"The only one I have, and I hesitate to use it because it could easily backfire—is to warn Maureen that if she ever tells anyone what Alex told her in confidence, I will seek charges against her for withholding evidence of a crime; I could, you know, because she admitted to me that Alex told *her* before he told you Father. But, like I say, I would be on shaky ground and it could backfire."

After the mass, Sara hosted a brunch at a restaurant near St. John's Cemetery where Alex would be buried beside his parents the next day in a private service. Typically, everyone who attends the Funeral Mass is invited to the brunch, but why Maureen decided on coming was unclear. In any case, neither Father Mike nor Sergeant Arrondondo had an opportunity to speak with her before she went through the line formed by Sara, Dolores, Maria and Francine, along with their respective husbands, and who were hosting the brunch and accepting condolences from those who had earlier been at the church.

When it came to Maureen, she introduced herself as a friend from long ago, back when they lived in the convent, making certain to include her maiden name. Dolores, standing next to Sara, followed through with, as is typical in a receiving line when you see someone you've not seen in years, "How have you been...nice to see you, thank you for coming...I see Arlene Stern occasionally so I am somewhat up-to-date with the convent kids that Alex has kept in contact with all these years," and finished with "I hope we get a few minutes later-on to renew our acquaintances."

As Maureen moved along, Sara whispered to Dolores, "Who was that?" and Dolores answered with a brief, "She is the sister of a boy that disappeared from the convent a long time ago." Sara's response was "Oh," but Father Mike, who was watching from a distance, could tell that the answer was not accepted adequately. Clearly Sara had picked up on the phrase *kept in contact with all these years.*

Father had promised Alex he would intercede for him with Sara if need be; thus—paying constant attention to the two women, was important to him. He wanted to be close enough to prevent any conversation that would hurt either Sara or her memory of Alex.

He had an opportunity to speak privately with Maureen after she subsequently made her way to a corner of the room and where she was standing by herself. Father walked up to her and said, "Hello Maureen, it is nice to see you after all these years. Hopefully you are well?"

"Yes, and the same goes for you Father," Maureen answered, "your sermon was moving. It touched me—it made me sad but it lifted me up again. Alex and I have known each other for most of our lives; of course you know that Father—he was my best friend and I shall miss him."

"Yes, I am aware of the relationship you two had. If it is any consolation, you were his best friend as well. You may know that Alex was with me when he died. He told me many things.

Actually he had asked me to hear his confession, so perhaps he knew he was not going to be on earth much longer—one never knows about the mystery of how that all plays out—but I can safely tell you that he had the fondest regard for you, as I am sure you had for him."

There was a moment of silence where it appeared Maureen was deciding what, if anything, she should say in response. Father Mike saw in front of him a strong, private, capable woman who could readily go through life without needing anyone, or could just as easily be surreptitiously dependent—on Alex, for example. There was no doubt in his mind that here was a complex woman, not simple to figure out, and if you thought you had come to a conclusion it could easily be an untrustworthy one in that regard.

"So I suppose if he was confessing his sins he told you about us?"

"Well, it *was confession*, so you will have to excuse me for not answering that question. However, it does not prevent you from telling me what you have on your mind, does it?"

"I cannot explain our relationship Father, I don't believe in sin. Of course there are bad people in this world so they are sinners, but that is not what we are talking about, is it? I do not know the last time I admitted to anyone that I am a truly lonely person, but I have compensated by not allowing myself to love anyone, including Alex. We were not lovers and one of my greatest fears is that Alex's wife, and to a lesser extent the rest of his family, will misconstrue our relationship. Does that make sense Father?"

"Of course it does Maureen. But isn't it up to you what others will find out?"

"No, I don't think so. It is difficult to keep a relationship secret—so yes, there are others who know, so I feel I must somehow explain to Sara so she can disregard anything else she may hear. I owe it to Alex, to her, to my husband and, to some extent to myself.

Dolores walked up to Father Mike and Maureen and said, "Thank you for that lovely sermon Father. I don't know which is more difficult, when someone dies suddenly or when there is a lingering illness. Unfortunately for our family we are going to have to deal with both. You comfort us Father, I hope you will be there for us again."

She turned to Maureen and said, "As I mentioned earlier, I've kept in touch with Arlene Stern all these years, and so I hear bits and pieces about some of the other convent kids. It seems Arlene has a propensity for keeping in contact with some, and when one of them keeps in contact with someone else, it ends up that Arlene knows a little about several of the kids but not very much about any one of them. Do you know what I mean?"

"Of course I do," Maureen answered, "please don't misunderstand, but I was never very friendly with any of them so I don't necessarily look forward to hearing about them." There followed a few seconds of silence, then Maureen added, "I am here because Alex and I were two who remained friends; we've been to each other's wedding, we've leaned on each other for support in times of difficulty, and have been able to laugh our way through hard times; and that's all there was to it."

Father Mike had to admire how well Maureen handled this first of many explanations of hers and Alex's relationship. In looking at Dolores inquisitively, he felt assured that she understood the subtle hint—don't kiss a frog if you don't believe in princes.

She immediately changed the subject, as if to sustain Father's impression. "Since the parish is going to be building a new church, I was thinking of having a reunion of the convent kids. It isn't like I wasn't paying attention to what you just said, but perhaps you could make an exception and join us. I know there are those who would like to see you and perhaps as a favor to me you'll think about it?" Dolores dug around in the small purse she was carrying and pulled out a card. "Here is my telephone number, if you would call me I will put you on the list to send more information."

"I will give your invitation some thought...I see they are asking us to take our seats and I am sitting over there," Maureen indicated a table in the corner. "It was nice talking to you Dolores, and again, please accept my sympathy." She nodded to Father Mike and went to sit for the brunch that was about to be served.

✢ ✢ ✢

Later on Sara, in making the rounds of the tables where her guests were seated, was able to quietly ask Maureen if she recently met Alex for dinner in New York and, "...Did you notice anything out of the ordinary or did he mention if he had felt ill recently..." trying to fill in the missing pieces to her husband's sudden death.

Maureen answered, "Yes, he invited me for dinner and no, I did not notice anything unusual." In that moment though, Sara's suspicions were confirmed and her eyes watered and she swallowed hard. Maureen noticed. "Please Sara, can you come with me right now—please? I need to talk to you...alone." They walked out to the hallway where there was some privacy.

"Sara, Alex and I have known each other since we were in the convent together. If you are thinking there was anything between us you would be doing yourself, him and me a disservice. There was nothing between us. He *loves* you, his children and his family...he *liked* me—please don't confuse the two."

Unfortunately Sara could not prevent herself from asking, "Were you lovers?"

"No," Maureen answered. "Long ago, in one of the many discussions we had together, and I will treasure those times forever, Alex told me about an Italian phrase he had picked up somewhere. It became our *ism*: Vivere per il momento and it means *Live for the moment;* my advice to you, in his memory and for yourself, is to consider making it yours as well." Maureen gave Sara a little kiss on her cheek.

As she was leaving the hallway, she turned to Sara as if to add, "It is the prudent thing to do," and left the restaurant.

The Dies Irae

*"That day of wrath, that dreadful day,
shall heaven and earth in ashes lay,
as David and the Sybils say."*

Made in the USA
Charleston, SC
06 August 2011